MIDNIGHT FOR
CHARLIE BONE

MIDNIGHT FOR
CHARLIE BONE

CHILDREN OF THE RED KING

BOOK 1

JENNY NIMMO

ORCHARD BOOKS
AN IMPRINT OF SCHOLASTIC INC.
NEW YORK

Text copyright © 2002 by Jenny Nimmo
First published in 2002 in Great Britain by Egmont Books Ltd.

ISBN 0-439-48839-7

12 11   03 04 05 06 07

Printed in the U.S.A.   40
First Scholastic paperback edition, September 2002

Cover illustration © 2002 by Chris Sheeban
The text type was set in 11-pt. Diotima Roman.
The display type was set in Latino-Rumba.
Book design by Marijka Kostiw

Another one
for Myfanwy,
with love
—J. N.

CONTENTS

PROLOGUE

Long, long ago a king arrived in the North. They called

him the Red King because he wore a scarlet cloak and

his shield was emblazoned with a burning sun. It was

said that he came out of Africa. This king was also a mar-

velous magician and each of his ten children inherited

a small part of his power. But when the king's wife died,

five of his children turned to wickedness and the other

five, seeking to escape the corruption that surrounded

their evil siblings, left their father's castle forever.

Brokenhearted, the Red King vanished into the

forests that covered the kingdoms of the North. He did not go alone, however, for he was followed by his three faithful cats — leopards to be precise. We must never forget the cats!

The manifold and fabulous powers of the Red King were passed down through his descendants, often turning up quite unexpectedly in someone who had no idea where they came from. This is what happened to Charlie Bone and to some of the children he met behind the grim, gray walls of Bloor's Academy.

CHARLIE HEARS VOICES

On a Thursday afternoon, just after tea, Charlie Bone saw smoke. He happened to be looking out of his window when a dark cloud lifted above the autumn trees. The wind blew it south and it moved through the sky like a great, floating whale.

Somewhere, on the other side of the city, there was a fire. Charlie could hear a fire engine racing toward it. He had no idea that in mysterious and unexpected ways he was connected to it and would soon be drawn to the place where it had begun.

Charlie slept well, got up the next morning, and went to school. After school, Charlie and his friend, Benjamin Brown, walked home together, as usual. The cloud of smoke had gone, but the sky was stormy and dark. A fierce wind sent red and gold leaves racing down Filbert Street.

Benjamin crossed the road to number twelve, while Charlie stopped at number nine. Most of the people who lived at number nine complained about the large chestnut tree in front of it—how dark it made their rooms, how damp and creaky it was, and how it would probably fall on the roof one day and kill them all in their beds. Needless to say, no one at number nine did anything about it. Complaining to one another was as far as they went. They were that sort of family. Or, rather, those sorts of families.

As Charlie ran up the steps to his front door, the tree sighed and rained a handful of chestnuts on his head. Luckily his thick, wiry hair softened the blows. Thick hair had its uses, though not many. Charlie was always being told to smarten himself up, an impossible task for someone with hair like a hedge.

"Hello, grandmas!" Charlie called as he stepped into the hall.

There were two grandmas at number nine: Grandma Jones was Charlie's mother's mother, and Grandma Bone was Charlie's father's mother. Grandma

Jones was round and cheerful and bossy, while Grandma Bone spoke only to complain. She rarely smiled and nothing made her laugh. Her hair was thick and white, and she wore long, stiff dresses in shades of black, gray, or brown (never pink, which was Maisie's favorite color). Grandma Jones liked to be called Maisie, but Charlie wouldn't have dared to call Grandma Bone by her first name, which was Grizelda. She liked to remind people that, before she had married Mr. Bone, she had been a Yewbeam. The Yewbeams were an ancient family, their history littered with artistic people and others who had more unusual talents, such as hypnotism, mind-reading, and bewitchery.

Charlie knew he had disappointed Grandma Bone by being ordinary. Even worse, in her eyes, he was quite happy to be ordinary.

When Charlie came home from school it was always Maisie who gave him a wet kiss on his cheek and pushed something to eat under his nose. Today Maisie had a large bump on her forehead. "Silly chestnut," she told Charlie.

Grandma Bone was always sitting in a rocker by the stove, criticizing Maisie's cooking or the state of Charlie's hair. Today the rocker was empty. That was the first unusual thing.

It was Benjamin's tenth birthday on Saturday and Charlie had decided to make him a birthday card instead of buying one. He'd taken a photo of Benjamin's dog, Runner Bean, smiling or, to be more precise, showing his long, incredibly yellow teeth.

Charlie had asked his mother to get the photo enlarged at Kwik Foto on her way home from work. He intended to draw a balloon saying HAPPY BIRTHDAY, BENJAMIN! above Runner Bean's head.

The second unusual thing was about to happen.

At five minutes past four, Charlie's mother came in with a box of overripe apples and rhubarb. "They'll make a lovely cobbler," she said, dumping the box beside Charlie's plate and kissing his shaggy head. Amy Bone worked part-time in a greengrocer's shop, so there was always plenty of fruit and vegetables at number nine.

Charlie leaned away from the rotting fruit. "Have you got my photo, Mom?" he asked.

Amy Bone poked around in her shopping bag and found a large orange envelope. She put it on the other side of Charlie's plate.

Charlie opened the envelope and revealed — not Runner Bean. Nothing like Runner Bean.

It was at this moment that Grandma Bone appeared. She hovered in the doorway, fingering her neck, touching her silver-white hair, and pulling at her stiff black skirt. She looked somehow as though she were on the brink of fulfilling her destiny. And in a way she was, though, at sixty-five, you could be forgiven for thinking it was a bit late.

The photograph that Charlie now held showed a man holding a baby. The man sat on an upright chair. He had thinning, grayish hair and a long, mournful face. His crumpled suit was black and his thick pebble glasses gave his pale gray eyes a lost marble-like stare.

Instead of pushing the photograph back into the envelope, Charlie continued to gaze at it. In fact, he couldn't tear his eyes away from it. He began to feel dizzy and his ears were filled with mysterious sounds, like the hiss and swish of voices on the radio when you can't pinpoint the right frequency.

"Oh," he said. "Um, what . . . ?" His own voice seemed far away, trapped behind a kind of fog.

"What's wrong, Charlie?" asked his mother.

"Is something happening?" Grandma Bone crept forward. "Aunt Eustacia rang me. She had one of her premonitions. Are you a proper Yewbeam, after all?"

Maisie glared at Grandma Bone while Charlie pulled his ears and shook his head. If only the horrible muffled buzzing would stop. He had to shout in order to hear himself. "They've made a mistake at the shop. Where's Runner Bean?"

"There's no need to shout, Charlie." His mother looked over his shoulder. "My goodness; that's certainly not a dog."

"Ow!" wailed Charlie. But suddenly the mumbling

voices broke free of the buzz and made themselves clear.

First came a woman's voice, soft and unfamiliar: *I wish you wouldn't do this, Mostyn.*

Her mother's gone. I don't have a choice. This voice was definitely male.

Of course you do.

Will you take her, then? said the man's voice.

You know I can't, replied the woman.

Charlie looked at his mother. "Who said that?"

She looked puzzled. "Who said what, Charlie?"

"Is there a man in here?" he asked.

Maisie giggled. "Only you, Charlie."

Charlie felt clawlike fingers sink into his shoulder. Grandma Bone leaned over him. "Tell me what you hear," she demanded.

"Voices," said Charlie. "I know it sounds silly, but they seem to be coming from this photograph."

Grandma Bone nodded. "What do they say?"

"For goodness sake, Grandma Bone, don't be ridiculous," said Maisie.

Grandma Bone gave Maisie a withering look. "I am not being ridiculous."

Charlie noticed that his mother had gone very quiet. She pulled out a chair and sat down, looking pale and anxious.

Maisie began to bang pans about, muttering, "You shouldn't encourage it. It's all garbage. I won't have it..."

"Shhhh!" hissed Charlie. He could hear the baby crying.

The strange woman spoke again. *You've upset her. Look at the camera, Mostyn. And please try to smile. You look so gloomy.*

What do you expect? said the man.

A camera shutter clicked.

There. Shall I take another?

Do what you want.

You'll thank me, one day, said the woman behind the camera. *If you really intend to go through with this, it's the only thing you'll have to remember her by.*

Hmm.

Charlie noticed that a cat peeked from behind the man's chair. It was an extraordinary color: deep copper, like a flame.

From far away Charlie heard his mother's voice. "Shall I take the photo back, Charlie?"

"No," murmured Charlie. "Not yet."

But it seemed that the photograph had nothing more to say. The baby fussed for a moment and then was quiet. The gloomy man stared silently at the camera, and the cat . . . ? Was that a purr? Maisie was making such a noise with the pots and pans it was difficult to hear anything else.

"Hush!" commanded Grandma Bone. "Charlie can't hear."

"It's all nonsense," Maisie grumbled. "I don't know how you can just sit there, Amy, and let your crazy mother-in-law get away with it. Poor Charlie. He's just a boy. He's got nothing to do with those silly Yewbeams."

"He's got their blood," said Charlie's mother, quietly. "You can't get away from that."

Maisie couldn't. She closed her mouth in a tight little line.

Charlie was very bewildered. In the morning he had been an ordinary boy. He hadn't been touched by a magic wand or banged his head. He hadn't had an electric shock or fallen off a bus, or, as far as he knew, eaten a poisoned apple. And yet, here he was, hearing voices from a piece of photographic paper.

To set his mother's mind at rest, Charlie said, "I don't think it was anything, really. I just imagined it."

Grandma Bone leaned even closer and breathed into his ear, "Listen tonight. Things work better after midnight."

"He'll be asleep by then, I'll have you know," said Maisie, who had ears as sharp as a rabbit's. "It's all garbage."

"Hah!" retorted Grandma Bone. "Just you wait!" She walked away, leaving a scent of mothballs and mint drifting around the kitchen.

"I didn't hear anything," Charlie said when she had gone.

"Are you sure?" his mother asked anxiously.

"Honest. I was just doing it to tease Grandma Bone." He was trying to convince himself as well as his mother.

"Charlie, you're a wicked boy," Maisie said happily as she banged a meat cleaver into a meaty bone.

Charlie's mother looked relieved and opened the evening paper. Charlie slipped the photograph back into its envelope. He felt exhausted. Perhaps a bit of TV would help him to relax. But before he could escape, the doorbell rang and Grandma Bone could be heard saying, "It's Benjamin Brown, isn't it? Charlie's in the kitchen. And you can leave that mangy Baked Bean outside."

"It's Runner, not Baked," said Benjamin's voice, "and I can't leave him outside. It's raining."

"Dogs like rain," said Grandma Bone.

Benjamin and his dog appeared in the kitchen. Benjamin was a small, pale-faced boy with hair the color of damp hay. Runner Bean was a large, long-nosed dog also with hair the color of damp hay. For some reason Benjamin was always being picked on by other boys. People stole things from him, tripped him, and laughed at him. Charlie tried to help his friend but, sometimes, Benjamin was beyond help. Sometimes, in fact, Charlie thought that Benjamin didn't even notice that he was a victim. He lived in a world of his own.

Runner Bean, smelling the meaty bone, rushed straight to Maisie, and began to lick her ankles.

"Get off me!" she yelled, swiping him on the nose.

"You are coming to my party, aren't you?" Benjamin asked Charlie.

"Of course I am," said Charlie, immediately feeling guilty about the birthday card.

"Good, because I'm getting a game that needs two people to play it."

Charlie realized that no one else would be at Benjamin's party. This made him feel even more guilty. Runner Bean began to whine, almost as if he guessed that he wouldn't be appearing on Benjamin's birthday card.

"I'll be there," said Charlie cheerfully. He hadn't

bought a present yet. He would have to rush out to the store before he began his quest. But what quest was that? Something seemed to be hijacking Charlie's thoughts.

"Want to come for a walk with Runner?" Benjamin asked hopefully.

"OK."

Maisie shouted something about supper as Charlie and Benjamin left the house, but the wind howled around their heads and a clap of thunder drowned her words. Runner Bean yelped as a chestnut hit his nose, and Benjamin managed to smile at last.

As the two boys and the dog ran into the wind, leaves flew in their faces and stuck to fur and clothes. Charlie felt better in the open air. Perhaps it really had been a trick of his imagination. He hadn't heard voices at all, it was just some silly nonsense that he'd made himself believe, and Grandma Bone had encouraged him, just to annoy Maisie and upset his mother.

"Yes," Charlie cried happily. "It's all garbage."

"And leaves," said Benjamin, who thought Charlie meant the litter being blown down the street.

"And leaves," sang Charlie. He saw a newspaper flying toward him and stuck his foot out to catch it. But the paper lifted in a sudden gust and wrapped itself around his waist. As he pulled it away from him, a picture on the front page caught his eye.

A mean-looking boy stood on the steps of a gray building. He had a long, narrow face and a wispy mustache grew above his thin upper lip. His dark hair, parted in the center, had been drawn back into a ponytail.

"What's that?" asked Benjamin.

"Just a boy," said Charlie, and yet he had the suspicion that this wasn't just any boy.

Benjamin leaned over Charlie's arm and read, "Manfred Bloor, age seventeen, was rescued from a fire at Bloor's Academy yesterday. Manfred said he was lucky to be alive."

"No, he didn't," said Charlie breathlessly.

"What do you mean, he didn't?" asked Benjamin.

"He didn't say that," Charlie murmured, and he suddenly sat on the ground, with his back to the wall. He held the paper at arm's length, dismayed by the words that were creeping out of the picture.

Someone's going to pay for this.

"How'd you . . . ?" Benjamin began.

"Shut up, Ben," cried Charlie. "I'm listening."

"What to?"

"Shhh!"

As Charlie stared at Manfred Bloor, he heard a lot of shouts and then a woman's voice broke through the others, *Are you accusing someone, Manfred?*

You're right, I am, said a husky voice.

Why do you think it wasn't an accident?

The husky voice again. *I'm not stupid, that's why.*

A man said, *The fire department told us a candle was probably blown over. Don't you believe this?*

ENOUGH! Whoever said this had such a deep and chilling voice, Charlie dropped the paper. It whirled away and flopped into the gutter.

"Charlie, what's going on?" asked Benjamin.

Charlie gave a deep sigh. "I'm hearing voices," he said.

"Oh, no." Benjamin sat beside him, and Runner Bean crouched beside Benjamin. "What sort of voices?"

Benjamin never, ever said, "That's garbage." He took life seriously, which wasn't always a bad thing.

Charlie told Benjamin about the photograph of Runner Bean that had gotten mixed up with a man and a baby. "It was going to be a surprise birthday card for you," said Charlie, "and now it won't be. I'm sorry."

"Doesn't matter," said Benjamin. "Go on about the photograph."

Charlie explained that he'd heard voices when he looked at the man and the baby. He'd even heard the baby cry and maybe a cat purring.

"Weird," breathed Benjamin.

"I made myself believe I'd just imagined it," said Charlie, "but when I saw the newspaper, it happened again. I could hear reporters talking to that boy on the front page. I could hear his voice, too. He sounded kind of mean and sly. And then someone said,

'Enough!' and that was the worst voice I ever heard in my whole life."

Benjamin shivered and Runner Bean whined in sympathy.

The boys sat, side by side, on the damp pavement, not knowing quite what to do. The wind flung leaves at them, and thunder rumbled in the distance.

It began to rain. Runner Bean nudged Benjamin and whined. He hated getting wet. And then, during a particularly loud clap of thunder, a man appeared in front of the boys. He was wearing a dark raincoat and his wet hair was plastered over his forehead in wide, black bands.

"It's raining," the man announced. "Had you not noticed?"

Charlie looked up. "Uncle Paton!" he said in surprise.

Uncle Paton was Grandma Bone's brother. He was twenty years younger than she was and they didn't get along. Paton led a secret life, even eating apart from the others. He never went outside in daylight.

"You're wanted at home," Uncle Paton told Charlie.

Charlie and Benjamin stood up and shook their cramped legs. This was the third unusual thing to happen today. It wasn't nearly dark enough for Uncle Paton to venture out.

Charlie wondered what could possibly have happened to cause such drastic action.

THE YEWBEAM AUNTS

I t was difficult to keep up with Uncle Paton. He swept through wind and rain as if he wore hip boots.

"I've never seen your uncle outside in the daytime," Benjamin panted. "He's a bit strange, isn't he?"

"A bit," agreed Charlie, who was rather in awe of his peculiar uncle. He hurried as Uncle Paton had already arrived at the steps of number nine.

Benjamin fell behind. "Something's up with your family," he called to Charlie. "I hope you can still come to my birthday."

"Nothing can stop me," said Charlie, reaching his uncle.

"No dogs," said Uncle Paton, as Benjamin and Runner Bean came leaping up to them.

"Aw, please?" asked Benjamin.

"Not today. This is family business," Uncle Paton said sternly. "Go home."

"OK. Bye, then, Charlie." Benjamin trailed away, followed by Runner Bean, his ears down and tail between his legs. A real hangdog.

Uncle Paton ushered Charlie into the kitchen and then disappeared upstairs.

Charlie found his mother and two grandmothers sitting at the kitchen table. Maisie looked very put out, but a secret smile played on Grandma Bone's thin lips. Charlie's mother was nervously stirring a cup of tea. Charlie couldn't imagine why. His mother didn't use sugar.

"Sit down, Charlie," said Grandma Bone, as if she were about to put on a show entirely for his benefit.

"Don't let the Yewbeams get at you!" Maisie whispered. She took Charlie's hand and patted it.

"What's going on?" asked Charlie.

"The Yewbeam aunts are coming," said his mother.

"Why?" asked Charlie.

The Yewbeam aunts were Grandma Bone's three unmarried sisters. Charlie only saw them at Christmas, and he'd formed the impression that they were deeply disappointed in him. They always left a strange assortment of gifts: paint sets, musical instruments, masks and cloaks, and even a chemistry set. Charlie had found none of these things the least bit useful. He liked soccer and TV, and that was about it.

Grandma Bone leaned across the table. Her eyes sparkled mysteriously. "My sisters are coming to assess you, Charlie. And if it is found that you are worthy — that you are, as I suspect, endowed — then they will provide the necessary funds to send you to Bloor's Academy."

"Me? At Bloor's?" Charlie was aghast. "It's for geniuses."

"Don't worry, love. You won't pass the test," said Maisie confidently. She got up muttering, "Of course, it's old Maisie who has to do all the preparation for our Lady Mucks, isn't it? I don't know why I bother."

There was to be a dinner for the aunts, Charlie's mother explained. The best silver, the finest crystal, and the treasured china, would be carried up from the cellar and laid in the chilly dining room, a room that was only ever used when the Yewbeam aunts came. Maisie was defrosting chicken and fish and goodness knows what else, as fast as she could.

Charlie would have been worried if he hadn't been completely convinced that he wouldn't pass the aunts' test. He remembered how he'd tried to paint a picture for them and failed miserably. How he'd unsuccess-fully attempted to play a violin, a flute, a harp, and a piano. He had put on the masks they provided: ani-mals, clowns, pirates, cowboys, and spacemen, but only managed to act the part of Charlie Bone. Finally, it had to be admitted that he was not gifted.

So as he waited for the great-aunts to arrive, Char-lie was not as fearful as he should have been.

Benjamin, on the other hand, was extremely fear-ful. Charlie was his best friend, his only friend. Any-thing that happened to Charlie would, indirectly, happen to him. Sinister events were closing in on his friend. Benjamin sat by his bedroom window and watched Charlie's house. As darkness fell the street-lights came on and lights winked in the building behind the chestnut tree: in the basement, the attic, and all the bedrooms. What was going on?

The wind intensified. Thunder and lightning coincided. That meant that the storm was right above. Benjamin clung to Runner Bean, and the big dog hid his face in Benjamin's sleeve.

The street was now deserted except for three shadowy figures. On they came, a line of black umbrellas hiding all but the hems of three dark coats and six boots: four black and two red. In spite of the wind, there was a strange rhythm in their movements, almost as if a dance were taking place beneath those wide umbrellas. The figures stopped beside the chestnut tree, as Benjamin feared they would. And then they climbed the steps to Charlie's house.

For the first time in his life, Benjamin was glad to be himself and not Charlie Bone.

At number nine the table was set, and damp logs smoldered in the fireplace. When the doorbell rang, Charlie was sent to answer it. The three great-aunts swept into the house, stamping their feet on the tiled floor and shaking out their wet umbrellas. Their coats were hurled across the hall, landing on Charlie as if he were a coatstand.

"Pick them up, boy," commanded Aunt Lucretia, as Charlie scrambled beneath the wet garments. "They're valuable moleskin, not rags."

"Now, don't be harsh, Lucretia," said Aunt Eustacia. "Charlie's got a secret to tell us, haven't you, dear?"

"Um," mumbled Charlie.

"Don't be shy." Aunt Venetia, the youngest, came swaying up to him. "We want to know, *everything.*"

"Yewbeams, come in. Come in!" Grandma Bone called from the dining room.

The three sisters sailed through the door: Lucretia, the eldest, first, Venetia, the youngest, last. Snatching glasses of sherry from Grandma Bone, they gathered around the dwindling fire, shaking their damp skirts and patting their abundant hair. Lucretia's white as snow, Eustacia's iron-gray, Venetia's still black and folded around her head like raven's wings.

Charlie backed away and made for the kitchen where Maisie and his mother were busy around the stove.

"Take the soup in, will you, Charlie?" asked his mother.

Charlie didn't want to be alone with the great-aunts, but his mother looked hot and weary, so he did as she asked.

The soup tureen was very heavy. Charlie could feel the glint of Yewbeam eyes following him around the long dining room table. He put the tureen on a mat and ran to get the bowls before Grandma Bone could complain about the drop of soup that had spilled over.

When everything was ready, Grandma Bone rang a bell, which Charlie thought was rather silly. Everyone could see that the meal was on the table.

"Why do we need a bell?" he asked.

"Tradition," snapped Grandma Bone. "And Paton has no sense of smell."

"But Uncle Paton never eats with us."

"Today," said Grandma Bone emphatically, "he will."

"And there's an end to it," said Maisie with a grin, which soon faded when the four sisters glared at her.

Uncle Paton arrived looking irritated, and the meal began. Maisie had done her best, but ten minutes was rather short notice to create a meal of any distinction. The soup was salty, the chicken dry, and the pudding had a sad, drowned look. No one complained, however. They ate fast and heartily.

Maisie and Charlie's mother cleared the table. Paton and Charlie helped. And then it was time for the assessment. Charlie discovered that his mother was not allowed to be present. "I won't go in there without you!" he said. "I won't."

"Charlie, you must," said his mother. "The Yewbeams have a lot of money. I have nothing."

"It beats me why you want Charlie to go to that ridiculous academy," said Maisie.

"For his father's sake," said Charlie's mother.

Maisie clicked her tongue and said nothing more.

Charlie's father was dead, so why did it matter so much? His mother wouldn't tell him. She gave him a little push toward the dining room and in he went.

"I want my mom in here, or I won't do it," said Charlie.

"My, my, a boy who wants his mother," Aunt Venetia cooed.

"A boy who wants his mother is a baby," said Aunt Lucretia sternly. "Time to grow up, Charlie. This is a Yewbeam affair. We don't want distractions."

At this point Uncle Paton tried to slip away, but his oldest sister called him back. "Paton, you're needed. Do your duty, for once."

Uncle Paton reluctantly slid into the chair she indicated.

Charlie was made to sit on one side of the table, facing the four sisters; Uncle Paton sat at the end.

Charlie wondered how the assessment would be conducted. There appeared to be no musical instruments, no masks or paintbrushes on the table. He waited. They watched him.

"Where did he get that hair?" Aunt Lucretia asked.

"His mother's side," said Grandma Bone. "A Welshman." She spoke as if Charlie were not there.

"Ah!" The three great-aunts sighed, disapprovingly.

Aunt Lucretia was fumbling in a large leather bag. At last she drew out a brown paper package tied with black ribbon. She tugged the ribbon and the package fell open, revealing a pile of ancient-looking photographs.

Grandma Bone pushed the package over to Charlie, and the contents fanned out across the table.

"What am I supposed to do with these?" asked Charlie, who had a very good idea what they wanted him to do.

The great-aunts smiled encouragingly.

Charlie prayed that nothing would happen; that he could just glance at the dusty-looking collection and look away before he heard voices. But, one quick look told him that the people in the photographs were making a great deal of noise. They were playing instruments: cellos, pianos, violins. They were dancing, singing, laughing. Charlie pretended not to hear. He tried to push them away from him, toward Aunt Lucretia. She pushed them back.

"What do you hear, Charlie?" asked Grandma Bone.

"Nothing," said Charlie.

"Come on, Charlie, try," said Aunt Venetia.

"And don't lie," said Aunt Eustacia.

"Or we'll make you cry," snarled Aunt Lucretia.

That made Charlie angry. He wasn't going to cry for anyone. "I don't hear nothing," he said, shoving the photographs away.

"Anything," said Aunt Lucretia, shoving them back.

"You don't hear anything. Not nothing. Grammar, boy. Has no one taught you?"

"He clearly needs to attend the academy," said Aunt Eustacia.

"Just look at them, Charlie, dear," said Aunt Venetia sweetly. "Just for one minute, and if nothing happens, we'll leave you in peace and just . . ." she waved her long white fingers, "melt away."

"All right," Charlie said grudgingly.

He thought he could get away with it; just look at the photographs and block out the sounds. But it didn't work. The sounds of cellos, pianos, sopranos, and great gusts of laughter came bursting out at him, filling the room. The great-aunts were talking to him, he could see their thin lips working away, but he couldn't hear their words above the dreadful clamor of the photographs.

At last Charlie seized the pile and flung them, face down, onto the table. The sudden silence was a wonderful relief. The great-aunts stared at him, quietly triumphant.

It was Aunt Venetia who spoke first. "There, that wasn't so bad, was it, Charlie?"

Charlie realized he'd been tricked. He'd have to watch out for Aunt Venetia in the future. She was obviously more cunning than her sisters. "Who are all those people, anyway?" he asked miserably.

"Your ancestors, Charlie," said Aunt Lucretia.

"Yewbeam blood ran in all their veins. As it does in yours, dear clever boy." Her attitude had changed completely. But Aunt Lucretia being nice was just as scary as Aunt Lucretia being nasty.

"You can go now, Charlie," said Grandma Bone. "We have things to discuss. Arrangements to make for your future."

Charlie was only too glad to go. He leaped up and marched to the door. As he went he caught sight of Uncle Paton's face. He looked sad and far away, and

Charlie wondered why he hadn't said a word the whole time he'd been there. Paton gave Charlie a quick smile and then looked away.

Charlie hurried to the kitchen where Maisie and his mother were eagerly waiting for the results of his assessment.

"I think I've passed," he told them glumly.

"Well, I'll be," said Maisie. "I thought you'd get away with it, Charlie. Was it the voices?"

Charlie nodded miserably.

"Those crazy Yewbeams." Maisie shook her head.

Charlie's mother, however, was not so unhappy. "The academy will be good for you," she said.

"No, it won't," said Charlie. "I don't want to go. It's a boring old place for geniuses. I won't fit. It's halfway across the city and I don't know anyone there. Suppose I refuse to go, Mom?"

"If you refuse . . . all this could disappear," said his mother, waving in the general direction of the kitchen cabinets.

Charlie was astounded. Were his great-aunts

witches, then? Making houses disappear at the touch of a wand, or maybe an umbrella?

"Do you mean the house could disappear?" he asked.

"Not exactly," said his mother. "But our lives would change. Maisie and I have nothing. Not a bean. When your father, Lyell, died, we were at the mercy of the Yewbeams. They provide for everything. They bought the house, they pay the bills. I'm sorry, Charlie, you'll have to go to Bloor's if that's what they want."

Charlie felt very tired. "OK," he said. "And now I'm going to bed."

He had forgotten about the orange envelope, but when he got to his bedroom, there it was on his pillow. His mother must have rescued it from the piles of food and dishes on the kitchen table. Charlie decided not to take a second look at the man and his baby. He would take the photo straight back to Kwik Foto tomorrow and maybe get Runner Bean in exchange.

When his mother came up to say good night, Charlie made her sit on his bed and answer a few questions. He felt he deserved to know more about himself before he set foot in Bloor's Academy.

"First, I want to know what really happened to my father," Charlie said. "Tell me again."

"I've told you so many times already, Charlie. It was foggy, he was tired. He drove off the road and the car plunged into a quarry that was a hundred meters deep."

"And why aren't there any photos of him around? Not one."

A shadow passed across his mother's face. "There were," she said, "but one day, when I was out, they all disappeared. Even the tiny picture in my locket."

Charlie had never heard about this. "Why?" he asked.

At last his mother told him the truth about the Yewbeam family; how horrified they'd been when Lyell fell in love with her, Amy Jones, an ordinary girl with no exceptional talents. In a word, unendowed.

The Yewbeams forbade the marriage. Their laws

were ancient and strong. The women could marry whomever they chose, but every male with Yewbeam blood must marry an endowed girl. Lyell broke the rules. He and Amy Jones had eloped to Mexico.

"We had a wonderful honeymoon," sighed Charlie's mother. "But when we came home I knew that Lyell was worried. He hadn't escaped them after all. He was always looking over his shoulder, running from shadows. And then, one foggy night, when you were two years old, he got a phone call. A summons, really. Grandma Bone was ill, he had to go to her immediately. So he got in his car and . . . drove into a quarry." She gazed into the distance for a moment and murmured, "He wasn't himself that day. Something had happened. It was almost as if he were under a spell."

She wiped away a very small tear. "I don't think Grandma Bone has an ounce of love in her," she said. "As far as the Yewbeams were concerned, when Lyell died it was just the end of an unfortunate episode. But they were interested in you, Charlie. Suppose you turned out to be endowed? They realized they would have to take care of you until they found out. So they gave me a house and let Maisie move in. And then Grandma Bone arrived. To watch us. Uncle Paton came shortly after that, because . . . well, I suppose he didn't have anywhere else to go. I was grateful for everything, until the photos vanished. It was something I just couldn't understand. Grandma Bone denied having touched them, of course."

Charlie listened to his mother's story and put two and two together. "I know why the photos vanished," he murmured. "Grandma Bone didn't want me to hear what my father had to say."

But, Charlie, you were only two," said his mother. "She didn't know that you would have this funny gift for hearing voices."

"She guessed," said Charlie. "It's probably in the family."

His serious face made his mother smile. She kissed him good night and told him not to worry about the

Yewbeams. "And don't worry about Bloor's Academy either," she said. "After all, your father went there."

"And did he have a talent?" asked Charlie.

"Oh, yes," said his mother, from the door. "But not your sort of talent, Charlie. He wasn't endowed. He was a musician."

When she had gone, Charlie couldn't sleep. He had too much on his mind. It was unsettling to think he was part of such a peculiar family. He wanted to know more. Much more. But where to begin? Perhaps Uncle Paton could provide a few answers. He didn't seem as heartless as his sisters.

The storm blew itself out. The rain stopped. The wind died and the cathedral clock struck midnight. On the twelfth stroke, Charlie felt a sudden, strange breathlessness. Something was happening to him. It was as if he were passing through a moment when he might live or die. He thought of Lyell, the father he couldn't remember.

The moment passed and Charlie found himself

wide awake and restless. A few minutes later, he heard Uncle Paton creak downstairs and go to the kitchen for a snack. Charlie had grown used to his uncle's nighttime ramble. It always woke him up. Usually he would just turn over and go back to sleep. Tonight he jumped out of bed and got dressed.

When his uncle left the house, Charlie crept downstairs and followed him. He'd often wanted to do this but he'd never had the courage. Tonight was different; he felt confident and determined. Paton moved fast. By the time Charlie had closed the front door, very softly, behind him, his uncle was about to turn a corner. Keeping close to the houses, Charlie ran to the end of the street.

Paton paused and looked back. Charlie shrank into the shadows. The street they had turned onto was lit by small bell-shaped lamps that cast a soft glow on the wet cobblestones. Here, the trees grew closer, the walls were higher. It was a quiet and mysterious place.

Paton Yewbeam was on the move again, but now

his purposeful stride had become an aimless stroll. Soon, Charlie, hopping from tree to tree, found himself only a few paces behind his uncle.

A chill wind whistled near Charlie's ears and he began to wonder if his midnight stalking was going to come to anything. Uncle Paton hadn't turned into a vampire or a werewolf after all. Perhaps he just felt happier in the dark. Charlie was about to turn and creep back home when his uncle suddenly stopped. He was standing about a meter away from a lamppost and a strange sort of humming came from him. Not humming, exactly, because Charlie couldn't actually hear it. It was more like a feeling of humming, as though the air around his uncle were charged with soundless music.

The light in the lamp grew brighter, so bright that Charlie could hardly look at it, and then, with a little crack, the glass shattered and shining fragments fell to the ground.

Charlie gave a low gasp. He rubbed his eyes. Perhaps it was just coincidence. His uncle standing there, while a power surge made the light in the lamp too hot for the glass.

Paton moved on and Charlie followed, still hiding behind the trees. His uncle slowed down as he drew level with another lamppost, but this time, although the light became fierce and bright, Paton walked past before the glass could shatter. And then, without looking back, he said, "Why are you following me?"

THE FLAME CATS

Charlie froze. He couldn't believe his uncle had seen him. But then the question came again, "Charlie, why are you following me?"

Charlie walked out from behind a tree. "How did you know?" he asked in a whisper.

Paton turned to look at him. "I haven't got eyes in the back of my head, if that's what you're thinking."

"No, I didn't think that," said Charlie. "But how?"

"I saw you, dear boy, as I turned the corner. To tell the truth I was half expecting it. I don't suppose you could sleep after that dreadful evening." Paton gave a grim smile.

"Is that your talent, Uncle Paton?" Charlie asked. "Brightening the lights?"

"Pathetic isn't it? I ask you, what use is it? I wish you hadn't seen." Paton regarded his lean fingers. "Come on, let's get you home; I've done enough for tonight." He held Charlie's hand and they began to walk home.

Charlie saw a new side to his uncle. Not many people could boost a light just by being there. In fact, as far as he knew, no one had ever done such a thing before. Lights played a big part in the nightlife of a city. Uncle Paton could have a wild time downtown, where lights winked and glittered on every surface.

"Have you ever — you know — done what you just did to lots of lights?" asked Charlie. "Like in a place where all the theaters and movies and clubs are?"

For a moment Charlie thought that Paton wasn't going to reply. Perhaps he shouldn't have asked. And then his uncle murmured, "Once, long ago, I did it for a girl I knew."

"Wow! Was she impressed?"

"She ran away," said Paton sadly, "and never spoke to me again."

"I see. Wouldn't it be safer if you went out in the daytime, Uncle Paton? I mean, there aren't as many lights on."

"Huh! You must be joking," said his uncle. "Every shop window has a light in it. There are lights everywhere. And people can see me in the daylight. Besides, it's become a habit. I just don't like daylight and won't be caught in it."

They had reached number nine, and Charlie hurried back to bed before anyone else in the house woke up. He fell asleep almost at once and dreamed that Uncle Paton had turned up the light in every star, until they all exploded, like fireworks.

In the morning, Charlie woke up with a nasty sinking feeling. Whether he liked it or not, he would soon be going to Bloor's Academy. Just thinking about it made him feel ill. He could only manage one slice of toast for breakfast. The eggs and bacon Maisie put in front of him were left untouched.

"He's worried, aren't you, love?" clucked Maisie. "Those miserable Yewbeams. Why should you go to that nasty big school? We'll get you some chocolate at the shops. That'll cheer you up."

Grandma Bone was not present. She always had breakfast in her room. And Paton only ate at night, as far as Charlie knew.

He glanced at his mother, who was miles away in some kind of reverie. "Will I have to wear a special uniform?" he asked.

His mother looked up with a start. "A blue cape," she said. "The musicians wear blue. Sapphire, a lovely color."

"But I'm not a musician," said Charlie.

"Not strictly speaking," his mother agreed. "But they won't have a department for your talent, Charlie. You'll be put into music, like your father. Take your school recorder. I'm sure that will do."

"Will it?" Charlie was doubtful. He'd never been good at music and only played his recorder when he was forced to. "When will I have to start?"

"After this semester," his mother told him.

"So soon?" Charlie was horrified. "In the middle of the year? Before Christmas?"

"I'm sorry, Charlie," his mother said regretfully. "The Yewbeams think it would be best. They say there's not a moment to be lost, now that you . . . now that they are certain."

"Poor little guy," Maisie muttered.

It had begun to rain again and Maisie pulled on a bright pink raincoat. Charlie's mother took an umbrella from the closet. She didn't like wearing raincoats.

"We won't be long at the shops," she told Charlie. "Do you want me to take that photograph back?"

Charlie had almost forgotten Benjamin's birthday card. For some reason he was reluctant to lose the photo just yet.

"No," he said. "But could you buy a birthday card for Benjamin? I don't think I'll be using Runner Bean after all."

When Maisie and his mother had gone, Charlie ran upstairs to get the orange envelope. He had just opened it and had pulled out the photo when the doorbell rang. No one answered it. Grandma Bone was out, apparently, and Uncle Paton wouldn't even answer the telephone during the day.

Still holding the photograph, Charlie went down to open the door.

A very strange man stood on the step. Stranger still

were the three cats, winding themselves around his legs.

"Onimous and Flames," said the man. "Pest control." He produced a card from the inside pocket of a furry-looking coat.

"Ominous?" asked Charlie.

"Not at all," said the man. "Onimous. Quite different. Orvil. Orvil Onimous." He gave Charlie a big smile, revealing sharp, bright teeth. "I believe you have a problem here. Mice?" He gave a funny sort of leap and landed beside Charlie.

"I don't know," said Charlie. He'd been told never to let a stranger into the house. But this one was in already. "Did someone send for you?"

"Something did. I can't tell you what it was, just yet. You might not believe me."

"Really?" Charlie was intrigued.

The cats had followed Mr. Onimous and were now prowling around the hall. They were most unusual-looking cats. The first was a deep copper color, the second a bright orange, and the third a fierce yellow. The copper cat seemed to know Charlie. It stood on its hind legs and rattled the kitchen doorknob.

"Have patience, Aries," said Mr. Onimous. "Will you never learn?"

Aries had managed to turn the knob. The kitchen door swung open and he ran inside, followed by the other two cats.

"Sorry about this," said Mr. Onimous. "He's an impulsive fellow, is Aries. Leo's a bit pushy too, but Sagittarius has lovely manners. Excuse me, I'd better keep an eye on them."

Before Charlie had time to turn around, Mr. Onimous had slipped past him and hopped into the kitchen, calling, "Flames, don't let me down. Do it nicely."

All three cats were now pacing before the pantry. Charlie remembered the rotting fruit, and before the cats could break through another door, he opened it and let them in.

A fierce pouncing, leaping, and screaming began. The pantry was apparently full of mice. Not for long.

The cats caught one mouse after another, depositing their bodies in a neat line along the wall.

Charlie backed away. He hadn't known there were any mice at all in the pantry. Why hadn't Maisie or his mother noticed? Perhaps they had all arrived this morning, drawn by the smell of old fruit. Charlie was rather fond of mice and wished he didn't have to watch the row of little gray bodies grow longer and longer.

When the line was fifteen mice long, the cats appeared to have finished the job. They sat down and vigorously washed their immaculate fur.

"How about a cup of coffee?" asked Mr. Onimous. "I feel quite exhausted."

As far as Charlie could tell, Mr. Onimous had hardly lifted a finger, let alone done anything exhausting. The cats had done all the work. But Mr. Onimous was now sitting at the kitchen table, looking eagerly at the kettle, and Charlie didn't have the heart to disappoint him. He was still holding the photograph, so he put it down and went to fill the kettle.

"Ah," said Mr. Onimous. "Here we have it. This explains everything."

"What does?" Charlie looked at the photograph that Mr. Onimous was now holding up to the light.

Mr. Onimous pointed to the cat at the bottom of the photograph. "That's Aries," he said. "It was quite a few years ago, but he doesn't forget. He knew you'd spotted him. That's why he led me here."

"Pardon?" Charlie felt weak. He sat down. "Are you saying that Aries," he pointed at the copper-colored cat, "Aries knew I'd seen his photo?"

"It wasn't quite like that." Mr. Onimous scratched his furry-looking head. His pointed nails were in need of a good cut, Charlie noticed. Maisie would never have let anyone get away with nails as long as that.

The kettle boiled and Charlie made Mr. Onimous his coffee. "What was it like, then?" he asked, putting the cup before his visitor.

"Three sugars, please," said Mr. Onimous.

Charlie impatiently tossed three spoonfuls of sugar into the coffee.

Mr. Onimous beamed. He took a sip, beamed again, and then, leaning close to Charlie, he said, "He knew you were connected, Aries did. And so you are; you have the photograph. These cats aren't ordinary. They know things. They chose me because I've got a special way with animals. They lead me here and there, trying to undo mischief, and I just follow, helping where I can. This case," his finger came down on the man holding the baby, "this is one of the worst. Aries has always been very angry about it. Time and again he's tried to put it right, but we needed you, Charlie."

"Me?" asked Charlie.

"You're one of the endowed, aren't you?" Mr. Onimous spoke softly, as if it were a secret, not to be spoken out loud.

"They say so," said Charlie. He couldn't help but look at the photograph, with Mr. Onimous' finger stuck so accusingly on the man's face. And as soon as he looked, he began to hear the baby crying.

Aries ran over to him and, placing his paws on Charlie's knees, let forth an earsplitting yowl. His cry was immediately taken up by orange Leo and yellow Sagittarius. The noise was so painful, Charlie had to press his hands over his ears.

"Hush!" commanded Mr. Onimous. "The boy's thinking."

When the yowling had died down, Mr. Onimous said, "You see. You are connected, Charlie. Now tell me all about it."

Although decidedly odd, Mr. Onimous looked kind and trustworthy, and Charlie was badly in need of help. He told Mr. Onimous about the mix-up with the photographs, the voices, the horrible Yewbeam aunts and their assessment, and their decision to send him to Bloor's Academy. "And I really don't want to go there," finished Charlie. "I think I'd almost rather die."

"But, Charlie boy, that's where she is," said Mr. Onimous, "the lost baby. At least, that's what the cats seem to think. And they're never wrong." He stood up. "Come on, cats, we've got to go."

"You mean the baby in the photograph was lost?" asked Charlie. "How can you lose a baby?"

"It's not for me to say," said Mr. Onimous. "You take that photo where it belongs, and perhaps they'll tell you."

"But I don't know where it belongs," said Charlie, beginning to panic. Mr. Onimous was slipping away without helping at all.

"Use your head, Charlie. That's an enlargement, isn't it? Find the original and you'll find a name and address."

"Will I?"

"Without a doubt." Mr. Onimous smoothed the pile on his coat, turned up his collar, and made for the front door.

Charlie stood up, uncertainly, questions bubbling in his head. By the time he reached the open door, all that could be seen of his visitor was a small disappearing figure, followed by a flash of hot colors, like the bright tail of a comet.

Charlie closed the door and ran upstairs. Seizing the orange envelope, he shook it fiercely and out fell a small photograph—the original of the enlargement downstairs. He turned it over and there, sure enough, was a name and an address, written in bold, flowing letters:

Miss Julia Ingledew
3 Cathedral Close

Where was Cathedral Close, and how was he to get there? He would have to leave the house before Maisie and his mother got home. They would never agree to his roaming off on his own, to a place he didn't know. And if he didn't act now, he might not get back in time for Benjamin's party. But he'd have to leave a message, or his mother would worry.

As far as he could remember, Charlie had never been inside his uncle's room before. A DO NOT DISTURB sign hung permanently on the door. Recently, Charlie had begun to wonder what Paton did inside all day. Sometimes a soft tapping could be heard. Usually there was silence.

Today, Charlie would have to ignore the sign.

He knocked on the door, hesitantly at first, and then more vigorously.

"What?" said an angry voice.

"Uncle Paton, can I come in?" asked Charlie.

"Why?" asked Paton.

"Because I have to find somewhere, and I want you to explain to Mom."

There was a deep sigh. Charlie didn't dare open the door until his uncle said coldly, "Come in, then, if you must."

Charlie turned the doorknob and peered inside. He was surprised by what he saw. His uncle's room was overflowing with paper. It hung from shelves, dripped from piles on the windowsill, covered Paton's desk, and lapped like a tide around his ankles. Where was the bed? Under a blanket of books, Charlie guessed. Books lined the walls, from floor to ceiling, they even climbed around the desk in teetering towers.

"Well?" asked Paton, glancing up from a mound of paper.

"Please can you tell me where Cathedral Close is?" Charlie asked nervously.

"Where do you think? Beside the cathedral, of course." Paton was a different person in daylight — chilly and forbidding.

"Oh," said Charlie, feeling foolish. "Well, I'm going there now. But could you tell Mom? She'll want to know, and . . ."

"Yes, yes," murmured Paton, and with a vague wave, he motioned Charlie away.

"Thanks," said Charlie, closing the door as quietly as he could.

He went to his room, hurriedly pulled on his jacket, and tucked the photos, in their orange envelope, into his pocket. Then he left the house.

From his bedroom window, Benjamin saw Charlie walking past with a determined expression.

Benjamin opened his window and called, "Where are you going?"

Charlie looked up. "To the cathedral," he said.

"Can me and Runner Bean come?" asked Benjamin.

"No," said Charlie. "I'm going to get your present, and it's got to be a surprise."

Benjamin closed the window. He wondered what sort of present Charlie could buy in a cathedral. A pen with the cathedral's name on it? Benjamin had plenty of pens.

"Still, I don't really mind," he told Runner Bean. "As long as he comes to my party."

Runner Bean thumped his tail on Benjamin's pillow. He was lying where he wasn't supposed to, on Benjamin's bed. Luckily, no one but Benjamin knew about it.

The cathedral was in the old part of the city. Here the streets were cobbled and narrow. The shops were smaller, and in their softly lit windows, expensive clothes and jewelry lay on folds of silk and velvet. It seemed like a very private place, and Charlie felt almost as though he were trespassing.

As the ancient cathedral began to loom above him, the shops gave way to a row of older houses. Number Three Cathedral Close, however, was a bookshop.

Above the door a sign in olde worlde script, read INGLEDEW'S. The books displayed in the window were aged and dusty looking. Some were bound in leather, their leaves edged in gold.

Charlie took a deep breath and went in. A bell tinkled as he stepped down into the shop, and a woman appeared through a curtained space behind the counter. She wasn't as old as Charlie expected, but about the same age as his mother. She had thick chestnut hair piled up on her head, and kind brown eyes.

"Yes?" asked the woman. "Can I help you?"

"I think so," said Charlie. "Are you Julia Ingledew?"

"Yes." She nodded.

"I've come about your photograph," said Charlie.

The woman's hand flew to her mouth. "Goodness!" she said. "Have you found it?"

"I think so," said Charlie, handing over the orange envelope.

The woman opened the envelope and the two photos fell onto her desk. "Oh, thank you," she said. "I can't tell you how glad I am to have these."

"Have you got mine?" asked Charlie. "My name's Charlie Bone."

"Come through," said Miss Ingledew, motioning Charlie to follow her through the curtain.

Charlie walked cautiously around the counter and through the curtain in the wall of books. He found himself in a room not unlike the shop. All books again, packed tight on shelves or laying in piles on every surface. It was a cozy room; for all that; it smelled of warm, rich words and very deep thoughts. A fire burned in a small iron grate and table lamps glowed through parchment-colored shades.

"Here we are," said Julia Ingledew, and from a drawer she produced an orange envelope.

Charlie took the envelope and opened it quickly. "Yes, it's Runner Bean," he said. "My friend's dog. I'm going to make a birthday card with it."

"A lovely idea," said Miss Ingledew. "More personal. I always like personal. It shows one cares, doesn't it?"

"Yes," said Charlie uncertainly.

"Well, I'm very grateful to you, Charlie Bone," she

said. "I feel you should have a reward of some sort. I haven't got much cash about, but I wonder..."

"It doesn't matter," said Charlie, a little embarrassed, though he could have used a little money to buy Benjamin's present.

"No, no, really. I think you're just the person. In fact I feel that these have been waiting just for you." She pointed to a corner and Charlie saw that his first impression of the room had been mistaken. It was not filled entirely with books. A table in one corner was piled high with boxes: wooden boxes, metal boxes, and big cardboard cartons.

"What's in those?" asked Charlie.

"My brother-in-law's effects," she said. "All that is left of him. He died last week."

Charlie felt a lump rising in his throat. He said, "Um..."

"Oh, dear. No, not his ashes, Charlie," said Miss Ingledew. "They're his—what shall I call them—inventions. They only arrived yesterday. He sent them by courier the day before he died. Goodness knows why he left them to me." She got one of the boxes, removed the lid, and took out a metal robotic-looking dog. "It's no good to me," she said. "Do you want it?"

Charlie thought of Runner Bean, and then of Benjamin. "Does it do anything?" he asked. Because inventions usually did something.

"Of course. Let me see." She pulled down the dog's tail. It barked twice, and a voice said, "I am number two. You have already pulled my tail, so you know how to make me play. To fast-forward press my left ear. To rewind press my right ear. To record press my nose. To stop pull my right foot up. To replace tapes open my stomach." The voice that gave these instructions was familiar to Charlie.

"Any use to you?" asked Miss Ingledew. "Or would you like to see the others?"

"It's perfect," said Charlie. "Brilliant. But the voice, is it your...?"

"Yes. My brother-in-law, Dr. Tolly. The device was one of his earliest, but he never bothered to sell it. Once a thing was made, that was it. He was a lazy man, Charlie. Clever, but lazy."

"It's him in the photo, isn't it?" Charlie didn't mention that he'd recognized the voice. How could he?

"Yes, that's Dr. Tolly. He did something terrible once." Miss Ingledew's mouth closed in a grim line.

"Why did you want his photo, then?" asked Charlie.

The bookseller darted him a quick look, as if she were sizing him up. "It's the baby I want," she said at last. "It's all I have to remember her by." And suddenly Miss Ingledew was telling Charlie about the dreadful day when her sister Nancy died, just before her daughter's second birthday, and how a few days later, Nancy's husband, Dr. Tolly, had given his daughter away.

"I didn't think you could give children away," said Charlie, horrified.

"You can't," said Miss Ingledew. "I was sworn to secrecy. I should have taken her, you see. But I was selfish and irresponsible. I didn't think I could cope. Not one day has passed, since then, when I haven't regretted my decision. I tried to find out whom she'd been given to, where she had gone, but Dr. Tolly would never tell me. She was lost in a system of lies and tricks and forgery. She'd be ten years old now, and I'd give anything to get her back."

Charlie felt very uncomfortable. He was being drawn into a situation he didn't much like. If only he hadn't heard the voices in the photograph. How could he possibly tell Miss Ingledew that three cats thought the lost baby was at Bloor's Academy. She would never believe him.

In a shadowy corner, a grandfather clock struck twelve and Charlie said, "I think I'd better go home now. Mom'll be worried."

"Of course. But take the dog, Charlie, and"— she suddenly darted to the table and withdrew a long silver case from the bottom of a pile—"will you take this one as well?"

She didn't wait for an answer, but plunged it into a bag marked INGLEDEW'S BOOKS. Handing the bag to

Charlie, she said, "You can put the dog in as well, there's just enough room."

The bag was unbelievably heavy. Charlie carefully placed the dog, in its box, on top of the metal case. Then he stumbled to the door, wondering how on earth he would manage to heave the bag all the way home.

Julia Ingledew helped him up the step and opened the shop door, which gave another melodious ring.

"I hope you don't mind my asking," said Charlie, "but what's in the case?"

The answer was rather surprising. "I don't know," said Miss Ingledew. "And I'm not sure I want to. Dr. Tolly exchanged it for his baby. Whatever it is, it can't be worth as much as a baby, can it?"

"N-no," said Charlie. He put the bag on the ground.

"Please take it, Charlie. You look like just the right person. I've got to get it out of the house, you see." She lowered her voice and darted a quick look down the street. "And can I ask you to keep it a secret, for now?"

"That's a bit difficult," said Charlie, even more reluctant to take the strange case. "Can't I even tell my best friend?"

"Tell no one who you wouldn't trust with your life," said Miss Ingledew.

THE INVENTOR'S CASE

Before Charlie could think of anything to say, the bookseller gave him a brief wave and then closed her door. He was alone in the shadowy street with something that had been exchanged for a baby.

Why hadn't Miss Ingledew opened the case? What could be inside? Charlie began to talk to himself as he struggled over the cobblestones and several people glanced at him suspiciously. Perhaps they thought he had stolen the bag. He turned a sharp corner and nearly fell over a big, shaggy dog.

"Look out!" cried Charlie, dropping the bag. "Runner Bean, it's you!"

Runner Bean jumped on the bag and licked Charlie's face.

"Get off!" said Charlie. "That's valuable."

Benjamin came hurrying up to them. "Sorry," he panted. "I couldn't stop him."

"Were you following me?" asked Charlie, who was quite pleased to see Benjamin.

"Not really. I was just taking Runner for a walk. I think he must have got your scent." Benjamin stared at the impressive black bag. "What's in there?"

"Your birthday present," said Charlie, "but you'll have to help me carry the bag. It weighs a ton."

"Wow. What? No I mustn't ask," said Benjamin shyly.

Charlie had to confess that there was a mysterious something else in the bag, but after a quick peek, Benjamin said he didn't mind at all that he was going to get the small cardboard box, instead of the large metal case.

"It's a funny place to come for a present," Benjamin remarked, with a backward glance at the looming cathedral.

"I didn't know I would find one," said Charlie. "I came here to look for Runner Bean's photo." He told Benjamin about the strange lady bookseller and the mysterious case the lazy inventor had sent her.

Taking a handle each, the boys began to carry the black bag home. They didn't notice that they were being followed. If they had looked behind them, they might have seen that a weasely red-haired boy, badly disguised as an old man, was hiding in doorways and then creeping up on them.

Runner Bean growled softly and nudged the bag, trying to hurry the boys. It was very troubling to the dog. There was something behind him and something in the bag that weren't right.

As Charlie and Benjamin turned onto Filbert Street, Runner Bean whirled around and ran toward the stalker, barking furiously. The red-haired boy jumped away from him and fled up the street.

"What was that all about?" asked Benjamin as the dog came bounding back.

Runner Bean couldn't explain.

When they reached Benjamin's house, Charlie asked his friend if he would take the bag inside with him. He didn't want Maisie or Grandma Bone poking their noses into it.

Benjamin looked dubious. "I don't know. Where will I put it?"

"Under the bed or something. Please, Benjamin. My grandmas are always in my room, but no one seems to hassle you."

"OK," he said.

"Don't open your present until I come back," he told Benjamin. "I'd better go home now, or there'll be trouble."

Charlie was about to turn away when he heard a hollow knocking from inside the bag. Benjamin looked up, rather scared, but Charlie pretended he hadn't heard and ran down the steps. He walked into the kitchen where his two grandmothers were arguing fiercely. When Charlie appeared they glared at him.

"Charlie Bone!" screamed Maisie. "How could you? You awful boy. How did this happen?" She pointed at the row of dead mice. Charlie had completely forgotten about them.

He explained how Mr. Onimous and the cats had leaped into the house before he could stop them. "And then I had to rush out and exchange the photo," he waved the orange envelope. "I'm sorry I forgot about the mice."

"Yellow cats, orange cats?" said Grandma Bone, with a catch in her voice. Charlie could have sworn that she was afraid.

"Well, I suppose they did a good job," said Maisie, beginning to forgive Charlie. "I'd better clean this up."

Grandma Bone was not in a forgiving mood. "I knew it," she muttered angrily. "You brought them here, you wretched boy. You're like a magnet. Bad blood mixed with endowed. It never works. I won't rest easy until you're shut up in Bloor's."

"Shut up? You mean I won't be coming out?"

"Weekends," snapped Grandma Bone. "Unfortunately."

Out she swept, her black boots rapping on the floor like drumsticks.

"I didn't know that I would be shut up," cried Charlie.

"Nor did I, love," puffed Maisie, busily disinfecting

the floor. "What do I know of these fancy schools? Your mother shouldn't bring home so much produce. Beats me how the pest control knew about it. I never told them."

"The cats," said Charlie. "They knew."

"You'll be telling me next that cats can fly," muttered Maisie.

Perhaps those cats can, thought Charlie. Aries, Leo, and Sagittarius were not ordinary cats, that was for sure. And Charlie had a suspicion that Grandma Bone knew this. But why was she afraid of them?

He went to his room to make the birthday card. But he found it hard to concentrate. The card went crooked, he left the "h" out of "birthday," and then the speech balloon slipped over Runner Bean's ear. Charlie flung down the scissors. Ever since he'd discovered he could hear photographs, his world had been turned upside down. If only he'd been able to keep quiet about the voices, he wouldn't have had to go to a horrible school where he'd be imprisoned for weeks at a time, with a lot of weird children who did peculiar things.

He heard his mother come in and call to Maisie. If only she would take his side and fight the Yewbeams. But she seemed to be afraid of them. Somehow, Charlie would have to fight them himself.

Maisie had cooked vegetable spaghetti for lunch. Charlie wondered about the mice in the pantry, but kept his thoughts to himself. His mother had bought him a sapphire blue cape, which she made him try on as soon as the spaghetti was finished. The cape reached almost to Charlie's knees. It had slits at the sides for his arms and a soft hood that hung down the back.

"I'm not going to wear a cape in the street," said Charlie, "and that's final. Everyone'll laugh at me."

"But Charlie, there'll be other children wearing them," said his mother. "And some will be in purple or green."

"Not in our part of town," said Charlie, pulling off the cape. "They'll all be from the Heights."

The Heights sprawled up the side of a wooded hill that looked down on the city. The houses were tall and grand and the people in them lacked for nothing. The large gardens were full of flowers that seemed to bloom all year.

"I know for a fact that not every child will come from the Heights," said Charlie's mother. "There's a girl just two streets away, Olivia Vertigo, she was in the papers. She'll be in drama, so you'll see her in a purple cape."

"Hmh!" muttered Charlie "If you mean Dragon Street, that's just as smart as the Heights." He decided he'd tuck the cape under his jacket until he got to the academy.

Even Maisie was beginning to give in. "It's really cute," she said of the blue cape. "Such a nice color."

Charlie grudgingly took the cape up to his room and stuffed it in a drawer. (Later his mother would come up and carefully hang it in the closet.) Then he put Benjamin's birthday card in the orange envelope and ran downstairs. "I'm going to Benjamin's birthday party now," he called to his mother.

Runner Bean greeted him with a loud barking. He wouldn't even let Charlie through the front door.

"What's the matter with Runner?" he shouted as Benjamin came bounding down the stairs.

"It's that case you left," said Benjamin. "He hates it. I pushed it under the bed like you said, but Runner growled and snarled and tried to pull it out again. He's chewed up the bag and scratched the lid with his claws."

Charlie managed to squeeze past the door while Benjamin hauled Runner Bean away. Finally, the dog gave a great howl, ran down the hall, and banged through his doggie-door into the back garden.

Now that Charlie had arrived, Benjamin wanted to open his present. He ran upstairs to get it.

There was absolutely no sign that a party was about to take place. Benjamin's parents worked every day of the week and Saturdays as well. Charlie wished he'd asked Maisie to make a cake for his friend, but he'd had too much on his mind.

"It looks really exciting," said Benjamin, shaking the box. "Come on, let's go into the living room."

No sign of a party here either.

Benjamin sat on the floor and opened the box. "Wow! A dog!" he said.

Charlie pulled the dog's tail and Dr. Tolly's voice rapped out the instructions.

Benjamin was so excited he could hardly speak. At last he managed to say, "Thanks, Charlie. Thanks. Wow, thanks!"

"I should have gotten you a new tape," said Charlie, "then you'd have..."

He was interrupted by Runner Bean, who tore into the room barking madly. He paced around the metal dog, glaring at it, and then he began to whine.

"He's jealous," said Benjamin. "That's all." He flung his arms around Runner Bean, saying, "I love you, Runner. You know I do. I couldn't live without you."

The big dog licked Benjamin's face. He was everything to Benjamin: mother, father, brother, and grandparent. He was always there when Benjamin's parents were out. And the boy could go anywhere, at any time of day or night. As long as Runner Bean was with him, he was safe.

Charlie gave Benjamin the birthday card. "I made it after all," he said.

Benjamin didn't notice any of Charlie's mistakes. Gazing at the picture, he told Charlie it was the best card he'd ever had in his life. And then Runner Bean looked up at the ceiling and howled.

Tap! Tap! Tap! The sound was faint but definite. Benjamin's room was right above them.

"It's that metal case," said Benjamin. "I wish you'd take it away. There could be a bomb in it, or something."

"Miss Ingledew didn't look like a terrorist," said Charlie. "Nor did Dr. Tolly."

"How do you know?" said Benjamin. "Terrorists are good at disguises. Let's go and have a look."

Runner Bean followed the boys upstairs, growling softly. This time he wouldn't even come into the bedroom.

Charlie pulled the bag from under the bed and, together, the boys drew out the metal case. The tapping had stopped. Charlie undid the clasps on either side of the handle, but the case wouldn't open. It was locked, and the key was missing.

"Didn't that woman tell you what was inside?" asked Benjamin.

Charlie shook his head. "She said she didn't want to know. Whatever it is, it was swapped for a baby. Her very own niece."

"A baby?" Benjamin's mouth dropped open. "That's terrible."

Charlie was beginning to feel guilty. "We'll put it in the closet under the stairs," he said. "You won't hear it there. And then I'll go back to Miss Ingledew and ask her for the key."

They dragged the bag downstairs and hid it behind a pile of old clothes that Benjamin's mother had dumped in the closet. When they'd closed the door, Runner Bean stood beside the stairs howling mournfully. Benjamin could only stop him by saying "Do you want out!?" very loudly.

It was getting dark but there was still no sign of Benjamin's parents. Benjamin seemed more resigned than upset. "I'll make my own cake," he said. And he did. It was a chocolate cake and he stuck ten candles in the top, and then he and Charlie sang "Happy Birthday." The cake was a bit crumbly but very good.

It was half past seven when Charlie looked at his watch. He knew he should be going home, but he didn't want to leave Benjamin alone, not on his birthday. So he stayed another hour, and they played hide-and-seek with Runner Bean, who was brilliant at it.

At half past eight, Benjamin's parents still hadn't come home, so Charlie decided to take his friend back for one of Maisie's hot meals. There was only one egg and a pint of milk left in Benjamin's fridge.

"How was the party?" asked Maisie, when two boys and a dog walked in.

"Great," said Charlie, "but we're still a bit hungry."

"There was a peculiar boy around here a couple of

hours ago," said Maisie. "He was pretending to be an old man but anyone could see he was a boy. He said you'd got some case of his mixed up in the wrong bag and he wanted it back. Well, I looked in your room but all I could find was a bag of shoes. The boy was very put out. He wouldn't believe me. A nasty piece of work, he was. Now you two run off, while I get some food on the table."

Outside the kitchen door, Charlie whispered, "Don't tell anyone about the bag, and especially not the case."

"Why not?" asked Benjamin.

"Because it was given to me and I feel sort of responsible," said Charlie. "I think we should keep it safe until we know more about it." He decided not to tell Benjamin about Mr. Onimous and his cats, just yet.

At that moment Grandma Bone appeared at the top of the stairs. "What's that dog doing here?" she asked, glaring at Runner Bean.

"It's Benjamin's birthday," said Charlie.

"So?" she asked coldly.

Runner Bean barked up at her and before she

could say anything more, Charlie dragged Benjamin back into the kitchen.

"Grandma Bone's in a mood," Charlie told Maisie.

"Isn't she always?" asked Maisie. "She'll calm down once you're at Bloor's."

Charlie hadn't wanted to break this news to Benjamin on his birthday, but now it was out and Charlie felt like a traitor.

Benjamin stared at him accusingly. "What's Bloor's?" he asked.

"It's a big school near the Heights," Charlie explained. "I don't want to go there, Ben."

"Then don't."

"He has to, dear. His mom's bought the uniform," said Maisie. She put two plates of baked beans and sausages on the kitchen table. "Now come and eat. It may be your birthday, but you look half-starved, Benjamin Brown."

Benjamin sat down, but he had lost his appetite. He slipped a sausage to Runner Bean when Maisie wasn't looking.

"I won't be going until after the semester," Charlie told his friend.

"Oh." Benjamin stared at his plate, unsmiling.

Unfortunately, Charlie's mother chose that moment to walk in with Charlie's pajamas. "No more patched pajamas for you, Charlie," she said. "The Yewbeams are providing a whole new set of clothes for the academy."

"Pajamas?" Benjamin looked up. "Are you going to sleep there?"

"I'll be back on the weekends," said Charlie.

"Oh." Benjamin shoveled a few beans into his mouth and then stood up. "I'd better go home now. Mom and Dad'll be back."

"Shall I come . . . ?" Charlie began.

"No. It's OK. I've got Runner."

Before Charlie could say another word, Benjamin and Runner Bean walked out. The dog's tail and ears drooped dejectedly, always a sign that his master was in low spirits.

"Funny boy," Maisie remarked.

"I think I ought to see if he's OK," said Charlie. "After all, it is his birthday."

But when he opened the front door, he was just in time to see Uncle Paton walking away from the house. And this gave Charlie an idea.

"Uncle Paton, can I come with you?" called Charlie, racing after his uncle.

"Why?" Paton had stopped to put a large bundle of letters into the mailbox.

"Because . . . because . . ." Charlie caught up with his uncle. "Well, I wanted to ask you to come somewhere with me."

"And where is that?"

"To a bookshop. It's near the cathedral, and I don't want to go there on my own—it's a bit spooky."

"A bookshop?" Paton was interested, as Charlie hoped he would be. "But, Charlie, even a bookshop will be closed at this time of night."

"Yes, but I think there will be someone in this shop, even if it's closed," said Charlie and he found himself telling his uncle about Miss Ingledew and the locked case. After all, he had to trust someone, and instinct told him that Paton was on his side, even if he was a Yewbeam.

A mysterious gleam had entered Paton's dark eyes. "So you want this lady bookseller to give you a key? Tell me, Charlie, where is the case?"

Charlie hesitated. "I don't want anyone to know," he said. "Someone's already come looking for it. But if you really. . ."

Paton held up his hand. "You're wise to keep it a secret, Charlie. Only tell me when you feel the time is right. Now, let's go find this bookshop."

They traveled through narrow side streets, where Paton's talent for boosting the lights wasn't so conspicuous. As they entered the deserted streets near the cathedral, lamps flickered rhythmically, now bright, now dim, as if they were part of a magical display.

A CLOSED sign hung behind a glass panel in Ingledew's door, but there was a low light in the window, illuminating the antique leather-bound books.

Paton gazed at them, hungrily. "I ought to get out more," he murmured.

Charlie pressed the bell.

A distant voice said, "We're closed. Go away."

"It's me, Charlie Bone," said Charlie. "Could I see you for a moment, Miss Ingledew?"

"Charlie?" Miss Ingledew sounded surprised, but not too angry. "It's rather late."

"It's urgent, Miss Ingledew—about the case."

"Oh?" Her face appeared at the small glass panel in the door. "Wait a minute, Charlie."

The light in the shop went on. A chain clanked, bolts slid back, and the door opened with a familiar tinkle.

Charlie stepped down into the shop, followed closely by his uncle.

"Oh!" gasped Miss Ingledew, retreating. "Who is this?"

"My uncle, Paton," said Charlie and, looking at his uncle, realized why Miss Ingledew seemed a little put out. Paton was very tall and very dark, and in his long black coat he did look rather sinister.

"I do hope I haven't alarmed you," said Paton extending his hand. "Paton Yewbeam at your service."

Miss Ingledew took the hand, saying nervously, "Julia Ingledew."

"Julia," repeated Paton. "Lovely. My nephew asked me to accompany him."

Charlie couldn't decide whether his uncle sounded pompous or shy. Perhaps a bit of both. "I've come about the key, Miss Ingledew," he said. "The key to that case you gave me."

"Key? Key?" She seemed confused. "Oh, I think they came with the, er... I'll have a look. You'd better come through to my, er... Or people will think we're open again." She gave a flustered laugh and disappeared through the curtains behind the counter.

Charlie and his uncle followed. The little room behind the bookshop glowed with mellow colors, and Paton's eyes roamed excitedly over the rows of books.

Miss Ingledew had obviously been reading when they arrived, for a large book lay open on her desk.

"The Incas," observed Paton, reading the chapter heading. "A fascinating subject."

"Yes," said Miss Ingledew, still agitated. She had found a small tin of keys that she proceeded to empty onto the desk. Most of the keys had labels attached to them, but some did not. "How am I to tell?" she asked. "There are so many. Charlie, I think you'd better take all the keys that aren't marked and see which one fits. I'm afraid that's all I can suggest."

"All that could be expected," said Paton.

Miss Ingledew frowned at him, put a pile of keys in a plastic bag, and handed them to Charlie. "There. Bring them back when you've tried them," she said.

"Thanks, Miss Ingledew." Charlie took the keys and, as there seemed to be nothing left to say, or do, he led the way back through the curtains.

Miss Ingledew came after them to bolt and lock the door, but as Charlie and his uncle stepped into the street, Paton suddenly asked, "May I call again, Miss Ingledew?"

"Of course," said Miss Ingledew, taken aback. "It's a shop. I can hardly stop you."

"No." Paton smiled. "But, after dark?"

Miss Ingledew looked rather alarmed. "On Fridays, I'm open until eight," she said, and closed the door.

For a moment Paton stared at the door as if he were transfixed, and then he turned, suddenly, exclaiming, "What a very charming woman." And his intense humming caused the nearest lamp to burn so fiercely, a fine shower of glass fell out. It landed on the cobbled street with a soft, musical tinkle.

TRAPPED IN THE DARK

"Uncle Paton, you're a vandal!" said Charlie.

A rich, throaty chuckle echoed down the narrow street. Charlie had hardly ever heard his uncle laugh before.

"Someone's going to get blamed for this," he said seriously, "and I bet it won't be you."

"Of course not," said Paton. "Come on, dear boy. We'd better get back before your poor mother starts to worry."

As they sped through the city, Charlie had to keep taking little runs in order to keep up with his uncle's long strides.

"The faster I go the more energy I burn," explained Paton, "so there's less left over for—accidents."

"Can I ask you something, Uncle Paton?"

"You can ask, but I might not answer," said Paton.

"When did it happen? I mean, can you remember

when you found out that you could make the lights brighter?"

Paton said wistfully, "It happened on my seventh birthday. I was so excited I shattered all the light bulbs —there was glass everywhere—children were screaming and pulling pieces out of their hair. They all went home early and I was left confused and unhappy. I didn't realize that I had caused it all until my sisters told me. They were very pleased. 'Thank goodness he's normal,' they said, as if shattering glass was normal and being ordinary was not. My parents were overjoyed. I had no other talents, you see. They let me finish everybody's ice cream, and then I was sick."

"Did you mind," asked Charlie, "being a Yewbeam, when you found out that it meant being different?"

Just a few doors from number nine, Uncle Paton came to a halt. "Look, Charlie," he said gravely. "You'll find that it's just a question of managing things. If you keep quiet about your talent, then all will be well. Keep it in the family, as they say. And never use it for frivolous reasons."

"Benjamin knows about the voices," Charlie confessed. "But he won't tell anyone."

"I'm sure he won't," said Paton, moving on again. "He's an odd little fellow. For all we know he too might be a child of the Red King."

"The who?" asked Charlie.

Paton sprang up the steps of number nine. "I'll tell you about him another time," he said. "By the way, I wouldn't mention the bookseller to Grandma Bone, if I were you." He opened the front door before Charlie could ask why.

Behind the door stood Grandma Bone, her face like thunder. "Where have you two been?" she demanded.

"None of your business, Grizelda," said Paton, striding past her.

"Are you going to tell me?" she asked Charlie.

"Leave the boy alone," said Paton, marching up the stairs. A second later his door closed with a bang.

Charlie ran into the kitchen before Grandma Bone could question him again. His mother was alone, reading a newspaper.

"I was with Uncle Paton," Charlie told her, "just walking."

"Oh." She looked anxious. "I suppose you know about his — what he does?"

"Yes. It's OK, Mom. It doesn't worry me. In fact, it's a relief to know there's someone else in the family who can — do something peculiar." Charlie couldn't stifle a yawn. Today, he'd walked farther than he'd ever walked in his life — and faster. "I think I'd better go to bed," he said.

He was about to fall asleep when he remembered the keys in his jacket pocket. He felt they should be well hidden. Grandma Bone would probably search his room tomorrow. She was already suspicious. Why did she have to know absolutely everything? It wasn't fair. He put the keys in the toe of one of his soccer shoes. Hopefully, she wouldn't want to look in such a smelly place.

Next morning, after breakfast, Charlie collected the bag of keys and put them back in the inside pocket of his jacket. Unfortunately, there was a loud jangling noise when he leaped down the last three steps of the stairs. This happened just as Grandma Bone was coming out of the kitchen.

"What's that noise?" she asked.

"My pocket money," said Charlie.

"No it isn't. Show me what you've got tucked in your jacket."

"Why should I?" Charlie asked very loudly. He hoped that someone would come and rescue him.

"Have you got my paper, Charlie?" asked Uncle Paton, peering over the railing.

"Not yet," said Charlie gratefully.

"He's not going anywhere until he shows me what he's hiding," said Grandma Bone.

Uncle Paton gave a sigh of irritation. "I've just given the boy a handful of coins for the newspaper. Really, Grizelda, don't be so childish."

"How dare you!" For a moment Grandma Bone looked as if she were about to burst with indignation.

Charlie seized his chance. He leaped past the fuming figure and ran out of the front door. Just before he slammed it behind him, he heard Grandma Bone say, "You'll regret this, Paton!"

Charlie raced across the road to Benjamin's house. He had to ring the bell several times before the door was opened.

"What do you want?" Benjamin was still in his pajamas.

"I've got the keys to the case," said Charlie. "Can I come in?"

"Mom and Dad are asleep," said Benjamin gloomily.

"I won't make a noise, I promise."

"OK." Benjamin reluctantly let Charlie into the house. Then, in bare feet, he padded to the closet under the stairs. "You can do it," he said, opening the door.

"Don't you want to see what's in the case?" said Charlie.

"No."

"Don't be like that, Ben," Charlie begged. "It's not my fault that I'm going to that horrible school. You don't think I want to, do you? I can't do anything about it or Mom and Maisie'll be turned out on the street."

"Will they?" Benjamin's eyes widened.

"Grandma Bone owns the house. And yesterday, when my aunts got to hear about me and the photograph voices, they came and gave me a test. If I don't do what they want, they'll turn us out. Mom and Maisie haven't got a penny."

Benjamin gasped. "So that's what your horrible visitors were doing?"

Charlie nodded. "They said I've got to go to the academy because I'm endowed—you know, the photo thing. I tried to pretend I wasn't, but they tricked me. They gave me such noisy photographs I couldn't even hear my own voice."

"Mean things," Benjamin said contritely. "I'm sorry, Charlie. I thought you'd been keeping secrets from me."

"No way. I just didn't want to break the news on your birthday," said Charlie.

There was a low bark from above and the boys

looked up to see Runner Bean, sitting halfway down the staircase. He seemed reluctant to come any farther.

"Come on, Runner. Come and see what's in the case," coaxed Benjamin.

Runner Bean couldn't be coaxed. He whined softly, but didn't move.

"Suit yourself," said Benjamin. He opened the closet door and stepped inside. Charlie was about to follow, when Benjamin said, "It's gone."

"Are you sure?" Charlie didn't like the sound of this.

"I put it behind a bag of clothes. The bag's gone and so is the case." Benjamin crashed around in the closet, moving brooms and boxes, lifting books, kicking at boots. "It's not here, Charlie. I'm really sorry." Benjamin emerged from the closet.

"Go and ask your mom where's she's put it," said Charlie.

"I can't. She gets really angry if I wake her up on Sunday morning." Benjamin began to bite his lip.

Luckily, before Benjamin could get too upset, Runner Bean distracted him by rushing down the stairs and leaping to the back door. He stood on his hind legs, planted his paws on the glass pane, and barked furiously.

The boys ran to the door, reaching it just in time to see a bright flash disappear behind a tree.

"The flames," breathed Charlie.

"Flames? What flames?" asked Benjamin.

Charlie told him about Mr. Onimous and his cats.

"Oh, cats," said Benjamin. "No wonder Runner's in such a state."

Charlie would always wonder if what happened next had anything to do with Mr. Onimous' three flames. For it was the cats that caused them to run to the back door. And if they hadn't they would never have heard the faint tapping that came from behind another door, a door right beside them.

"What's in there?" asked Charlie.

"The cellar," said Benjamin. "It's dangerous. The steps are rotten. We never go in there."

"Somebody does." Charlie opened the door. At his feet there was a very small amount of floor and then a dark nothingness. Charlie cautiously stepped through the door and looked down. He could just make out a rickety-looking stepladder leading down into the darkness. A faint tap came from the bottom of the steps and then it stopped.

"There's a light," said Benjamin, pressing a switch inside the door.

A lightbulb, hanging from the ceiling of the cellar, lit a dusty, almost bare room. And now Charlie could see how precarious the steps were. Some were cracked and others had completely fallen away.

"Dad keeps saying he's going to fix them, but he never has time," said Benjamin.

"I'm going down," Charlie announced. He could see the bright silver case laying beside the last step.

"Don't," said Benjamin. "You'll have a terrible accident and it'll be my fault."

"No it won't." Charlie began to descend. "I've got to open that case."

"Why?" wailed Benjamin. Runner Bean gave an accompanying howl.

"I want to know what's in it before I get to the academy. Whoops!" Charlie's foot slipped. He turned to cling to one of the stronger steps and continued the rest of the way holding on to the sides of the ladder, while his feet found the steps that could still bear his weight. In this way, with a few cracks and slithers, he managed to reach the cellar floor.

"Bring the case up here," said Benjamin, kneeling as close as he dared.

Charlie was already trying to fit the first key into the lock. "I think I'll do it down here," he said. "You never know what might come out of it."

The first key didn't fit, neither did the second. No sound came from the case and Charlie began to wonder if the strange tapping hadn't been the water pipes or even a rat under the floorboards. He tried the third key but had no luck with that either.

Miss Ingledew had given Charlie ten keys and, as he tried the fifth, he had a feeling that none of them would fit the silver case. Some of them were too large even to go into the lock. With a sigh, Charlie pulled out the sixth key.

"No luck?" asked Benjamin.

"Zilch," said Charlie. "It's freezing down here. I think I'll . . ."

He was interrupted by a loud rap on the front door. Runner Bean barked and Benjamin stood up. "What shall I do?" he said in a panicky voice.

"Better see who's there before your parents wake up," Charlie advised. "And shut the cellar door, in case whoever it is comes into the house."

Charlie didn't mention the light, but in his anxiety Benjamin thoughtlessly turned it off before he closed the cellar door.

"Hey!" Charlie whispered as loud as a whisper could get.

Benjamin had gone. Charlie was alone in the dark. He could see neither the case nor the keys. He could feel them, though, and as he ran his hand over the rippled surface of the case, he noticed that there was a small indentation in the side. Slowly his fingers traced the words: TOLLY TWELVE BELLS.

Benjamin's mind was racing as he went to open the door. He tried to imagine who would be on the doorstep so early on a Sunday morning. Should he let them in, and if he did, could he get back to Charlie who, he now realized, he'd left in the dark?

Benjamin opened the door, just a little, and peered around it. A woman stood on the step. She had black hair and she wore a dark, sleek-looking coat. Although she'd been half-hidden by an umbrella the last time he saw her, Benjamin had a very good idea who she was. He recognized the red boots. It was one of Charlie's Yewbeam aunts.

He said, "Yes?" but didn't open the door any farther.

"Hello, dear!" The woman had a sticky, sweet sort of voice. "You must be Benjamin."

"Yes," said Benjamin.

"Is my great-nephew here? Charlie? I know he's a friend of yours." She smiled sweetly.

Benjamin was saved the trouble of answering

immediately because Runner Bean gave a deep, throaty growl.

The woman laughed halfheartedly. "Oh, dear. He doesn't like me, does he?" she said.

Benjamin had come to the conclusion that he must on no account tell this Yewbeam person where Charlie was. "He's not here," he said. "I haven't seen him since yesterday."

"Really?" The aunt raised a long black eyebrow. She wasn't smiling any more. "How strange. He said he was coming to see you."

"No, he didn't," said Benjamin.

"Oh, and how would you know?" She had lost every ounce of her sweetness.

"Because he'd be here if he had," said Benjamin, without a moment's hesitation.

At this moment, Runner Bean began to bark quite ferociously, and Benjamin was able to close the door in the woman's face. When he'd locked and bolted it, he peeked through the spyhole and saw the woman glaring in at him, her face was white with rage.

Benjamin jumped away from the door and tiptoed back to the cellar. "Charlie," he whispered, opening the cellar door. "It's one of your aunts."

"No!" Charlie's harsh whisper swam out of the darkness. "Turn the light on, Ben."

"Sorry." Benjamim pressed the light switch and looked down to see Charlie kneeling beside the case.

"Which aunt is it?" asked Charlie.

"She's got black hair, a long dark coat, red boots, and a white face," Benjamin said softly.

"Venetia," breathed Charlie. "She's the tricky one."

"She doesn't look as if she's going to move off our front step. You'd better go out the back way."

But Charlie had four more keys to try before he gave up in disgust. None of them fitted. "I've got to find it," he cried.

"Shh! She'll hear you," Benjamin warned.

"I'm coming up." Charlie began to climb the steps. It was harder this time. Some of the steps had broken on his way down, and in some places he had to pull himself up with his hands. "Ouch!" he gasped as a splinter speared his thumb.

"Shhhhh!" hissed Benjamin.

At last Charlie reached the top step and, together, the boys crept down the passage to the front door.

Benjamin pressed his eye to the spyhole. "She's gone," he said.

"I don't know if that's worse or better," said Charlie. "She could be anywhere, waiting to pounce."

"Go through the garden at the back, and then you can look over the wall and see if she's there," suggested Benjamin. "You'll have a better chance that way."

"Good thinking," said Charlie.

They went to the back door with Runner Bean barking excitedly, expecting a walk.

"Your parents can sleep through a lot of noise," Charlie remarked.

"They're tired," said Benjamin, and then he asked, "Why is it so important to open the case? Can't we just leave it locked up forever? We could dump it in a garbage can or something."

"No way," said Charlie. "The thing inside it was there when the baby was swapped. It's bound to help Miss Ingledew get her back. We've got to keep it safe."

"Suppose it's something horrible that no one wants?"

Charlie had considered this, but decided that it was something someone wanted very much. Why were his aunts so interested? Why was a boy with red hair asking for it?

"Someone wants it, all right," said Charlie, "but they're not going to get it until I find the baby and, according to Mr. Onimous, the baby is at Bloor's Academy." He opened the back door, jumped down the steps, and raced across the garden.

Benjamin watched his friend dash through the gate without bothering to look either way. He was bound to be caught by that horrible aunt. Benjamin sighed. Sometimes Charlie didn't think too carefully about what he was doing.

Runner Bean looked so disappointed about the walk he hadn't had that Benjamin decided to make him a big breakfast. The thought of grilled sausages made him feel hungry himself.

In the middle of the kitchen table, there was a white card with the words ORVIL ONIMOUS AND FLAMES printed in gold lettering.

How and when did the card get there? And why?

Charlie had reached the end of the alley behind Benjamin's house. He was now in the street where he'd first seen his uncle boosting the lamps. A quick glance to left and right told him his aunt was not in the street.

"Maybe I've fooled her," muttered Charlie. He ran up to Filbert Street, turned the corner, and—

"Got you!" said a voice.

Aunt Venetia sank her long nails into Charlie's shoulder. "You're coming with me, little boy," she cooed nastily. "We've got something to ask you. And if we don't get the right answer, you'll be sorry. Very sorry."

A RUINED SCHOOL BREAK

Aunt Venetia marched Charlie home with her nails pressed firmly into his neck. Charlie ducked and wriggled all the way but he couldn't escape those steely claws.

Grandma Bone was waiting for them in the hall, her face as hard as stone.

"Well done, Venetia. One needs young legs to catch a villain."

"Villain?" protested Charlie. He glanced at Aunt Venetia's red boots. Her legs weren't so very young. She was cunning, that was all.

Grandma Bone prodded him into the kitchen, where he sat and rubbed his neck.

His mother looked up from her newspaper. "What's going on?"

"We've been a wicked and deceitful boy," said Grandma Bone. "Haven't we, Charlie? And a liar to boot."

"Have not," muttered Charlie.

"Oh, yes, I think we have." Grandma Bone sat opposite him and glared into his face. "He's got a case that doesn't belong to him, but he can't open it."

Before Charlie could stop her, Aunt Venetia had plunged her hand into his pocket and pulled out the bunch of keys. "What are these?" she asked, rattling them over his head.

"Charlie, whose are they?" asked his mother.

"No one's. That is—a friend gave them to me. They're just a game."

"Liar," snarled Grandma Bone.

"Don't call him that," said Charlie's mother angrily. "How do you know it's not true?"

"My dear Amy, I know a lot more about your son than you do," Grandma Bone said coldly. "He was given a case by someone who should have known better. Someone who didn't rightfully own it, and the stupid boy has hidden it, probably in Benjamin's house."

"I don't know what you're talking about," said Charlie. He refused to answer any more questions and eventually Grandma Bone gave up.

With a sinister smile, Aunt Venetia dropped the keys onto the table. "Better take them back where they belong," she said, almost sweetly.

Charlie grabbed the keys.

"You haven't heard the last of this," warned Grandma Bone.

"Leave him alone," said Charlie's mother.

"Perhaps we will for a while." Grandma Bone gave Venetia a knowing look. "We have other fish to fry."

To Charlie's great relief, the two sisters put on their hats and gloves and swept out into the street; to bother someone else, no doubt. If Benjamin was their intended victim, they'd never get past Runner Bean.

"Charlie, what's going on?" his mother asked when they were alone.

"It's nothing, Mom. Grandma Bone wants to know everything, but I've got a right to my secrets, haven't I?"

"Of course. But this seems a rather serious sort of secret. Can't you tell me what it is?"

His mother looked so concerned, Charlie hated not telling her the truth. He decided to let her know at least a small part of his problem.

"It's about a baby," he began.

His mother gasped, "A baby!"

Charlie wished she wouldn't look so frightened. "It's all right, I haven't stolen one or anything. It's not even a baby now, she—it's a girl—she's about the same age as me. When she was a baby her mom died and her dad swapped her for something else . . ."

"What?" his mother's hand flew to her mouth.

"It's horrible, isn't it? Anyhow, her father's just died and her only living relative wants to see her again, but she can't find her. So I'm going to."

"You, Charlie? You can't go around looking for lost children. This girl could be anywhere."

"Ah, but I think I know where she is. I can't tell you any more yet, Mom. I'm sorry. You won't say anything to Grandma Bone or the aunts will you? I don't think they're on our side exactly."

"I agree," his mother said wistfully.

"I'm going to find this girl, Mom," Charlie said earnestly. "It's funny but I suddenly feel it's something I've got to do."

To Charlie's dismay his mother's eyes began to look glittery and tearful. "How like your father you are," she said gently. "I'll keep your secret, Charlie. But take care. They're very strong, you know, the people you're up against." Her quick look at the window told Charlie exactly whom she meant.

The doorbell rang and, thinking Maisie had forgotten her key again, Charlie's mother sent him to open the door.

He didn't find Maisie on the doorstep; instead he found a boy with a twinkling sort of face. He was a little taller than Charlie, his hair was a bright shiny brown, and his eyes almost the same color.

"I'm Fidelio Gunn," said the boy. "They asked me to

help with your music. I'm going to be your tutor. Aren't you the lucky one?"

Charlie was speechless. "It's Sunday," he said at last.

The boy's grin almost reached his ears. "I'm too busy during the week. Can I come in?" He held up a violin case.

Charlie pulled himself together. "Who sent you?"

"Bloor's, of course," the boy said cheerfully. "I'm told your music needs work." His grin grew even wider.

"My music doesn't exist," said Charlie, grinning back.

The strange boy stepped into the foyer without being asked. "Where's the piano?" he said.

Charlie showed him into the room that was only used for Yewbeam visits. At the far end an upright piano stood against the wall. No one had ever touched it as far as Charlie could remember.

Fidelio opened the lid with a bang and ran his fingers across the keys. A real tune emerged, a rather beautiful one.

"Needs tuning," said Fidelio, "but it'll do. Does anyone play it?"

Charlie found himself saying, "Perhaps my father did. I don't know. He's dead now."

"Oh." For the first time since he'd arrived, Fidelio looked serious.

"It happened a long time ago," said Charlie hastily.

Fidelio's smile returned. He pulled out the piano stool, sat down, and played loud and merrily.

"What are you doing?" Charlie's mother stood in the doorway, her face a ghostly white.

"Hello!" said Fidelio. "I'm Fidelio Gunn. I've come to teach Charlie music."

"Why?" asked Mrs. Bone.

"Because he's one of the endowed, and although he'll probably never be a musician, he can't come to the academy knowing absolutely nothing, can he?" Fidelio gave Mrs. Bone a heartwarming smile.

"I suppose not," said Charlie's mother faintly. "No one has played that piano, since—for a very long time."

She cleared her throat, which had gone rather husky, and said, "You'd better go on then," and went out, closing the door behind her.

Charlie wasn't sure he liked people knowing he was endowed. "How did you know about me, being— you know—?" he asked Fidelio.

"If you're going to be in the music department and you can't play a sausage, then you must be one of them," said Fidelio. "The rest of us are geniuses!"

Charlie was intrigued. "Are there many of us?"

"Not many," said Fidelio. "I don't know you all. Some of you are actually talented as well as endowed. What can you do, by the way?"

Charlie didn't feel ready to talk about the voices. "I'll tell you some other time," he said.

Fidelio shrugged. "That's OK. Now, let's get on with the music."

They began with "Chopsticks" and, to Charlie's great surprise, after only a few horrible mistakes he actually managed to play some base notes with both hands while Fidelio picked out the tune.

At the end of an hour, Charlie could play scales in several different keys and even an arpeggio. Fidelio was a very noisy teacher. He hopped around Charlie, tapping his feet, rapping the piano, and shouting out the beat. Finally, he took out his violin and began to accompany Charlie. They made a great sound.

"Got to go now," sang Fidelio, flourishing his bow. "I'll be back next Sunday." He pulled a bunch of papers out of his music case and handed them to Charlie. "Study these and learn the notes. OK?"

"OK." Charlie's head was still ringing with music as he saw Fidelio out.

That afternoon Charlie set to work on the papers Fidelio had left with him. He soon realized it would be easier to learn the notes while he was sitting at the piano, but he had only pressed a few keys when Grandma Bone burst in, demanding to know why he was making such a racket.

"I've got to learn if I'm going to be in the music department, haven't I?" said Charlie.

Grandma Bone sniffed and then laid a large file on

the dining room table. "When you've finished with music, you're to start on that," she said.

Charlie didn't like the look of the thick, black file. Printed in gold on the cover were the words BLOOR'S ACADEMY. "What is it?" he asked.

"Work," said Grandma Bone. "Questions. You're to answer every question in the file. I shall check your answers at the end of each day. If they're wrong, you'll have to do them again. I expect them to take at least a week."

"That's not fair," spluttered Charlie. "It'll take all of my vacation."

"Hardly." Grandma Bone smiled. "You've got a computer, haven't you? Just think how much you'll know in just a week. You'll be almost clever, won't you, Charlie?"

"I don't want to be clever," Charlie grunted.

"If you don't answer those questions, you'll have a very bad time at Bloor's, I can assure you. You don't want to start off on the wrong foot, do you?" Still wearing her unpleasant smile, Grandma Bone left the room.

Charlie could hardly believe his bad luck. He opened the file and scanned the lists of questions. There were five hundred and two of them, and, at a quick glance, Charlie didn't know the answer to any of them. They were all about ancient history and unheard-of places and people. The worst ones were mathematical and scientific. Even with a computer it would take him ages to get even halfway through.

Charlie groaned. He left his music and carried the black file upstairs. As he passed his uncle's door he had an idea. He knocked, hesitantly.

"What?" asked a familiar, angry voice.

"It's me, Uncle Paton," said Charlie. "I'm sorry to disturb you but I've got a really bad problem and I need some help."

"Come in, then," his uncle said with a sigh.

Charlie walked in. Uncle Paton's room looked, if anything, more chaotic than before. He even had bits of paper stuck to his sleeves.

"What's the problem?" Paton asked.

Charlie took the file to his uncle's desk. "Grandma

115

Bone says I've got to answer all these questions in a week. There are more than five hundred of them."

His uncle whistled and said, "A tall order, Charlie."

"How can I do it, Uncle Paton?"

"You'll need a lot of paper."

"Please. Be serious," Charlie said miserably.

"I take it you're asking for my help," said Paton. "If that's the case, then I can't leave my work today. But tomorrow I'll certainly do what I can for you. My general knowledge is considerable. We'll make short work of this, I'm sure," he tapped the black file. "Now take the nasty-looking thing away and leave me in peace."

"Thanks, Uncle Paton. Thanks, thanks!"

Filled with gratitude, Charlie bounced to the door, but this time, before he left he couldn't stop himself from asking, "What exactly is your work, Uncle Paton?"

"I'm writing a book," his uncle said without looking up. "I have always been writing it, and probably always will be."

"What's it about?"

"It's a history, Charlie." Paton was now scribbling

furiously in a notebook. "A history of the Yewbeams and their ancestor, the Red King."

There it was again, the Red King. "Who was he?" Charlie asked.

"Who was he?" Paton stared at Charlie as if he weren't really seeing him, as if his thoughts were far away. "One day I'll be able to tell you more. For the moment, all I can say is that he was a king—who disappeared."

"Oh." Charlie decided it would be best to disappear while his uncle was still in a good mood. He shut the door, very quietly, behind him.

Uncle Paton kept his word. Every day he joined Charlie in his room and together they worked their way through the long list of questions. Paton hadn't been exaggerating about his general knowledge. It was considerable.

Charlie worked on one hundred questions a day; that way, his uncle told him, he'd be finished by Friday night and could have a free weekend before he went to the academy.

In the evenings Grandma Bone allowed Charlie to open the piano and play the notes Fidelio had given him to memorize. But one day, he forgot. He was so hungry he went to the kitchen and began eating bread and butter. After a few bites his head sank to the table and he fell asleep. He woke up to find Grandma Bone holding his head up by his hair. "Music, Charlie!" she barked at him. "No supper until you've done your music."

Charlie dragged himself to the piano. Grandma Bone watched him like a hawk until he'd pulled out the piano stool and sat down. He was so tired he could barely make his fingers move; so he didn't try. He sat back and, folding his arms across his chest, he murmured, "If my father were here he could teach me. I suppose he was the last person to play this piano properly."

Grandma Bone was about to walk away but, all at once, she said, "Your father had a grand piano. It stood in the center of a large, bright room. The only things in the room were the piano and Lyell, your father.

118

Through the long windows there was a view of the lake, but your father never looked at it. He gazed at his music while his fingers found the notes. And he would cast his spell."

"And then what happened?" Charlie asked bravely.

He could almost hear the click in Grandma Bone as she snapped out of her reverie. "He broke the rules, Charlie. That's what happened. Beware it doesn't happen to you."

She was gone in a second and Charlie found that he was now wide awake. In half an hour he managed to memorize so many notes he could read a simple tune and even play it.

Ever since he had been tricked into betraying himself, Charlie had avoided looking at newspapers or magazines. He didn't want to hear voices. He didn't want to eavesdrop on private conversations or listen to people's secrets. Every time his mother opened a newspaper he would turn his head away. But Maisie said his gift should be used, for fun if nothing else. Eventually she persuaded Charlie to listen in on a photo of her favorite film stars: Gregory Morton and Lydia Smiley.

The photo had been taken beside a swimming pool and at first Charlie could only hear a faint splashing sound. He was about to push the magazine away, hoping that he'd lost his unwelcome talent, when a voice said, *You'll have to lose weight, darling. You're bursting out of that bikini.*

It must have been the photographer's voice, because Gregory Morton swore horribly and said, *You leave my girl alone, you great ***!!! I like 'em chubby, it's . . .*

Lydia Smiley swore even more than Gregory and said, *That's it. I've had it with you guys. You can both ***!!!*

Charlie repeated what he'd heard to Maisie and his mother. They laughed so much that tears ran down their faces. Charlie didn't think it was that funny but Maisie's laugh was so infectious, he too began to giggle.

"Oh, Charlie, do some more," begged Maisie. "Come on, how about this one?" She pushed the magazine back to Charlie, pointing at a picture of the prime minister and his family.

Charlie had barely glanced at it when the door burst open and Grandma Bone marched in. She guessed, immediately, what had been going on and, striding to the table, she swept up the magazine and thrust it under her arm.

"How could you?" she yelled, glaring first at Maisie and then at Charlie's mother. "This boy is endowed," she jabbed Charlie's head with a long finger, "and you are encouraging him to abuse his gift."

"I was only. . ." Charlie began.

"I know what you were doing," Grandma Bone said coldly. "Sitting in the kitchen and having a good laugh is not the right attitude. You don't deserve your gift, you stupid boy, but seeing as you've got it, you're now responsible for improving it. Improve, respect, foster your inheritance—don't waste it on trashy, foolish affairs. Save it for important things."

Charlie was about to say that prime ministers were important, but thought better of it. He only had two days and two hundred questions to go, and he didn't want to spoil his chances of a free weekend.

"I don't see why Charlie shouldn't have a bit of fun now and then," said Maisie indignantly. "He's my grand-son too."

"More's the pity," snapped Grandma Bone. "Charlie, get back to work."

Charlie scurried upstairs to his room, leaving Maisie and Grandma Bone shouting insults at each other.

He was about to sit at his desk when he caught sight of Benjamin crossing the road. Charlie waved and opened his window.

"What's going on?" called Benjamin. "I haven't seen you for days. I keep ringing your bell but no one will let me in."

Charlie lifted the black file. "I've had five hundred questions to do," he told Benjamin. "Only two hundred to go now, and I get a free weekend. How's the you-know-what?"

"Bad," said Benjamin. "It's still making a noise. One of your horrible aunts came around. She was pretending to be collecting for charity, but I knew her. She was just like the other one, only older."

"You didn't let her in?" asked Charlie anxiously.

"No. Runner gave his killer growl and she left."

"Good old Runner. I've got to get back to work now, Ben." Charlie gave a huge sigh. "See you on Friday when I've finished the questions."

"OK." Benjamin gave a forlorn wave. "It's been a funny vacation. I haven't seen anyone. Think I'll take Runner to a movie."

"*Heart of a Dog* is on at the multiplex," said Charlie. "He'd enjoy that." He closed the window and went back to his questions. But he found it almost impossible to concentrate. He kept thinking about the silver case. What was in it? And why were the Yewbeams so anxious to get it?

HYPNOTIZED!

On Friday night Grandma Bone marked Charlie's last hundred questions. He'd checked them very carefully with his uncle and he was sure that all his answers were right. But Grandma Bone wore such a grim expression as she read Charlie's messy handwriting, his heart began to sink.

It was very hot in his grandmother's room, and Charlie had to stand beside a heater while Grandma Bone sat at a small table in front of him. Her skinny legs stretched under the table toward the heater and Charlie couldn't help noticing that two bony toes had poked their way through the holes in her socks. He began to feel sick.

At last his grandmother placed a small reluctant check beside the last line on the last page. She looked up. "Your writing is a disgrace," she said.

"But did I get the answers right?"

"You did." She sniffed and blew her nose. "Did you cheat?"

"Cheat?" said Charlie. "N-no."

"You don't seem very sure."

"Of course I'm sure," said Charlie. "I mean, I was supposed to look them up, wasn't I? Or use my computer. And I did."

"Here are ten more questions." She handed him a sheet of paper. "You may sit at my table and answer them here, where I can keep an eye on you. They're easy, so you won't need to look them up."

"But that wasn't the deal," wailed Charlie. "It's not fair."

"Life isn't fair," said Grandma Bone. She waltzed over to her large, lumpy bed and lay back on the pillows. "Go on—the sooner you start, the sooner it will be over."

Charlie silently ground his teeth. All the questions were mathematical problems. He gave a low groan and began. The first two problems took him ages but he had just begun to work out his third answer when he heard a snort from behind him.

Grandma Bone had fallen asleep. Her mouth was wide open and a deep grunting noise was coming from it. Charlie tiptoed to the door, opened it very quietly, and crept out into the passage. There was a tiny *click* as he closed the door, but Grandma Bone didn't wake up.

Without bothering to put on a coat, Charlie sneaked out into the street and ran across to Benjamin's house. As he leaped up the steps, he could hear Runner Bean barking, and then three ear-splitting shrieks. Charlie rang the bell.

He was aware of an eye on the other side of the spyhole, and then the door was opened.

Charlie was amazed to see, not Benjamin, but Mr. Onimous standing before him.

"The very one," said Mr. Onimous with a little hop. "We've been waiting for you. Come on, come on!"

As Charlie stepped into the house, there was another furious bark.

"Now then, Broad Bean," called Mr. Onimous. "Be polite. My flames don't like rude dogs." He took little leaps down the passage until he reached the cellar door. Behind the door Benjamin stood with his hand on Runner Bean's collar. Runner Bean kept lunging over the rickety steps; his growl had turned into an angry whine.

Charlie soon saw why. At the bottom of the steps, Mr. Onimous' three cats were circling the metal case. Aries suddenly gave an eerie snarl and jumped on the case. Leo, his tail lashing, attacked the lock with his claws, while Sagittarius bit one of the clasps.

"Come on, my flames," called Mr. Onimous. "You can do better than this. Show us what you're made of."

The cats looked up at him, their strange eyes glittering, and then they did something extraordinary. They began to run around the silver case. Nose to tail, they formed a circle, and as they ran, the circle brightened until it became a fierce light. Faster ran the blazing creatures, and soon there were no cats to be seen, but only flames crackling around the metal, licking, burning, scorching. The smell of burning filled the cellar and Charlie and Benjamin began to cough. Runner Bean leaped away, howling.

It was no use — when the flames had died down and the cats became cats again, the case remained locked.

"You'll have to find the right key, Charlie," Mr. Onimous said. "Dr. Tolly knew what he was doing when he sealed that case. Perhaps he meant for it to stay locked forever."

The three cats leaped up the fragile steps with ease. Charlie could feel the heat still crackling in their fur as they brushed against his legs.

"They're a great comfort on a cold night," said Mr. Onimous. "Any chance of a coffee?"

While they drank the rather strong coffee Benjamin had made, Mr. Onimous told Charlie that it was he who had put the case in the cellar in the first place. "I came in while young Benjamin was over at your place," said Mr. Onimous. "It was his birthday, I gather. Not much cake left was there?"

"How did you get in?" Charlie asked suspiciously.

"Benjamin's good mother let me in," said Mr. Oni-mous. "She'd just come home. Well, we'd seen this lady, me and the flames, this very dark lady with red boots, collecting old clothes. We knew she'd be at the door of number twelve pretty soon, asking for old clothes. Ben's mom would've opened the little closet and the red-booted lady would've seen the case and Ben-jamin's mom, bless her, would've said, 'Take it, dear. It's garbage for all I know.' And once she'd got it, well that would be the end of it, wouldn't it?

"But it was me and the flames Mrs. B let into the closet, on the pretext of a mouse-search, you under-stand, and while she was making me a nice cup of cof-fee, the flames suggested I tip that case into the cellar, see?"

"How can cats suggest things?" asked Benjamin.

"With their eyes, Ben," said Mr. Onimous, "and their mewing voices, and their swishing tails, and clever claws." He stood up and, wiping his small hairy hands on his coat, he said, "Charlie, I want to wish you luck.

It's not easy changing schools at the best of times, and Bloor's Academy isn't an easy place. What you have to do will be difficult and dangerous, but remember, you've been chosen to rescue a life that's been stolen. What a grand way to begin a career!" He held out his pawlike hand.

Charlie shook it.

Benjamin asked, "Who chose him?"

Before Mr. Onimous could reply, Charlie said, "Has it got something to do with a red king?"

"Everything," said Mr. Onimous.

He wouldn't say another word, but hopped to the door and was away up the street. The two boys watched his small, fleet body disappearing around a bend, followed by the tail of burning-bright cats.

"We never asked him how he knew about the case in the first place," said Benjamin.

"There's a lot I keep forgetting to ask Mr. Onimous," said Charlie. "He's the quickest person I've ever met."

Dr. Tolly's case was safe for now, but how long would it take the Yewbeams to get it? It would have to be moved to a safer place, somewhere they'd never think of looking.

Charlie had an idea. "Fidelio Gunn!" he said aloud.

"What's that?" said Benjamin.

"A boy," said Charlie. "My music teacher. Come over on Sunday and you can meet him. Fidelio will help. I know he will."

Benjamin looked doubtful. "We ought to find the key first."

Charlie agreed. "We'll go first thing tomorrow."

Grandma Bone had left the house to visit her sisters when Charlie got home. She didn't get back until very late, and so any unpleasantness about unanswered questions was avoided.

Next morning, Maisie was the only one up when Charlie crept downstairs. "You go and enjoy yourself, Charlie," she said, tucking a banana into his pocket. "Have as much fun as you can before it's too late."

Charlie didn't think fun was the right word to describe what he would be doing. It felt too serious. But he didn't tell Maisie.

Benjamin was waiting outside number twelve. He had left Runner Bean to guard the case. Miserable howls dogged them all the way up the street. "We won't be long, will we?" Benjamin asked guiltily.

Charlie wasn't sure. It was another cold, dark day. Now and again flurries of hail and sleet would beat into their faces, and they had to walk with their heads bent to avoid the stinging slaps of ice.

The crowds were thin and the road approaching the cathedral almost deserted. But, as they drew near to Ingledew's, two figures emerged from the veil of sleet, boys of about sixteen or seventeen. They stopped when they saw Charlie and Benjamin and moved slightly apart, filling the narrow pavement. As Charlie stepped into the street to avoid them, one of them said, "Charlie Bone?"

Charlie shuddered. He'd heard that voice before. He looked up and recognized the boy who had glared out at him from the newspaper: Manfred Bloor.

"Where are you going, Charlie Bone?" asked Manfred.

"None of your business," said Charlie, sounding braver than he felt.

"Oh, no?" The other boy gave a high-pitched snicker.

"It is my business," said Manfred. "But I know already. You're going to a bookshop called Ingledew's where you'll beg Miss Ingledew to look for a key, a key to a certain case that doesn't belong to you, or to her."

Charlie said nothing. He leaped around Manfred and jumped into the road, but Manfred's hand shot out and clamped itself on Charlie's arm. The other boy, a weasely red-haired individual, grabbed hold of Benjamin.

"I've got bad news for you, Charlie," Manfred said in a cold, toneless voice. "You won't be going to any bookshop. And you won't be getting a key! No one's going to open that case until it's handed over to me."

"I don't know what you're talking about," said Charlie, trying to twist out of Manfred's grip.

"We just want to buy a book," added Benjamin.

"You won't find any kids' books at Ingledew's," said the red-haired boy.

"Let go of me!" shouted Charlie. "I can go where I want. You've no right to stop me." He brought up his free hand and gave Manfred a blow on the ear, but the taller boy seized both of Charlie's hands and, squeezing them tighter and tighter, forced him to the ground.

"Look at me!" Manfred commanded.

Charlie looked. He couldn't help himself.

"Look into my eyes," came the sinister whisper.

Manfred's eyes were like shining coals, black and fathomless. Charlie stared at them, repelled and fascinated. He felt himself sinking, deeper and deeper. And now he was drowning, for he couldn't get his breath. The world outside Manfred's coal-black eyes began to disappear, and Charlie found himself inside another world: inside a car to be precise.

The car was traveling at great speed through a forest, and Charlie appeared to be driving. The coal-black eyes were beside him now, and the sinister voice repeated, "Look at me!"

There was a sudden, violent jolt and Charlie was being dragged from the car. He knelt on the rim of a great pit while the car — a blue one — tumbled over the edge. The silence of the forest was broken by the scream of birds and then, far, far below, came a low, echoey splash.

"Charlie! Charlie!"

Charlie opened his eyes and found himself sitting on the ground with his back against a lamppost. Benjamin was peering into his face.

"What happened to you?" Benjamin asked in a frightened voice.

"I don't know," said Charlie.

"You kind of went to sleep," Benjamin told him. "I've been shaking you for ages."

"Why did I go to sleep?" asked Charlie, feeling a bit foolish.

"It was when you looked into that boy's face," said Benjamin. "I think he must have hypnotized you."

"Who? When?" Charlie couldn't remember anything. "What am I doing here?"

"Oh, Charlie!" Benjamin wrung his hands. "You've forgotten everything. We were going to see Miss Ingledew to ask for a key, and then those two boys stepped in front of us, and one of them, the one with a ponytail, made you look into his eyes, and you went all funny and sleepy."

"Oh!" Charlie began to remember. He shivered. The air was painfully cold but the memory of Manfred's eyes was colder.

"Shall we go to the bookshop now?" asked Benjamin.

"I don't feel well," Charlie muttered, staggering to his feet. Benjamin had never heard his friend say such a thing. Charlie was always well. Benjamin was worried.

As the two friends walked home through the icy streets, Charlie began to murmur about driving through a forest and a blue car tumbling into a quarry. Benjamin thought Charlie was sleepwalking or had gone crazy. Nothing Charlie said made any sense until he suddenly stopped and, grabbing Benjamin's arm, he said, "That's what happened to my father, Ben. He drove into a quarry."

"Really?" said Benjamin. "I always wondered. In fact, sometimes I thought your father had just run away."

"No," said Charlie gravely. "He was murdered."

Benjamin didn't know what to say to this. Charlie's life had become, not only pretty complicated, but dangerous as well. They had reached Charlie's house by now, and Benjamin decided it would be best to let his friend have a rest. Besides, he could hear Runner Bean barking. He hoped he hadn't been barking for a whole hour.

"Let's talk about the case tomorrow," said Benjamin. "I'll come by when you have your music lesson."

"Music lesson?" Charlie looked puzzled.

"Fidelio Gunn," Benjamin said kindly.

"Hm." The color had begun to come back into Charlie's pale face. "Oh, yes. See you tomorrow, Ben."

Charlie dragged himself up the steps of number nine. It was quiet in the house. The smell of Maisie's cooking drifted into the hall, but instead of making Charlie feel hungry, it just gave him a stomachache.

He went upstairs and lay on his bed. This must be what people felt like after an operation, Charlie thought, as if they were not quite connected to the real world.

Manfred Bloor had known who he was. But how? Charlie remembered the photograph. When he had looked at it and heard those voices, Aries the cat had peeked out and seen him. Somehow a connection had been made, even though eight years had passed. Could it be that when he saw Manfred in the newspaper, Manfred had seen him, too, and known who he was?

Charlie decided to try an experiment. Somewhere he had a photograph of Benjamin; it had been taken on the same day as the photo of smiling Runner Bean. Charlie rummaged in a drawer and pulled out Benjamin's startled face. The camera flash had taken him by surprise.

Charlie stared at his friend's face. For a moment

Benjamin just stared back, and then a voice said, *Charlie, I don't like having my photo taken.*

In the background a dog barked and then Charlie's own voice could be heard, saying, *Smile, Benjamin. Go on. You look great. Really!*

That was it. No more voices. Just the sound of a dog panting heavily and then a long, doggish yawn.

At number twelve, Benjamin had just opened a large container of strawberry yogurt. He was about to plunge his spoon in when Charlie's face appeared floating among the strawberries. It turned Benjamin's stomach over. He put the container back in the fridge.

"It's gone bad," he told Runner Bean. "We'll have cheese instead."

Runner Bean was glad to hear this. He wagged his tail happily.

Charlie's mom woke him up for his lunch, but after that he fell asleep again. At teatime Maisie asked him if he felt ill, because he looked very peculiar and he hadn't touched his sandwich.

"Not ill," said Charlie. "I think I've been hypnotized."

Maisie and his mother laughed.

"Grandma Bone's on the warpath," said Maisie. "She wanted to see you about some questions, but then she got a phone call and took off to visit the Yewbeams."

After tea, Charlie fell asleep again. He didn't wake up until he heard his uncle creaking downstairs at midnight.

Charlie tiptoed down to the kitchen. His head felt much clearer and he was really hungry. He found his uncle sitting at the kitchen table eating cold chicken, green beans, and salad. There was a basket of rolls on the table and a bottle of wine. Paton's large wine glass was half full.

The only light in the room came from a single candle sitting on an ornate silver candlestick in the center of the table.

Uncle Paton squinted past the candle flame. Eventually he saw Charlie hovering in the shadow by the door.

"Come in, dear boy," said Uncle Paton. "Do you like chicken?"

"Do I?" Charlie pulled up a chair. "Right now I'd eat almost anything."

His uncle passed him a chicken leg on a plate and asked, "How was your day?"

"Horrible." Charlie told Paton about Miss Ingledew's keys, Manfred Bloor, and the nasty experience of being hypnotized.

Uncle Paton dropped his fork. "Do you mean to tell me that those boys were trying to prevent you from reaching the bookshop?"

"That's exactly what I mean," said Charlie. "Manfred's going to get the key from Miss Ingledew before I can, and then he's going to come looking for the case. Everyone seems to be looking for it."

"That sweet lady needs protection," Paton murmured. "Tell me, Charlie, why are you so determined to keep this troublesome case?"

"Whatever is in it was swapped for a baby. I want to swap it back again so Miss Ingledew can see her niece. It doesn't seem fair, does it, that the baby's only relative can't find her?"

"I wonder why it never occurred to that charming lady that she could have exchanged the case for the child?" Paton mused.

"She just got it," Charlie said. "Before that she was tricked, put off, and lied to. By the time she got the case, she'd given up searching."

"You do seem to know a lot," said Paton. He took his empty plate to the sink. "Charlie, you're going to be out of action next week, so I shall return the keys to Miss Ingledew for you. If she finds the right one, I shall give it to you when you come home for the weekend. But I think you should show me the case. I want to be there when you open it. As a precaution."

"A precaution?" asked Charlie.

"Who knows what that thing contains?" said Paton. "An adult should be on hand. Don't you agree?"

"I suppose." Charlie was beginning to get a gnawing pain in his stomach again. This time it was because Paton had mentioned his being away for a week. Imprisoned at Bloor's Academy.

"Uncle Paton, why do I have to go to Bloor's just because I'm endowed?" asked Charlie.

"So they can keep an eye on you. They wouldn't dare let you go anywhere else, in case you start using your talents without their knowing it. They like to be in control."

"I suppose you went to Bloor's?"

"Of course," said Paton.

"And did you enjoy it?"

"'Enjoy' is not the word I'd use. I got by. I kept my head down and they left me alone, more or less." Paton sighed. "I suppose that's always been my trouble. I've kept my head down when, occasionally, I should have put it up. Oh, well. Perhaps it's not too late."

There was a creak outside—the door flew open with a bang and the light came on. Grandma Bone stood on the threshold. She glared at Charlie, saying, "What's this? A midnight feast? Bed, Charles Bone! You'll finish those questions in the morning. School on Monday. How are you going to cope without sleep?"

"Good night, Grandma! Good night, Uncle Paton!" Charlie scurried past his grandmother. As he climbed the stairs he could hear her shouting at Uncle Paton.

"What's going on here, Paton? I can't trust you any-more. Whose side are you on? Answer me!"

BREAKING THE RULES

Benjamin and Fidelio arrived on Charlie's doorstep at the same time. Benjamin knew immediately that the cheerful-looking boy was Charlie's music teacher. For one thing, he was carrying a music case in one hand and a violin case in the other. And, he just looked musical. They introduced themselves and Fidelio rang the bell.

Grandma Bone opened the door. "Go away," she said to Benjamin. "Charlie's going to have a music lesson. You'll be in the way."

"No he won't," said Fidelio. "We're going to play a trio. Benjamin is essential."

"A trio?" Grandma Bone raised a thick gray eyebrow. "I don't believe it."

Benjamin began to turn away but Fidelio grabbed his arm. "We need him, Mrs. Bone," Fidelio insisted. "Dr. Saltweather, who is head of music, said we were to have some group playing so Charlie can get used to joining in with the class."

"Hmph. The lies you children tell. It's beyond belief." But she couldn't have been quite sure it was a lie, because she let Benjamin come in.

Charlie was already practicing his scales when Fidelio and Benjamin arrived.

"You've improved," said Fidelio. "We're going to make a lot of noise today because all three of us are going to be playing." He opened his music case, pulled out a flute, and handed it to Benjamin.

"I don't know how to..." Benjamin began.

"You soon will," said Fidelio.

Sure enough, in less than ten minutes, Benjamin was playing the flute. The three boys made a great deal of noise. Charlie expected Grandma Bone to come storming in at any minute, but she never did. It was a wonderful feeling to bang away and sing your head off, all in the cause of learning. He waited until Fidelio took a break before he broached the subject of the case.

When Fidelio put his bow down at last, Charlie said

quickly, "We have a problem, Fidelio. And we wondered if you could help us."

"Probably," said Fidelio eagerly. "Go ahead."

Charlie told him about the locked case and the keys. He omitted the part about the baby. He didn't know Fidelio well enough for that, yet.

"So you want me to hide this case for you," said Fidelio. "That's easy. Our house is full of instrument cases. I can hide it under the others."

"The thing is, we're being watched," said Charlie. "My aunts already know it's in Benjamin's house. So we've got to find something big to carry it in."

"I'll bring my dad's xylophone case," said Fidelio. "It's gigantic. Funny you should say you're being watched. I could swear I saw Asa Pike on the other side of the road today. He was in disguise, as usual. He's in drama, but he can't act. Anyway, he was dressed in this long coat and funny hat, and he was wearing a false mustache. But I always know Asa when I see him — he's got those yellowy, wolfish eyes."

"And red hair?" asked Charlie. Manfred's friend had yellow eyes.

"That's him. He's Manfred Bloor's slave. He'd do anything for him. Sell his own mother, probably."

Charlie told Fidelio about the hypnotizing episode.

"I've heard rumors about Manfred," Fidelio said gravely. "They say if you get on the wrong side of him you can be . . . damaged forever. I'd advise you to keep out of his way."

The door opened and Grandma Bone poked her head in. "I presume you've finished," she said.

"You presume right, Mrs. Bone," said Fidelio. He began to gather up his instruments and sheets of music. Charlie and Benjamin saw him to the door, but before Fidelio walked away, he said. "See you tomorrow, Charlie. And you very soon, Benjamin!"

Charlie looked up and down the street before closing the door. There was no sign of Asa Pike, or anyone in a long coat and a false mustache. Turning to Ben, he whispered, "Did you see my face yesterday, at about teatime?"

Benjamin, very surprised, said, "I saw you in my yogurt. It made me feel sick."

"Sorry, it was just an experiment."

Benjamin tried to guess what sort of an experiment it was, and then decided he didn't really want to know.

Grandma Bone allowed Benjamin to stay for tea, but he was sent home early so that Charlie could pack his bag and prepare himself for his first day at Bloor's Academy.

"You won't have to take much," said Charlie's mother as she laid out the new pajamas. "You'll be home again on Friday."

Charlie wished he hadn't been given pajamas with teddy bears on them, but he didn't like to seem ungrateful so he kept quiet about it. He packed a clean shirt, his toiletries, spare socks and underwear, and the blue cape.

"I think you're supposed to wear this, Charlie," said his mother, pulling out the cape. "I've sewn your name at the back in green thread, see. I'm afraid it's the only color I had."

Charlie pushed the cape back again. "I'll take it out when I get there," he said.

Tomorrow, as it would be his first day, his mother was going to take him to the academy entrance. The paperwork for registration had all been completed by Grandma Bone. On Friday he would come home on the school bus and get off at the bus stop at the end of Filbert Street.

"There's something else you might want to take," his mother murmured. She left the room and when she came back, a few moments later, she was holding something wrapped in white tissue paper. "They said you were to wear a blue tie," she said, "and Grandma Bone has provided one, but . . ." She folded back the tissue paper and held up a bright blue tie. At one end of the tie, a small gold "Y" had been stitched in silk thread. "It was your father's," she told Charlie. "The 'Y' is for Yewbeam. Although your father's name was Bone, he had Yewbeam blood and that, it seems, carries a great deal of weight at Bloor's. The Yewbeams are re-lated to the Bloors, apparently."

"Related? Do you mean like cousins?" Charlie wondered why his mother hadn't mentioned such an important fact before.

"Distant cousins."

"Anything to do with a red king?" asked Charlie.

"Your father did mention him."

"So why did Grandma give me a tie without a 'Y'?"

"Perhaps you have to prove yourself first, Charlie. Perhaps they think you'll go astray—like Lyell did." She tucked the tie into Charlie's bag. "Anyway, you never know, you might need it."

When she had gone, Charlie took out the tie and examined it. The material was soft and shiny, silk or satin perhaps. He pressed it to his face and sniffed it. The tie smelled of the way his mother used to smell, when she still had nice things to wear. All her best clothes had worn out, and now, Charlie realized, his mother looked just a bit shabby.

The next morning, Maisie cooked Charlie such a

big breakfast it overflowed his plate. He managed to chew a bit of bacon, but that was all. His stomach was churning.

The kitchen seemed to be full of nervous people. Even Uncle Paton had turned up. "I'd drive you to the place, dear boy," he told Charlie. "But there's no parking to be had within a mile of the place. The staff are very possessive about their parking lot."

Everyone looked uncomfortable, knowing that Paton couldn't go out in daylight anyway, and then Grandma Bone said, "A taxi's been ordered. It's just turned up."

"I don't want to go in a taxi," cried Charlie. "I'll look like a nerd."

"You'll do as you're told," said Grandma Bone. "Now fetch your things."

With tears and kisses from Maisie, a wave from Paton, and a grim smile from Grandma Bone, Charlie and his mother were bundled into the taxi. They were dropped off on a side road leading to the academy, and walked through a medieval square where cobblestones surrounded a fountain of stone swans. Ahead was a tall gray building, ancient and imposing. The walls that flanked the square were five stories high, their windows dark rectangles of reflecting glass.

On either side of the huge arched entrance, there was a tall tower with a pointed roof, and when they reached the wide flight of steps up to the entrance, Charlie's mother suddenly stopped and stared up at a window in one of the towers. Her face was drained of color and, for a moment, Charlie thought she was going to faint.

"What is it, Mom?" he asked.

"I thought someone was watching me," she murmured. "Charlie, I must go now." She kissed him quickly and hurried away across the square.

Charlie became aware of other children arriving in buses at the end of the square. Before long he was surrounded by leaping, running, walking, and shouting children, all in capes of blue or green or purple.

"Charlie, put your cape on!" called a voice. "Or you'll be in trouble." Fidelio emerged through the bustling crowd. "You have a cape, haven't you? I forgot to mention it."

"Yes." Charlie pulled the cape out of his bag and put it on.

"Good, now come with me," said Fidelio. "Keep close. There's a bit of a mob on Monday mornings."

They were now in a paved courtyard and, as Charlie followed Fidelio, his eye was caught by one of the windows overlooking it. There was a long black stain on the gray wall beneath it.

"That's where Manfred nearly burned to death," Fidelio said in a harsh whisper.

"The fire?" asked Charlie.

They had reached a doorway where two huge doors, studded with bronze figures, stood wide open. Charlie stared at them in awe as he passed through. He found himself in a long stone hallway, and suddenly all the laughter and shouting died away. Only the sound of feet tapping on stone could be heard.

Keeping Fidelio in sight, Charlie made his way through the throng of children crisscrossing the hall and disappearing into doors on either side. Fidelio seemed to be making for the door with two long crossed trumpets hanging above it.

They were nearly there when there was a shriek and someone grabbed hold of Charlie's cape. He looked behind him to see a girl with purple hair sprawled on the stones. She was a very odd sight; apart from her purple hair and cape, she had a purple pattern on her forehead and she was wearing purple shoes with high stiletto heels and very pointed toes. Her backpack had fallen open, scattering books and pens in all directions.

"Sorry," said the girl. She began to giggle. "Shoes'll be my downfall, or falldown." She giggled even more.

Charlie was about to help her up, when a voice ordered, "Leave it, Bone!"

Asa Pike, also in purple, stood glaring down at the girl. "Olivia Vertigo, what are the rules? Recite!"

Scrambling to her feet, the girl chanted,

Silence in the hall,

Talking not at all,

Silence if you fall,

Never cry or call,

Blah! Blah! Blah!

Asa grabbed her arm. "Insolence isn't amusing," he barked. "Come with me." He began to drag her away.

"My books," wailed Olivia.

Charlie scooped up the scattered books and pens while Fidelio, putting a finger to his lips, found Olivia's purple backpack and helped Charlie fill it. As soon as they were through the door beneath the crossed trumpets, Fidelio said, "We can talk now."

They were in a large, tiled coatroom, with lockers covering two walls and coat hooks on the other two. A row of basins ran down the center of the room.

"What's going to happen to that girl?" asked Charlie.

"She'll probably get detention, a horrible lecture from Manfred, and then not be allowed to go home till Sunday. She's only been here a short while, but she's already had detention twice. She'd probably have been expelled if she weren't so brilliant at acting. I was sent into her class, once, to fetch Mr. Irving, and she was doing this solo piece—it was amazing."

Fidelio showed Charlie his locker and then took him to the oak-paneled Assembly Hall. A group of musicians stood on the stage, tuning their instruments.

"First we have the school hymn and then registration," said Fidelio.

Charlie followed him to the benches in the front row. Gradually, the hall filled up with girls and boys all wearing blue capes. There must have been about a hundred children between eleven and eighteen. Charlie thought he must have been the youngest, until a very small boy slipped in beside him.

"Hello," said the small boy. "I'm Billy Raven."

"I'm Charlie Bone," said Charlie.

The small boy smiled. He had almost-white hair and his eyes were a strange, dark red. "I'm an albino," he explained. "I don't see too well. But I hear very well."

"Aren't you a bit young for Bloor's?" said Charlie.

"I'm seven," Billy replied. "But I'm an orphan, so they took me in. Besides, I'm endowed."

"So am I," Charlie whispered.

Billy beamed at Charlie. "I'm glad," he said softly. "Now there are three of us."

Charlie didn't have time to ask who the third endowed musician was, because a tall man with white hair had walked onto the stage.

"Dr. Saltweather," whispered Fidelio, on Charlie's other side.

There were five other music teachers on the stage: two youngish women, an old man with glasses, a cheerful-looking man with lots of wiry hair, and someone whom Charlie found himself staring at—he had never seen such a blank sort of face. The man was tall and lean with black hair that he had apparently forgotten to comb. His expression didn't change once, even when the orchestra struck up and everyone else began to sing.

When assembly was over, Fidelio took Charlie to

a door beside the stage. A notice on the door said
MR. PALTRY — WINDS.

"I'll see you at break," said Fidelio. "I'm off to strings
now, and Miss Chrystal."

"Who were the other teachers on the stage?" asked
Charlie.

"Well, you've got old Mr. Paltry — don't envy you
there — then there's Mr. O'Connor, he does guitar and
stuff like that. The two ladies teach strings, and Dr.
Saltweather does brass and choir."

"What about the man at the end — the tall man?"

"Oh, Mr. Pilgrim." Fidelio grimaced. "He teaches
piano, but hardly anyone goes to him. He's too weird."

"Weird?"

"He never says anything. You don't know if you've
done well or not. My father taught me to play the
piano. He teaches in a normal school. I'd better go now.
I'm late."

So, Fidelio's father taught in a normal school. What
did that make Bloor's? Very interesting, Charlie thought.

He watched his new friend fly across the hall to another door, and then went in to face Mr. Paltry—Winds.

Mr. Paltry didn't like endowed children. He made this very clear to Charlie. Endowed children were a waste of his time. They had their own uncommon talents, but they were of no use to anyone, as far as Mr. Paltry could see.

At the end of an uncomfortable and unproductive lesson, Charlie was told to leave his cape in the coatroom and to go into the garden for a run.

"Where's the garden?" Charlie asked.

He thought this was a reasonable question, but Mr. Paltry seemed to find it very annoying. "Where do you think?" he snapped.

Luckily, Charlie found Fidelio in the coatroom. "Everyone has to have a run after the first lesson," he told Charlie. "Come with me."

The garden was hardly what Charlie would have called a garden. There was no end to it as far as he could see. There were no walls or fences either. The back of the academy overlooked a huge field where children ran or jogged in twos and threes and, some-times, alone. A deep wood surrounded the field and, in the distance, a gray, reddish-colored wall could be seen, disappearing into the trees. Fidelio told Charlie that this was the ruin.

"Hundreds of years ago it was a huge castle," he said. "But now it's just a ruin. Most of the roof has fallen in, but there are still some creepy passages and weird statues and crumbly steps. The trees have grown all around it and even inside it, and that makes it even more spooky."

"Have you been in there?" Charlie nodded at the sinister-looking wall.

"Have I?" Fidelio gave a grim smile. "Every winter, at the end of November, we have to play the ruin game. Everyone has to go in, whether they want to or not. Two years ago a girl went in and never came out."

Fidelio had begun to run around the field and Charlie, pacing beside him, asked, "Didn't they find the girl, then?"

"Never," said Fidelio. He lowered his voice. "And they

say it's happened before. Capes were found, but never a...a..."

"Body?" suggested Charlie.

Fidelio nodded. "They just disappeared."

Charlie glanced at the distant dark hedge and shuddered.

After a fifteen-minute run, the sound of a hunting horn rang out across the field, and the children began to troop back into the building.

"You've had your worst lesson," Fidelio told Charlie. "Nothing will be as bad as Mr. Paltry. It's English next, and I'll be in the same class, but first our capes. We're only allowed to take them off for games or running."

When Charlie got to the coatroom, his cape had disappeared. The only one left hanging on the hooks was a tatty garment with jagged tears in one corner.

"Put it on, Charlie," Fidelio advised. "It's better than nothing. Someone must have taken yours by mistake."

Charlie wouldn't wear the tattered cape. "It's not mine, and someone might come looking for it."

Fidelio looked anxious. "Go on, Charlie. Please wear it or there'll be trouble."

But Charlie wouldn't. He didn't realize what sort of trouble Fidelio meant. If he had, he might have done as his friend asked.

The English teacher, Mr. Carp, was a broad, red-faced man. As soon as Charlie walked in without his cape, Mr. Carp's small eyes fixed themselves on him. What, he wanted to know, was Charlie thinking of? Where was "the essential garment"?

"If you mean my cape, sir, I can't find it," said unsuspecting Charlie.

Mr. Carp carried a cane. He brought it down — *whack* — across his desk. "Out, boy!" he screamed.

"But, sir," said Fidelio. "It's not his fault."

"Shut up, Gunn!" shouted Mr. Carp. For a big man he had a very high voice. "You," he pointed his cane at Charlie. "Out this minute!"

Unwilling to cause any more trouble, Charlie left the room as quickly as he could. Once he was outside the classroom, however, he didn't know where to go.

So he just stood by the wall and stared down the long hall to the great doors that led to the outside world. The stone hall was freezing cold and the thought of spending the night at Bloor's Academy was becoming less and less appealing.

Just when Charlie thought the English lesson might be ending and Fidelio could come and help him search for his missing cape, someone came out of a door farther down the hall. It was Asa Pike.

The red-haired boy gave Charlie a slow, malicious smile and walked up to him.

"Well, if it isn't Charlie Bone," snickered Asa. "I see you've transgressed on your very first day."

"Trans what?" said Charlie.

"Did I ask you to speak?" Asa stopped smiling. "Where's your cape, Bone?"

"I don't know."

"Come and see the head boy." Asa locked his hand around the back of Charlie's neck and pushed him down the hall. Charlie saw that they were heading for a door marked PREFECTS.

Asa opened the door and pushed Charlie inside.

There were several older boys in the room, lounging in armchairs and sofas. Some of them glanced up at Charlie and then went back to their books or their conversations.

Beneath a window at the end of the room, there was a long desk, and behind the desk sat Manfred Bloor in a purple cape. There were two chairs on the other side of the desk. In one of them sat the girl with purple hair, swinging her feet. Asa pushed Charlie into the other chair. Olivia grinned at him.

"No cape," Asa announced.

Charlie quickly looked away from Manfred's stare. He didn't want to be hypnotized again.

Manfred said, "Has no one told you the rules, Charlie Bone?"

"No." Charlie looked over Manfred's head.

"They're sent to pupils before they come here. Didn't you get any?"

"No." Charlie stared through the window behind Manfred. "They were probably sent to my grand-

165

mother and she forgot to give them to me." It was quite likely that Grandma Bone had deliberately withheld the rules, thought Charlie, just to get him into trouble.

Manfred opened a red box file, extracted a piece of paper, and handed it to Charlie. "The rules. Study them. Learn them, Bone." He turned his attention to Olivia. "As for you, Olivia Vertigo, it seems that you can't learn. I'm giving you both detention on Friday night. Your parents will be informed. They can collect you on Saturday."

"You can't do that," said Charlie, leaping up. "It's my first week. My mom'll..."

"Mom?" said Manfred scornfully.

"Mom?" repeated Asa. "We don't talk about moms in here."

"Moms don't exist in here!" Manfred added darkly.

THE RED KING'S ROOM

Olivia and Charlie were marched to the door and thrust out into the hall.

"Now what?" asked Charlie glumly.

"Let's go to a coatroom where we can talk," whispered Olivia.

Charlie followed her down the hall and through a door beneath two golden masks, one smiling and the other sad.

The purple coatroom was far more interesting than the blue coatroom. It was full of strange costumes: hats with feathers, helmets, top hats, flowers, and masks hung from the walls; and the floor was littered with boots and shoes of every size and description.

Olivia kicked off her purple shoes and stepped into a pair of plain-looking pumps. "Do you think these will do?" she asked Charlie. Charlie shrugged.

"Don't look so gloomy. It's not that bad. I'm always

getting detention. I go exploring. I've already learned some very interesting things about this place."

"But what if I don't find my cape? I'll keep getting detention."

"I think I know who's got it," Olivia told him. "I went into your coat room to look for my backpack — the one you kindly rescued for me. It was break and the only person in there was this boy with a long face and droopy hair. He jumped when I went in, and he looked guilty and kind of secretive. He was holding a blue cape."

"Do you know his name?" asked Charlie.

"Gabriel something-or-other," said Olivia. "If he's swapped capes you'd better wear his until you can prove the other one is yours."

"Thanks, Olivia!" Charlie began to feel more optimistic. "I'll do that right now."

"See you at dinner," she called as Charlie dashed across the hall into the blue coat room.

When Fidelio came out of the English class he found Charlie wearing a very tattered blue cape.

"Glad you've come to your senses," whispered Fidelio. "Follow me to the blue cafeteria."

Charlie followed. The blue cafeteria was at the end of several long passages and Charlie tried to memorize his way by studying the paintings on the walls. It was important to know where food could be found. Most of the paintings were portraits of stern-looking men and women. They seemed to reach back through the ages, their clothes reflecting the centuries they had lived in. He began to recognize names: Raven, Silk, Yewbeam, Pike, and Bloor. History had never been Charlie's strong point, but he was sure these portraits were leading back to an age when people drew on walls.

At last they entered a big, steamy room that smelled of boiled cabbage. While they were in line for their food, Charlie told Fidelio about Olivia's visit to the blue coatroom.

"There was this boy looking guilty and holding a cape," said Charlie. "Olivia said his name was Gabriel something-or-other."

"Gabriel Silk," said Fidelio. "He does piano. I think he's endowed. He's certainly very odd."

"Odd?" asked Charlie.

Fidelio nodded at the dinner line. "That's him at the end."

Charlie saw a tall boy with a long face and droopy, mouse-colored hair. Everything about him looked loose and gangly, even his hands.

"He seems happier than usual," said Fidelio. "Oooops! Now he doesn't."

Gabriel had dropped the pile of books he was trying to carry under one arm, and was having great difficulty balancing his plate while he retrieved them.

"I wonder if that's my cape," said Charlie. "Mom sewed my initials in the back. She used green thread because she couldn't find any white."

"We'll try to get a look at it tonight," said Fidelio. "He probably won't take it off until then."

A plate containing something brown and green was shoved into Charlie's hands, and he followed Fidelio to an empty table. After a few mouthfuls, Charlie noticed that Fidelio seemed to be enjoying the rather disgusting cabbage and leaving the brown stuff.

"Vegetarian," explained Fidelio. "They never give us a meal we can eat. I expect you'd like my hash."

"Is that what it is? I wouldn't mind a bit. You can have my cabbage."

Just as they were swapping hash for cabbage Miss Chrystal—who taught strings—walked past their table.

"You know that's not allowed," she said with a smile.

Charlie had the impression that Miss Chrystal wasn't a very serious person. The smell of cabbage was momentarily drowned by her delicious flowery perfume.

"Sorry, Miss Chrystal," said Fidelio, grinning broadly. "This is Charlie Bone; he's new today."

"Hello, Charlie," said Miss Chrystal. "If I can be of any help, Fidelio knows where to find me." She bestowed another beaming smile on Fidelio and drifted away. It was good to know that there was at least one friendly teacher in the academy.

The rest of the day passed without any more unpleasant incidents. Charlie followed Fidelio from room to room, out to the cafeteria for tea, and then into the field for a last run before dark. But as the lights began to come on in the great, gray building, and a night sky filled the windows, he found himself thinking of home. And when they passed through the hall on their way to dinner, he pictured the cozy kitchen at number nine and a plate of Maisie's special spaghetti. He turned to look at the tall, solid doors that led to the outside world.

"It's no good, Charlie," whispered Fidelio. "They won't open until Friday. I've tried them."

"Were you homesick at first?" asked Charlie.

"Yes, but it didn't last. Friday comes soon."

"I'm not going home on Friday. I've got detention," said Charlie gloomily. "Manfred gave it to me."

"I don't believe it!" Fidelio was clearly shocked. "On your first day. Manfred's certainly got it in for you." Seeing Charlie's forlorn expression, he added quickly, "You're in for a surprise. We're about to meet the whole school. And the dining hall is quite something, I can tell you."

Fidelio was right. They walked together down the same echoing passages toward the blue cafeteria, and then farther. Now they were descending, very gradually, into a huge underground cavern, and Charlie noticed that children in green capes and others in purple were joining them. The crowd of children pressed toward a flight of steps, and then down and down into another long passage, this one leading to a vast hall.

"We're under the city," said Fidelio. "This is the oldest part of the building. It's where the Red King's descendants are supposed to have kept their prisoners."

The Red King again. "Who was the Red King?" asked Charlie.

Fidelio shrugged. "He built the ruined castle, that's all I know. I think he was OK but they say his children were a really bad group. Come on, we'll be late."

On either side of three extremely long tables, benches were filling up with children. Blue capes on the left, purple in the center, and green on the right. A prefect at each end was serving soup from a big steel container. Others were doling out hunks of bread.

At the end of the hall, on a raised dais, the academy staff sat around a fourth table, the High Table, Fidelio told Charlie. At last Charlie got his first glimpse of Dr. Bloor. He wore a black cape like the staff who taught subjects other than the three arts, but there was no mistaking him. He sat at the head of the High Table and he kept looking around at the mass of chattering children. He was a wide, powerfully built man with iron-gray hair and a straight, well-clipped mustache.

Under heavy, dark brows, Dr. Bloor's small black eyes scanned the three long tables and Charlie, almost bewitched, found himself following the big man's gaze until, eventually, their eyes met.

Dr. Bloor stood up. He walked off the dais and began to move down the aisle between the blue and purple tables. He never took his eyes off Charlie.

"What's the matter?" Fidelio nudged Charlie. "Don't you like the soup?"

Charlie couldn't answer. Dr. Bloor had reached him.

"Charles Bone!" It was the same chilling voice that had come leaking out of the newspaper. "A pleasure to have you here."

Charlie murmured feebly that he was glad to be at Bloor's, but he was hardly aware of what he was saying. Instinctively he was searching the broad face looming above him, and, to his astonishment, he found that photographs were not the limit of his endowment. Fear added another dimension. It allowed him to read faces. Charlie found that he knew, without question, who had taken Dr. Tolly's baby.

Maisie always said that a face told you a lot about a person. This one was beginning to tell Charlie more than he wanted to know. Quickly and deliberately, he closed his mind against it.

"Are you all right?" Fidelio asked Charlie. "You look as if you've seen a ghost."

Charlie watched Dr. Bloor's broad back receding. He stopped again and spoke to a girl in a green cape. She had long, pale hair and when she looked up, frowning, Charlie noticed that her wide gray eyes seemed confused and fearful.

"Charlie!" Fidelio nudged him. "What is it?"

"Who's that girl?" asked Charlie. "The one Dr. Bloor's talking to."

"Emilia Moon," said Fidelio. "She does art. She's quite good at it. Egg and chips are on the way up, so you'd better finish your soup or you won't get any. That's the rule."

Charlie slurped up the last of his soup, just as a plate of egg and chips reached him. He passed the empty bowl down the line to the end of the table where Billy Raven was stacking them up.

Emilia hadn't touched her soup. She was frowning at it as if she couldn't understand how it got there. Charlie felt he should warn her about the egg and chips, but she was too far away.

"Do we get pudding?" he asked Fidelio hopefully.

"You're joking. We get an apple if we're lucky," said Fidelio. "Or a pear."

They were lucky. A pear arrived in front of Charlie soon after the egg and chips.

When dinner was over and the last plates were being stacked, Dr. Bloor came to the front of the dais and clapped his hands. There was instant silence.

"I have an announcement to make," the doctor said solemnly. "A new boy has arrived to join the endowed. Charles Bone, stand up."

Feeling very hot, Charlie stood up. As three hundred pairs of eyes turned in his direction, his knees began to knock against each other.

"Charlie!" Dr. Bloor spoke his name as if it were a bad mistake. "After supper we have two hours of homework. Endowed children work in the King's room." He paused for several seconds, staring around at the silent and motionless crowd of children. And then, in a thunderous tone that made Charlie jump, he commanded, "Disperse!"

"Where's the King's room?" Charlie asked desperately, as Fidelio leaped up from the bench.

"Follow Gabriel," Fidelio advised, "or Billy Raven—

he's easy to spot. I've got to go now, Charlie. We have to be in our classrooms in three minutes. See you tonight!"

Fidelio was swept away on a tide of colored capes as children surged toward the end of the dining hall. Charlie searched frantically for Billy Raven's white head. But the tiny albino was hidden in the mass of jostling children. At last Charlie spotted him. He was weaving his way, very expertly, between the others, and it took Charlie some time to catch up with him.

"Hi!" said Charlie, grabbing the end of Billy's cape. "Can I come with you? I don't know where the King's room is."

"Not many people do," said Billy, grinning. "It'll take you a while to remember the way, but I'll be your guide as long as you want."

Charlie barely had time to murmur his thanks before Billy was off. First to the lockers to pick up books and pens, and then back across the hall, down a passage, turning a corner and leaping up a staircase. At last they arrived at a pair of tall black-painted doors. Billy pushed one of the doors and they stepped into a strange circular room. Ten children sat at a round table.

Manfred and Asa were there; Gabriel Silk sat between Emilia Moon and a plump, curly-haired girl who looked so normal it was hard to believe she was one of the endowed. A large, muscular girl contrasted strangely with the small, slight girl sitting next to her. Beside them, a dark girl with a long, sharp nose stared disdainfully at Charlie, and he felt his heart sinking. How much time would he have to spend with this unfriendly-looking bunch? He wished Fidelio and Olivia were part of the group.

Two boys sat with their backs to the door and one looked back as Charlie came in. He had chiseled, African features and the warmest smile Charlie had seen for a long time.

"This is Charlie!" said Billy Raven.

"Hi, Charlie, I'm Lysander," said the dark boy with the big smile.

Some of the girls introduced themselves. Dorcas

was plump and cheerful, Beth very large. Bindi was tiny, and Zelda had the long nose. Emilia Moon didn't even lift her head.

Charlie's relief at seeing a few friendly faces was short-lived.

"Sit down, Charlie Bone. And be quiet!" Manfred nodded at an empty chair on the other side of Emilia Moon. Billy sat beside Lysander.

As Charlie fumbled with his books, wondering where to start, he felt Manfred's coal-black eyes on him. He wanted to take a better look around the room, but dared not glance up until he was sure Manfred's dangerous stare was directed back at his book. When at last Charlie managed to take a quick look at his surroundings, he found someone else watching him, or rather goggling at him — the only person in the room whose face he hadn't seen.

The boy was older than Charlie, maybe twelve or thirteen. He had round startled eyes and his yellow hair stood up stiffly, as though an electric current had passed through it. Charlie frowned, hoping the boy would look away, but he didn't. In fact Charlie's fierce expression only seemed to intrigue him. In the end it was Charlie who had to look away.

Instead of starting his homework, his gaze slid up to the wall behind the yellow-haired boy. And there he was, the Red King. He stared out from a gold-framed painting, which must have been very old. The paint had cracked and faded so badly that the features on the long dark face were blurred and misty, except for the eyes — black and magnetic. The cloak he wore was a rich, velvety red and the slim crown on his dark hair had a mysterious golden sparkle.

"Charlie Bone!" Manfred's voice made Charlie start. "Why aren't you working?"

"I was looking at the Red King," said Charlie, avoiding Manfred's gaze. "It is the Red King, isn't it?"

"Of course! Get back to work!"

Manfred kept his eyes on Charlie, until Charlie opened his English book.

For the next two hours no one spoke. There were sighs and grunts, coughs and sneezes, all around Charlie, but no words. In a dark corner a clock ticked and chimed every quarter hour. Pages turned, pens squeaked, and Charlie was in danger of falling asleep.

At last the clock chimed eight o'clock and Manfred stood up. "You may go!" he said, and he walked out of the room with Asa loping behind him.

Charlie gathered his books together and went over to Billy Raven. "Who's the boy with the yellow hair?" he whispered.

The boy in question had just left the room with his green cape flying around him, as though caught by a mysterious breeze.

"Oh, that's Tancred," said Billy. "He can be a bit stormy. Come on, I'll show you the way to the dormitories."

Their journey took them up so many staircases and along so many passages, Charlie began to wonder if he'd ever find his own way back for breakfast. At last they arrived in a bleak, low-beamed room with bare floors and a single, dim light.

There were six beds, placed uncomfortably close

to one another, on both sides of the long room. The beds were narrow and covered with woolen blankets. There was a chair at the end of each one and a small cabinet against the wall between them. Charlie was relieved to see Fidelio sitting on a bed at the end of the room.

"Over here, Charlie!" Fidelio sang out. "You're next to me." He pointed to a bed.

Charlie went over and dumped his bag on a chair.

"Capes on the hooks beside us, the rest of your stuff in the drawers." Fidelio lowered his voice. "And look who's on your other side. You'll be able to get a look at his cape."

Charlie saw Gabriel Silk pushing clothes into a bedside cabinet. He didn't remove the cape, however, even when he went into the bathroom.

"Very suspicious," said Fidelio. "Have you got a flashlight?"

Charlie hadn't been thinking about flashlights when he packed his bag.

"A flashlight is an essential item," Fidelio told him.

"You can read after lights out and find your way around. It's so dark in here at night, you can't see a thing." He took a slim blue flashlight from a drawer and handed it to Charlie. "You'll need that to see the cape," he said. "Put it under your pillow."

Charlie was the last boy to get ready for bed. It took him some time to unpack his bag and find everything he needed for the night. He was embarrassed about the bears on his pajamas, but when he saw that somebody had squirrels on theirs, bears didn't seem so bad.

He had just hopped into bed when a hand came in the door and switched off the light. "Silence!" said a harsh female voice. The hand retreated, the door closed, and the dormitory was plunged into darkness.

There was something familiar about the voice, but Charlie couldn't quite place it.

"Who was that?" he whispered to Fidelio.

"Matron," said Fidelio, "the nearest thing a woman can get to a dragon."

There was a great deal of snuffling and rustling as the boys tried to get comfortable in their hard, narrow beds. Charlie waited until the noises had died down. In the bed beside him, Gabriel Silk was breathing deeply. He seemed to be asleep.

Charlie took out the flashlight and swung his feet to the floor. Making sure the flashlight was trained on the wall, he switched it on. The blue cape was right in front of him. He lifted it down from Gabriel's hook and saw the initials sewn inside the collar.

"It's mine," Charlie whispered.

Fidelio was sitting up in bed. "Take it," he said softly. "Quickly."

Charlie took Gabriel's tattered cape and replaced it with his own. He was about to hang the old cape on Gabriel's hook when there was a howl of panic.

"No!" cried Gabriel, leaping up and tearing at the cape. "You can't do this. Please! Please take it!" He flung the cape with the slashed corner on Charlie's bed.

Charlie laid the flashlight on his pillow where it cast a soft glow around his bed. "That one is yours," said Charlie. "I don't want it."

"You don't understand. I can't wear it, I can't. It's

full of... of horror. Its fear drags me down." Gabriel sank onto his bed and covered his face with his hands.

"What are you talking about, Gabriel Silk?" Fidelio asked in a harsh whisper. "Why should Charlie give you his cape?"

"Because I can't wear that one," Gabriel nodded at the older cape. "Something dreadful happened to the person who wore it before me. I can feel it, you see. It's like wearing a nightmare."

Charlie began to understand. "Is that your endowment, Gabriel? You can feel things that have happened?"

Gabriel nodded. "I get it from the things people have worn. It's horrible. If my clothes aren't brand new I get all these feelings that don't belong to me. Other people's worries. Sometimes I get happiness, but even that's no good because it's not true happiness and it doesn't last. At the beginning of the semester I had a brand new cape, but my gerbils attacked it and Mom had to get me a new one."

Charlie couldn't help being curious. "How many gerbils do you have?" he asked.

"Fifty-three," said Gabriel miserably. "They ate almost all of it. We haven't got much money so Mom asked the academy if they could give me a second-hand cape. They gave me that one."

By now the whole dormitory was wide awake. One of the boys at the end of the row said, "I bet it belonged to that girl who was lost in the ruin. She must have been pretty terrified."

"I think we should be quiet or Matron will come in and we'll all get detention," said another voice.

Charlie didn't know what to do. How could he make Gabriel wear someone else's nightmare?

"I'll do anything for you, anything," Gabriel whispered. "But please don't make me wear that cape."

Charlie took down his new cape and handed it to Gabriel.

"Thanks! Thanks, Charlie!" Gabriel hugged it gratefully.

"There is something you can do for me," Charlie said softly. He opened one of his drawers and took out the tie his mother had given him. "Can you tell me anything about the person who wore this?" He passed the tie to Gabriel.

Gabriel didn't ask any questions. He wound the tie around his neck and closed his eyes. He ran his fingers down the length of the blue silk and touched the small gold "Y" at the end of the tie. A shadow crossed his long face. "It's very strange," he murmured. "Whoever wore this tie was happy once, but now he's lost." He took the tie from his neck and ran it through his fingers. "I've never felt anything like this before. It's as if the person doesn't know who he is." He passed the tie back to Charlie.

At least his father had been happy once. Charlie assumed that "lost" meant dead. He put the tie in his drawer. He hadn't learned very much.

He was about to turn off the flashlight when a small figure appeared at the foot of Gabriel's bed; his white hair was a pale blur in the darkness.

"Can you tell me about this person?" Billy whispered. He put a long blue scarf on Gabriel's blanket.

Gabriel sighed but he didn't object. He draped the

scarf around his neck and once more closed his eyes. "Well, this person was always in a hurry," he said. "Here, there, everywhere. He just couldn't stop," he paused, "and now, I'm afraid, he's dead." He took off the scarf.

"Nothing else?" Billy Raven begged. "Didn't he say anything?"

"I'm sorry, it doesn't work like that," Gabriel said regretfully. "I don't hear voices. And when people die the messages get much weaker."

"I see. Thank you." Billy's sad voice echoed in the darkness as he tiptoed away.

Charlie turned off the flashlight, leaned over, and tucked it under Fidelio's pillow. Fidelio had fallen asleep. His quiet breathing made Charlie yawn and then, suddenly, he was wide awake. Something Gabriel had said didn't make sense.

"Gabriel," he whispered. "My father wore that tie. He died when I was two. Why did you say he was lost?"

"Because he is," said Gabriel's sleepy voice.

"Do you mean dead?"

"No, I mean lost. Definitely not dead."

Charlie stared into the darkness. He listened to the soft breathing that filled the unseen spaces all around him, knowing that he would be lying there, listening, for hours to come. "Not dead?" he whispered. "Gabriel, are you sure?"

"Quite sure," Gabriel murmured with a yawn. "Good night, Charlie!"

SKELETONS IN THE CLOSET

Charlie woke up with a dry throat and sore eyes. He had only slept for an hour. He resigned himself to wearing Gabriel's tattered cloak. After all, it wasn't going to give him nightmares.

Gabriel and Fidelio waited while Charlie tried to untangle his hedge of hair, but after five minutes they all agreed that Charlie's combing wasn't having much effect.

"If we don't go soon, we'll only get the burned pieces of bacon," Fidelio warned.

Charlie was starving. He threw down his comb and hurried down to breakfast with the others. He was glad of their company, for he'd never have found his way down to the bottom floor without them.

Gabriel was so happy wearing Charlie's cloak, he looked like a different person. In fact, he was all smiles. He even walked faster, now that he had cast off those horrible, frightening feelings.

Breakfast was oatmeal, burned bacon, and a mug of tea.

"Do we get this every day?" Charlie asked, trying to swallow a lump of oatmeal.

"Every day," said Fidelio.

Charlie tried not to think about Maisie's big breakfasts.

His second day at the academy was not as bad as his first. With Fidelio's help and sometimes Gabriel's, Charlie managed to find all his classes. On the third day he even found his way to the garden by himself.

Friday arrived. The day Charlie had been dreading. When classes were over he sat on his bed and watched Fidelio pack.

"What happens in here," Charlie asked, "when everyone else has gone home?"

"You're pretty much left to yourself," said Fidelio. "There's nothing to worry about. Manfred will be about, of course, but you won't be alone. Olivia's got detention too, remember, and Billy Raven never goes home, because he hasn't got one. I'll go and see

Benjamin and collect the case you want me to hide and at, let's see, half past eleven on Saturday, I'll come and wave to you. I'll give you the thumbs up if we've managed to move the case."

Charlie was tempted to tell Fidelio about the baby, but now wasn't the time. "How will I see you?" he asked glumly.

"Go to the music tower. Olivia will show you. I'll wave at the window facing the street on the second floor, and then you'll only have four hours to go before you're out."

Charlie sighed.

"Cheer up!" Fidelio patted Charlie's shoulder and picked up his bag.

Charlie followed his friend downstairs and watched him swing his bag toward the tall oak doors. They were open now, and children rushed through them, eager for a weekend of freedom.

Fidelio turned and gave a quick wave. He was almost the last to leave. Charlie had a desperate urge to rush through the doors before they closed. He took a few paces forward, glanced quickly around him, and increased his pace.

"Give up, Bone!"

Charlie whirled around. Manfred Bloor was standing in a shadowy recess halfway down the hall.

"Did you think no one was watching you, eh?"

"I didn't think anything," Charlie said.

"Take your homework to the King's room and stay there until you hear the dinner bell." As Manfred spoke, the two massive doors closed and his voice echoed across the empty hall.

"OK," Charlie muttered.

"Say, 'Yes, Manfred,' none of this 'OK' stuff."

"Yes, Manfred."

Charlie found Olivia and Billy chatting in the library.

"We don't have to be silent when Manfred's not here," Billy said happily.

Charlie wondered how Billy survived, imprisoned in Bloor's week after week, all alone in the dark dormitory when everyone else had gone home.

"Do you ever get out of here?" he asked Billy.

"I've got an aunt who lives by the sea, so I go there for the holidays," said Billy, "and I'm not lonely because there are . . ." he hesitated and said, almost under his breath, "there are always the animals."

"What animals?" asked Olivia. "I don't see any animals."

"Cook has a dog," said Billy. "It's very old, but it's friendly and there are — mice — and things."

"You can hardly talk to a mouse," said Charlie.

Billy was silent. He looked down at his book and began to read. The round lenses in his reading glasses made his eyes look like two huge red lamps. All at once he muttered, "Actually, I can."

"Can what?" asked Olivia.

Billy cleared his throat. "Talk to mice."

"Really?" Olivia closed her book. "That's fantastic. Is it your thing? You know, your endowment."

Billy nodded.

"Does that mean you can understand them as well?" asked Charlie.

Slowly and solemnly, Billy nodded again.

Charlie gave a low whistle. Benjamin had often said he wished he knew what Runner Bean was saying. "Could you come and talk to my friend's dog?" he asked Billy.

Billy didn't reply. He stared at Charlie with a bewildered expression.

"Perhaps that would be frivolous," said Charlie. "Sorry. I shouldn't have asked."

"Please don't tell anyone. I can't talk to everybody's pet. Animals have so many languages. It's very tiring listening to them."

Charlie and Olivia swore not to tell a soul. They returned to their books, but after a while Charlie became aware that Billy was neither working nor reading, he was just gazing into space.

"Can I tell you something?" Billy asked.

Olivia and Charlie both said, "Yes."

"It happened a week ago. I was on my way to the garden after tea. Manfred had been talking to someone. I don't know who it was, but I heard a girl crying in the prefects' room."

"Not me," said Olivia.

"Not you," Billy agreed. "But like I said, it was a girl, and she was crying, so I knew someone was in bad trouble. I suppose I'd slowed down a bit to listen, because Manfred suddenly stormed out and knocked me over. He told me I was blind and stupid and other horrible things, and that I was to go into the garden at once."

"So did you?" Olivia asked eagerly.

"My leg hurt," said Billy. "So I was a bit slow. I was limping down a passage when I heard the cats. There were three of them. 'Let us in,' they said. 'Quickly, Billy. Come to the door in the tower.'

"Which tower?" asked Charlie. "There are two."

"I guessed it would be the music tower. The other one hasn't got a door. I was afraid Manfred would see me but I couldn't ignore those cat voices. I limped and ran until I got to the tower. I crossed the empty room at the bottom and when I got to the door, I just unbolted it and let them in."

Charlie knew what Billy was going to say next, but he didn't interrupt.

"They were mighty strange cats." Billy's large ruby-colored eyes grew even wider. "They were like flames, red and orange and yellow. They thanked me, very politely, and then they told me the Red King had sent them."

"But he's been dead for hundreds of years," said Olivia.

"I asked the cats about that, but they just gave me a funny look and said, 'Of course,' and then they ran toward the stairs. Just before they vanished, the red one said, 'Leave the door, Billy!' so I did. I went into the garden as quickly as I could, but I'd only been there a few minutes when the fire bell rang. Manfred's room was on fire, and Manfred was in it."

"So it was the cats," breathed Charlie.

"They must have knocked a candle over," said Olivia. "Manfred's always got candles in his room. You can see them flickering from outside."

"Did they find out who let the cats in?" asked Charlie.

"They thought it was Mr. Pilgrim," said Billy, "because he's always in the music tower."

"So he got blamed!" said Olivia.

"Teachers don't get blamed," muttered Billy. "Do they?"

Before anyone could answer him, a voice outside the door said, "Silence in the King's room."

Olivia made a rude face at the door and Charlie tried not to laugh. Billy gave an anxious frown and went back to his homework.

When the dinner bell rang, at last, Charlie's stomach was rumbling. He always seemed to be hungry these days.

They made their way to the dining hall, but just before they went in, Olivia warned Charlie that they would be sitting at a table with Manfred. Charlie's heart sank. He'd been looking forward to dinner, but how could he enjoy it when he was trying to avoid Manfred's stare all the time?

"Has he ever — hypnotized you?" Charlie asked Olivia.

"Not yet. I'm not worth bothering with. I mean, I'm not endowed so I'm not a threat. I'm just a nuisance."

"He can't hypnotize me," Billy told them solemnly. "It's my eyes. He can't get past them." He smiled with satisfaction.

The dining hall was vast and echoey, and their footsteps rang out in the eerie silence as they made their way past empty benches to a table where Manfred sat, staring into a candle. Two places had been laid on his right side, one on his left. Charlie made sure he sat on the right, farthest away from Manfred.

Some of the teachers had gone home but Dr. Bloor was there, and so was Dr. Saltweather. Mr. Pilgrim sat slightly apart from the others; a small frown crossed his face when the children came closer, and yet he hardly seemed to see them.

Charlie reckoned it was one of the worst meals he'd ever eaten. It was bad enough, trying to avoid looking at Manfred, but the older boy wouldn't let them talk either. "You're not supposed to be enjoying your detention," he said sourly. So while they ate, there was no conversation to drown out the biting, chewing, gulping, and swallowing that went on.

At the end of the meal, when the plates had been stacked and cleared, they filed out of the dining hall as demurely as they could. But, as soon as the door closed behind them, Olivia said, "We've got two hours before bed. Where shall we start exploring?"

Charlie and Billy didn't have any ideas, so Olivia suggested the Da Vinci tower. Charlie wanted to know where it got its name, but Olivia shrugged and said, "It's always been called that. I think the art department used to use the room at the top, but now it's empty. Someone told me it wasn't safe. It's old and crumbly inside."

Charlie wondered why they were exploring an unsafe and crumbly building, but he didn't like to appear anxious. Besides, Olivia had made her mind up. She showed them a flashlight she'd hidden in the inside pocket of her cape, explaining that there might not be any lights in the tower.

It took them half an hour to find a likely-looking

way into the Da Vinci tower. There was a very small door at the far end of a passage on the third floor. "Same floor as my dormitory," Olivia told the others, "so if we're caught here, we've got an excuse."

The door was bolted but, surprisingly, not locked. Olivia slid back the bolts, which were stiff and very rusty.

"No one's been here for years," Charlie observed.

"Exactly. It makes it all the more interesting, doesn't it?" Olivia's eyes were sparkling. "Come on!"

The door creaked as she pulled it open. A dark passage curved away from them, disappearing around a corner hung with gray cobwebs. There was no light switch to be seen, nor any lamps or lightbulbs.

They crept through the door and found themselves walking on wide, dusty floorboards. A smell of damp, decaying things wafted out of the shadows.

"We'd better close the door," said Charlie, rather reluctantly.

"Must we?" asked Billy.

Olivia flicked on her flashlight and its powerful

beam lit up the passage before them. "It's OK, Billy," she said.

As Charlie closed the door something made it stick, and when he looked down to see what it was he noticed Olivia's shoes. She was wearing black patent leather shoes with very high heels. Charlie hoped they wouldn't meet too many old staircases.

As it happened, as soon as they'd passed the cobwebby corner, an old staircase was the first thing they met. It was the only way out of the passage. They would either have to climb up a steep curving spiral, or down a sequence of narrow, rocky steps.

"Let's go up," begged Billy. "It looks horrible down there."

"Intriguing though," murmured Olivia. She shone the flashlight into the dark shaft below them. There seemed to be no end to it.

"Up not down!" said Charlie, noticing Billy's anxious expression. He remembered that Billy couldn't see too well. "I'll go first, Billy you come right behind me, and Olivia last. That'll be safest."

Billy looked relieved and Olivia happily agreed. "You'll need the flashlight if you're going first," she said, passing it to Charlie.

The spiral steps were extremely narrow and uneven. Charlie practically had to crawl up them. He could hear Billy panting nervously behind him, and the occasional scrape of Olivia's shoes on the stone.

All at once there was a clatter, several muffled thumps, an echoing moan, and then a gruesome silence. It was quite obvious what had happened.

"Do you think she's dead?" Billy whispered.

The moan started up again, so at least that question was answered. But how badly wounded was Olivia?

"We'll have to go down backward, Billy," said Charlie. "Do you think you can?"

"Yes," Billy said uncertainly.

Slowly and carefully they retraced their steps. The moaning began to fade and Charlie called out, "Hold on, Olivia. We're coming." They had reached the small landing before the rocky steps plunged down into the shadows.

"I'll go first," Charlie offered. "Do you want to wait here, Billy?"

"No. Not alone." Billy quickly clambered after Charlie.

The rough staircase began to curve and Charlie, directing the flashlight downward, found Olivia at the bottom, huddled against an ancient-looking door.

"Are you OK?" was Charlie's first question.

"'Course I'm not. My knees hurt and I've bumped my head. I couldn't see where I was going, could I?"

Charlie didn't like to mention the high heels. "Shall we pull you up? Do you think you can stand?"

"I'll try." Olivia grabbed the door handle above her and gradually pulled herself upright. She must have been leaning rather heavily on the rotten door because there was a sudden crack and the old door fell inward with Olivia on top of it.

"Yeeeee-ooooo-ooow!" she yelled.

There wasn't much point in telling her to be quiet. Charlie scrambled after her. As he stepped onto the fallen door, the flashlight shone into the room beyond and Charlie saw something so extraordinary, he had to ignore Olivia for a moment and aim the light farther into the room.

"Wow!" he murmured. "It's amazing."

"What is?" Olivia rolled over and got to her feet. Now she, too, could see.

The room was full of armor, or rather pieces of armor. There were also pieces of metal figures. They lay on tables and chairs; they littered the floor and hung from the walls. There were shiny skulls with hollow eyes and terrible metal grins; steel fingers clinging to boxes; metal feet dangling from cabinets; arms, legs, ribs, and elbows all in tangled heaps on the floor. Worse than all that were the skeletons hanging from the ceiling.

"Ugh!" said Olivia. "It's like Frankenstein's workshop."

Billy, who had squeezed between them, asked, "Who's Frankenstein?"

"A doctor who made a monster out of a dead·man," Olivia told him.

"Dead pieces," Charlie corrected.

Olivia grabbed his arm. "Did you hear that?"

Charlie was about to ask what, when there came the thin *tip-tap* of approaching footsteps. They weren't coming from the rocky steps behind them, but from a door at the far end of the room.

"Quick!" Olivia pushed both boys off the fallen door and into a closet with a door standing slightly open. As soon as they were inside, she pulled the door shut, but not before they'd had a glimpse of the things in the closet.

Olivia and Charlie both clamped their hands over Billy's mouth. He was, after all, much younger than they were. And the closet was full of skeletons.

Charlie switched off the flashlight just as someone entered the room. A light came on. It shone through the cracks in the closet door and the children were painted, like zebras, in stripes of light and shadow. Olivia just managed to stop giggling. Squinting through a crack, Charlie saw Dr. Bloor moving between the stacks of armor and metal figures.

The shapes were now easier to see, and Charlie noticed that some were animals — dogs, cats, and even a rabbit. They're Dr. Tolly's, he thought. But how did they end up here, in a secret room in Bloor's Academy? Were they bought or given or stolen?

The big man swung around. He began to walk in the direction of the closet. As he passed a metal dog he picked it up and wrenched off the tail. He bashed the dog's body against a table. It broke apart and a stream of wheels, cogs, springs, and screws poured out. Dr. Bloor peered at the shiny heap, grunted, and then swept them off the table. He was obviously searching for something and angry because he couldn't find it. He turned his attention to the closet again, and walked purposefully toward it.

They hardly dared to breathe. Olivia, Charlie, and Billy clutched one another's hands. Olivia's long nails bit into Charlie's palm and he was on the point of yelling out, when a door opened with a loud squeak and a voice said, "I thought I'd find you in here."

CLUES AT LAST

"That old door's fallen in," said Dr. Bloor.

"Oh? Has someone been prying?"

"I doubt it. It's just the damp and old age."

"Mm. I wonder," said a familiar voice.

"All this junk Tolly sent us . . ." Dr. Bloor kicked at a metal arm, and it rolled across the floor toward the closet. "Tricks, all of it. Where's the real thing?"

"I told you, Dad. Miss Ingledew gave it to Charlie Bone."

"You can't be sure."

Olivia's grip relaxed and Charlie was able to drag his hand away from the painful nails. Billy had momentarily forgotten the skeletons hanging behind him and was now peering through the largest crack in the door. "It's Manfred," he whispered.

Charlie had already recognized the voice. "Shhh!" he whispered. "Listen."

"Of course I'm sure," said Manfred. "Asa was watch-

209

ing. He saw Charlie come out of Ingledew's with a large black bag. Who else would she give it to?"

Dr. Bloor grunted and lowered himself into an ancient-looking chair. Clouds of dust billowed around him as he sank into the cracked leather cushions. "Beats me how the boy knew where to go. How he knew it was at Ingledew's."

"It was the cats, naturally," said Manfred. "You know what they do—knock things off tables, distract people. Somehow the boy got hold of that photograph and then, of course, he had to take it back to the Ingledew woman. I bet you anything one of those cats got into Kwik Foto when they were packing. A moment's distraction and—poof—wrong photo in wrong envelope."

"I'll skin those animals alive if I ever get hold of them!" Dr. Bloor punched the arm of his chair and another cloud of dust whirled out. "The very smell they leave makes me feel ill."

"Sulfur," said Manfred.

"Age," said his father. "Nine hundred years of sneaking and meddling."

"And stealing and burning," said Manfred.

In the eerie gloom of the closet the three children gaped at one another. "Nine hundred years," mouthed Olivia.

Billy shook his head in disbelief. Charlie frowned and shrugged. Why not? he thought. Stranger things are happening every day in this place.

"Talking of burning," muttered Dr. Bloor. "Do we know for sure it was the cats?"

"I told you, I saw them under my window when I was trying to put out the flames."

"And you think the girl had something to do with it?"

"Of course. I'd just given her a good beating."

"You shouldn't have done that, Manfred," Dr. Bloor said sternly. "It won't help."

"I lost my temper. It makes me mad when she's not responding. She's waking up, you know. I can't keep her out for much longer." Manfred gave a sigh of im-

211

patience. "It's not as if I haven't got enough to do, keep-ing an eye on Pilgrim."

"And how is that little problem coming along?"

"I'm not sure. I may be imagining it, but I think he's changed since the boy arrived. Perhaps we shouldn't have brought him here."

"We had to, Manfred. Couldn't leave him out there once we knew he was endowed."

"I know. I know."

Inside the closet, Olivia made a face and pointed at Charlie. "You," she mouthed.

Charlie shrugged again. What Dr. Bloor and his sin-ister son mean? Who was the girl who was waking up? Why was Manfred keeping an eye on Mr. Pilgrim? He listened intently for clues.

But Manfred and his father were beginning to move away. It seemed that Charlie was not going to learn any more about himself or the waking girl. And then, just before Manfred left the room, he said, "It won't be long now. Asa's been very vigilant. He's pretty sure that kid with the dog is hiding it. We just have to get the parents out of the way and we'll have it."

"Manfred," Dr. Bloor's voice was distant now, but his words could be clearly heard. "It has to be destroyed before it wakes her up."

The light in the room went out and the door closed.

For a few seconds the three children remained silent. When they were sure they were alone, Olivia said, "Well, that was interesting, wasn't it?"

"Let's get out of here," said Charlie. "I've got a lot to tell you."

Billy was the first to leap out of the closet. He ran over the fallen door and up the rocky steps before the others had even dusted themselves off.

They needn't have bothered with the dusting. By the time they had crept out of the Da Vinci tower, they were, all three, covered in cobwebs again. Olivia had a swollen ankle and cuts and bruises on her knees, but she refused to make a fuss. Charlie was impressed. "I think you should see Matron," he said. "There might

213

be something nasty in all that dust, you know, an ancient bug or something."

"Matron? She's a dragon," said Olivia. "She's bound to ask me what I've been doing. I'll just hide my knees under some tights and Mom can deal with it tomorrow."

Billy reminded Charlie that he had something to tell them.

"You bet I have," said Charlie. "All that stuff Manfred and Dr. Bloor were talking about, well, it made everything that's been happening to me make sense."

Olivia suggested they go to her dormitory as it was closer than the boys'. "It's just three doors down this passage," she said. "We can get cleaned up before Matron starts her rounds."

She spoke too soon. Matron had already started her rounds. Just as they reached Olivia's dormitory, the door opened and Matron came out. Only then did Charlie discover why her voice had seemed familiar. Matron was Lucretia Yewbeam.

Of course, Billy and Olivia simply recognized her

as their school matron, but Charlie was so shaken he felt as though he'd gotten punched in the stomach. He took a desperate gulp of air and stuttered, "Aunt L-L-Lucretia!"

"Matron to you!" snapped Aunt Lucretia.

"I d-didn't know you were a matron," said Charlie, still in shock.

"We've all got to earn a living these days," said Matron Yewbeam.

Clearly puzzled, Olivia and Billy turned from Charlie to Aunt Lucretia and back again.

"You're all filthy," Matron went on. "Where've you been?"

Olivia was ready for this one. Without a moment's hesitation she said, "We were out in the garden and when we tried to come in, the door was locked, so we went around and found a window and climbed into this empty, really dirty room. Well, really we fell in, because the window was quite high."

Matron frowned. Did she believe Olivia? It was just possible that someone had locked the garden door.

She said, "I'd put you all on detention for another twenty-four hours, but as it happens I want my day off, too. So this time I'll let you off with a warning."

"Thank you, Matron," Olivia said gushingly.

"However!" Matron Yewbeam wasn't fooled that easily. "You can all go to bed, right now."

"But we've got another hour," Billy said bravely.

"It'll take you a whole hour to clean yourselves up," barked Matron. "Off you go, right now." She turned to Olivia. "And you'd better have those knees cleaned up!"

Leaving Olivia to Matron's far from tender care, Charlie and Billy made their way back to their own dormitory.

There was something to be said for an almost empty school, after all. The water in the taps was hot. So far Charlie had only managed to get one cold bath. Not that he enjoyed baths. But today he had the longest, hottest bath he could remember.

Five minutes after the boys had climbed into bed, there was a knock on the door and Olivia bounced in. She was wearing a white velvet nightgown with big purple flowers all over it, and her purple hair had turned a mousy brown.

"Matron made me wash it," she informed the boys. "It was just spray-on dye." She plopped herself at the foot of Charlie's bed. "So, what have you got to tell us?"

"It's like this," began Charlie, and he told them everything that had happened to him, from the moment he saw the photograph of the strange man and the baby, until he reached Bloor's Academy. "All the time I've been thinking that the thing in the case was valuable, a precious thing that could be exchanged for Miss Ingledew's niece, whoever she is. But it seems that Dr. Bloor just wants to destroy it."

"Before it wakes the girl up," added Olivia. "And the girl must be the stolen baby."

"So, in a way, what's in the case is still valuable," said Billy, "because of what it can do. It's like a kind of spell."

"Hmm." Olivia swung her legs. "Do you know what I think?" She didn't wait for them to ask. "I think Manfred's hypnotized her. Perhaps she's always been hypnotized, ever since she was stolen, or swapped, or

217

whatever. But it's wearing off a bit, so Manfred has to keep doing it, to make sure she doesn't wake up and run away, or remember who she really is."

"Olivia, you're brilliant," said Charlie. "To tell the truth, for a while, I thought it was you."

"Me? No way. I think I'd know if I was hypnotized." Olivia grinned. "I'm pretty sure I can find out who she is, though."

"How?" asked Charlie.

"Observation. I'm good at that. If the baby was swapped eight years ago and she was almost two, then she's going to be about the same age as us. She's bound to be endowed, because that's why Dr. Bloor would have wanted her. So, who fits the description? There aren't that many of you, are there?"

"Twelve," said Billy. "Five are girls. Zelda's too old, she's thirteen. So's Beth. That leaves Dorcas, Emilia, and Bindi."

"Can't be Dorcas," Olivia declared. "She's so cheerful. I've never seen anyone less hypnotized."

"It's Emilia," Charlie exclaimed. "Of course, it is.

Think about it. She always looks as if she's in a kind of trance, and she's afraid of Dr. Bloor."

"Who isn't?" asked Olivia. "But I think you're right. She's in my dormitory, so I'll keep my eyes open. Better go now. Good night, boys. See you in the morning." Olivia bounced off the bed and out the door.

She had hardly left the room when the voice of Lucretia Yewbeam barked, "Lights out!" And a white hand snaked around the open door and snapped off the light.

For a moment, both boys were silent. There were four empty beds between Charlie and Billy. On the other side of the room all the beds were empty. It gave Charlie the creeps. He wondered what it was like to be Billy, alone in this big, dark room every weekend.

"Billy," he whispered. "Next weekend, can you come home with me? Will they let you?"

"Oh, yes," said Billy eagerly. "I've been to Fidelio's house. So, I'm sure they'll let me come to yours."

"Good."

There was a creak, a soft shuffling, and a thin beam

of flashlight approached Charlie's bed. Charlie could just make out Billy's small figure in pale blue pajamas.

"Charlie, you know you said you can hear what people are saying in photographs?"

"Yes," said Charlie, uncertainly. "Sometimes."

A crumpled photograph was placed on his pillow.

"Can you tell me what these people are saying?" asked Billy. "They're my parents."

Charlie stared at the photo. He saw a young couple standing under a tree. The woman was wearing such a pale dress she looked like a ghost. She had blonde, almost white, hair. They were both smiling, but only with their mouths. The woman's eyes looked fearful, the man's angry.

The voice that suddenly erupted in Charlie's ear gave him such a jolt his head ducked forward as if he'd been hit.

Come on, smile for your little boy, Mrs. Raven. Is it so hard? There was no mistaking that cold, deep voice.

The young man said, *You'll never get away with this.*

Look at my son, Mr. Raven. Isn't he handsome, my little

Manfred? That's right. Look into his eyes. Like lovely shiny coals, aren't they?

"Can you hear anything?" asked Billy.

Charlie didn't know what to say. How could he leave Billy with those awful words? He decided to lie, but before he could speak something happened. Something that had never happened to him before. He began to hear the young man's thoughts.

We can still get away. We'll take little Billy and drive far away, where they'll never find us. I wish that boy wouldn't look at me like that. His eyes are like pitch!

"Well?" asked Billy anxiously.

"The woman . . ." Charlie's thoughts were racing. "The woman said, 'Be quick, I must get back to little Billy.' And the man said, 'Yes, our baby is very precious. He's going to be a star!'"

Even in the dim light, Charlie could see Billy's happy smile.

"Anything else?" asked Billy.

"No. Sorry."

"Did the person who took the photo say anything? I never found out who it was."

"They didn't say anything." Charlie handed the photo back to Billy.

"One day I might be adopted," said Billy. "I'll have parents again, and I'll be able to go home like everyone else." He crept back to bed and, in a few moments, he was fast asleep, the crumpled photo buried deep under his pillow.

Charlie lay awake for a long time, trying to puzzle out what was going on at Bloor's Academy. Babies had been stolen, children had vanished, and fathers too? A father he had thought was dead was still alive, but didn't know who he was.

"Uncle Paton," Charlie murmured. "He can find out. I bet he already knows a lot more than he admitted."

One more day and Charlie would be at home. Questions for Paton were already forming in his mind when he fell asleep at last.

MIND GAMES

At breakfast the next morning, Charlie was relieved to find that Manfred was absent from the table.

"He always sleeps late on the weekends," Billy told him. "He's up half the night, you can see his candles burning from our window."

"What's he doing?" Charlie murmured.

"Practicing sorcery," said Olivia, rolling her eyes.

The trouble was, Charlie thought, Olivia was probably right.

"So he won't be watching us all morning, either?" he asked.

"Oh, no," Billy assured him. "We'll have to go and work, of course. Our books will be all ready for us, and a sheet of questions to answer, but we can talk and draw or do anything we like as long as we stay there till twelve and finish the questions."

They made their way to the King's room, where Charlie found a sheet of very mean questions to answer. He was less than halfway through when he re-membered Fidelio. "I promised to go to the music tower at half past eleven," he told the others. "Fidelio's coming to give me a sign that he's moved the case."

"We'll cover for you," Olivia said brightly. "And if you haven't finished your questions you can copy my an-swers when you get back."

"Thanks," said Charlie gratefully. He remembered that he didn't know how to get to the music tower. It would take him ages to find the way. "Fidelio said you'd show me the way, but if you're covering for me . . ."

"I'll draw a map," said Olivia.

She kept her word. As Charlie struggled with his questions, glancing at the clock every five minutes, Olivia drew out a neat plan of the passages that led to the music tower. She pushed it over to him.

"Can you understand it?" she asked.

Charlie studied the map. "Yes. I go through the last door at the end of the hall."

"That's it."

"It's nearly half past," said Billy.

Charlie leaped up. "We'll say you've gone to the bathroom if anyone comes in," said Olivia.

Charlie walked to the door, opened it, and looked out. No one was there. He gave Olivia and Billy a quick wave, stepped out into the passage, and closed the door behind him.

Following Olivia's map he reached the main hall and raced toward a small arched door near the main entrance. The ancient-looking door seemed to be locked. Charlie's heart sank. He twisted the big iron ring that served as a handle and, at the third attempt, the door swung back. Charlie stepped into a dark passage and carefully latched the door behind him.

He realized that he was now in a part of the building below Manfred's room and he began to tiptoe.

The dark, stone passage led, at length, to an empty room at the bottom of the tower. Charlie saw the door that Billy must have opened to let the cats in. It was now firmly bolted. Opposite the door, a flight of stone steps ascended to the upper floors.

Charlie began to mount the steps that spiraled

upward, without rails or even a rope to cling to. He emerged at last into another empty room with two windows overlooking the square. He peered out. There was no sign of Fidelio. Perhaps he hadn't climbed high enough to get a good view. Charlie mounted a second set of steps, and then, without pausing on the next floor, climbed quickly up to the third. From here he could see the whole city. It was a bright, cold morning and, in the distance, the huge cathedral rose out of the mass of surrounding roofs like a magnificent monster, its golden spire twinkling in the sunlight.

Two figures suddenly ran past the fountain below and stopped when they reached the tower. They waved. Fidelio had brought Benjamin with him.

Charlie waved back. Had Fidelio managed to hide the case? Charlie lifted his right thumb to the window and shrugged. He spread his hands. Did they understand him?

Apparently not. Fidelio and Benjamin began to act in a very peculiar way. Benjamin pulled an imaginary cord, while Fidelio stuck his hand behind him and wagged it, like a tail.

Charlie shook his head and shrugged. What were they doing? It didn't make sense.

The two boys were obviously very excited about something, but Charlie wanted to know if the case was safe. He tried to make shapes with his hands, to mouth questions, "Is it safe? The case? Where is it?"

It was no use. Benjamin and Fidelio had something else on their minds. Whatever it was, Charlie would have to wait until tonight to find out. He gave another wave and was about to run down the steps when he heard footsteps below him. If he went through the door into the corridor he might find himself outside Manfred's room. The only way out was up.

As Charlie began to creep up to the fourth floor, distant music echoed down the narrow stairwell. Someone was playing a piano. Very beautifully. It was wonderful, rich, complicated music. The pianist seemed to be using every note on the keyboard, and Charlie was drawn toward the sound as though by a magic thread. He didn't stop at the fourth floor but continued upward, slowly now, and almost fearfully, because he found that it was impossible to stop. And he was afraid of what he might find when he reached the top of the tower.

The room he finally stepped into was not empty like the others. This room was full of music books. Piles of sheet music lay on the floor, shelves of leather-bound scores lined the walls: Mozart, Chopin, Beethoven, Bach, Liszt. Composers' names. Some were familiar to Charlie, others he'd never heard of.

Beyond a small oak door a stream of piano music rose and fell. Charlie touched the door handle. He twisted it and the door opened. He stood on the threshold and gazed into the room. It was empty, except for a huge black piano and the man sitting behind it: Mr. Pilgrim. The strange piano teacher looked straight through Charlie; he didn't even seem to be aware of the open door, although the draft caused several papers to float off the windowsill.

Charlie wasn't sure what to do. He stood there,

mesmerized, and then, at last, he stepped into the room and closed the door behind him. Mr. Pilgrim played on, now looking at his hands, now staring at the sky beyond the windows, his face blank, his eyes dark and unfathomable.

Far away the great cathedral clock began to chime out across the city. One, two, three... it was twelve o'clock, Charlie realized. He would be late. The others would wonder where he was. Manfred might come looking for him. He turned to go but, suddenly, Mr. Pilgrim stopped playing. He appeared to be listening to the chimes. When the clock struck twelve, Mr. Pilgrim stood up. He saw Charlie standing by the door and frowned.

"I... I'm sorry, sir, I got lost," said Charlie, "and your music was so... well, beautiful, sir, it kind of made me want to listen."

"What?" said Mr. Pilgrim.

"It made me want to listen, sir,"

"Oh."

"I'm sorry to intrude," Charlie murmured. "I'd better go now."

"Wait." The strange teacher stepped around the piano and came toward Charlie. "Who are you?"

"I'm Charlie Bone, sir."

"Charlie?"

"Yes."

Charlie saw a flicker of interest in Mr. Pilgrim's dark eyes, and then it was gone. "I see," he muttered. "You'd better run along."

"Yes, sir." Charlie was gone in a second. He leaped through the door and down the spiraling steps in half the time it took to climb them. He managed to reach the King's room without meeting anyone, except a janitor who grinned and gave him a large wink as he tore across the hall.

"What've you been doing?" asked Olivia when Charlie burst into the room. "Manfred's been in here twice, asking where you were!"

"What did you tell him?" said Charlie.

"I said what we agreed. That you were in the bath-room."

"Twice?" Charlie was worried.

"The second time I said you had a stomachache," Billy said gravely. "But I don't know if he believed me."

At that moment, Mr. Paltry came in, collected the books, and told the children to get ready for lunch.

Lunch was cheese sandwiches and an apple each. The staff that were on Saturday duty sat at the High Table, but Manfred and Dr. Bloor didn't appear.

"They have their meals in the west wing on the weekends," Billy said, "with Mrs. Bloor and the rest of the family."

Charlie was surprised. "There are more Bloors?"

"An old, old man," said Billy. "I've never seen him but Cook's dog told me about him."

"I bet you learn a lot from Cook's dog," Olivia remarked.

"I do," said Billy.

After lunch they were allowed into the garden and

Olivia insisted they walk close to the ruin. Billy wasn't too eager, but Charlie was curious.

"Come on, Billy," said Olivia. "We won't go in. We'll just take a look. I haven't played the ruin game, yet."

"Nor me," said Charlie.

"Nor me," muttered Billy, but he reluctantly followed the others up to the dark rust-colored walls. They were at least four meters high, Charlie reckoned, and massively thick. The great stones loomed out of the trees like the boundary of some lost and ancient city. The entrance was a wide archway, and beyond this they could see a mossy paved courtyard with five shadowy passages leading out of it.

Charlie thought of the girl who had vanished and shuddered. "What goes on in there?" he murmured.

Olivia guessed what was on his mind. "I'm going to make sure I'm never alone in there, not for one second. It gives me the creeps, wondering what happened to that poor girl. They say her cape was practically shredded to bits."

"It was a wolf," said Billy.

MIND GAMES

"A wolf?" Charlie and Olivia stared at him.

"Cook's dog told me," said Billy. "It never lies. Dogs don't. To be precise, it said the thing was a kind of wolf. It lives in the academy but it comes out to the ruin at night."

They found themselves looking up to the sky, which was already beginning to fill with evening clouds. Olivia took a step backward, and then she ran across the grass dramatically howling, "Nooooo! Noooooo! Nooooo!"

The others ran after her, laughing at her flying white legs and funny, high-pitched wailing, although Charlie secretly admitted that there was a bit of fright mixed up in all the laughter.

They burst through the garden door and ran straight into Manfred.

"Olivia Vertigo, go and pack," he said coldly. "Bone, come with me."

"Why?" asked Charlie, staring at the floor.

Manfred said, "Because I told you to."

Charlie was tempted to run up to the dormitories with Olivia. Soon his mother would be at the door. Surely, Manfred couldn't stop him from going home? On the other hand, perhaps he could.

Manfred turned away and snapped his fingers. Charlie grinned at his two friends and began to follow the older boy.

"Good luck!" Olivia whispered.

Manfred led the way to the prefects' room. Today it was empty and Manfred allowed Charlie to sit in one of the easy chairs, while he took his usual place behind the large desk.

"Don't look so petrified, Charlie!" Manfred attempted to smile but he wasn't very good at it. "I'm not going to eat you."

Charlie wasn't convinced. He kept his eyes on the floor.

"I just want to know where you've put the case Miss Ingledew gave you. It belongs to us, you see." Manfred's tone was soft and persuasive, but Charlie wasn't fooled.

"I don't know what you're talking about," he said.

"Of course you do, Charlie. It's no good to you. In fact it'll only bring you trouble. Come on, where is it?"

When Charlie didn't respond, Manfred began to get impatient. "Look at me, boy!" he barked.

Charlie kept his eyes on the floor.

"How long do you think you can keep that up?" sneered Manfred. "Come on, look at me. Come on, just a quick look. It won't hurt."

Charlie found his gaze being slowly drawn to Manfred's pale face. He couldn't stop himself. If Manfred managed to hypnotize him, all would be lost. He knew he would tell him everything. And then another thought occurred to him. Perhaps he could fight Manfred. If he read his face and listened to his thoughts, maybe he could break the older boy's control.

So Charlie looked at the thin, cold face and the coal-black eyes, and he tried to hear the voice of Manfred's thoughts. But no voice came. Instead a picture crept into his mind, a picture of a man playing a piano.

"Stop it!" Manfred commanded. "Stop doing this, Bone!"

But Charlie clung to his image, and now he could hear music, rich and fast and very beautiful.

"Stop it!" shrieked Manfred.

A glass of water whizzed past Charlie and smashed against the wall behind him. He leaped out of the chair as a large book came flying at him. The next missile Manfred picked up was a glass paperweight, but before he could throw it the door opened and Dr. Bloor looked in.

"What's going on?" he asked.

"He won't respond," hissed Manfred. "He keeps blocking me. He can play mind games too."

"Interesting," said Dr. Bloor. "Very interesting. You shouldn't get in such a state, Manfred. I've warned you. You must control yourself."

Charlie glanced at the wall. Broken glass lay across the back of the chair he'd been sitting in, and a large wet stain darkened the rose-colored wallpaper.

"Charlie, your mother's waiting," said Dr. Bloor. "Go pack, immediately."

"Yes, sir," Charlie said eagerly. He left the room as fast as he dared.

Billy was waiting for him in the dormitory. He wasn't alone. On the floor beside his bed lay the oldest dog Charlie had ever seen. It was very fat and its long brown face was so creased and folded it was difficult to make out where its eyes and mouth were kept. It was panting heavily, which wasn't surprising as it must have come up several staircases from the kitchen. Its smell reminded Charlie of his mother's rotting vegetables.

"Is it allowed in here?" said Charlie anxiously.

"No one knows about it," said Billy. "I'm left to myself most of the weekend, and even Matron goes home on Saturdays."

Charlie began to throw things into his bag. "I wish you could come home with me," he said. "It must be horrible in here at night."

"I'm used to it," said Billy. "I've got Blessed to talk to. We've got a lot to discuss today."

"Blessed?" Charlie regarded the wrinkled, dumpy creature at Billy's feet.

"It's a nice name, isn't it?" said Billy.

Charlie didn't argue. He would have liked to see just how Billy communicated with a dog, but he couldn't wait to get home. He said good-bye to Billy and raced down the many passages and staircases to the hall.

THE INVENTOR'S TALE

Mrs. Bone was sitting in one of the large carved chairs near the main doors. Charlie didn't see her at first because she was hidden behind Dr. Bloor's burly frame. He was talking to her very earnestly and Amy Bone looked as anxious as a schoolgirl who had just done something wrong. When she saw Charlie she gave him a tiny wave and smiled nervously.

Dr. Bloor swung round. "Ah, there we are then," he said, trying to sound cheerful. "I've just been telling your mother how well you've done in your first week, apart from the little—er—misdemeanor with the cape."

"Yes, sir." Charlie wondered how he was going to explain the torn cape to his mother. He would just have to hide it, he decided.

Mrs. Bone stood up, gave Charlie a quick peck on the cheek, and whisked him through the doors before any more could be said.

"Have a good weekend," called Dr. Bloor, ignoring the fact that the weekend was half over.

"Yes, sir," said Charlie, neglecting to add thank you.

His mother didn't mention the misdemeanor. "I hope you don't mind walking, Charlie. It's not quite dark enough for Paton to come out and I couldn't manage to find the taxi fare. And as you missed the school bus..."

"Sorry, Mom."

"It wasn't fair to give you detention on your first week," she said hotly. "But we'll forget it, shall we? Maisie's got all your favorite food."

Charlie already felt hungry.

They crossed the square with the fountain and walked down the alley that led to High Street. It was only when they were halfway down High Street that Charlie became aware of an old man keeping pace with them on the other side of the road.

Charlie knew who it was, immediately. The disguise was hopeless. None of the old man's clothes fitted properly and his white beard was obviously false. It just didn't match the bright red hair that stuck out at the back of the ratty old cap.

"Can you walk a bit faster, Mom?" asked Charlie. "We're being followed."

"Followed?" Mrs. Bone stopped and looked back. "Who's following us?"

"Just a boy," Charlie told her. "He's on the other side of the road. It's silly because he knows where I live. He just seems to like stalking people."

"Come on, Charlie!" Mrs. Bone grabbed Charlie's arm and pulled him down another narrow alley. "It'll take us longer this way, but I can't stand to be followed."

This had happened to his mother before, Charlie realized. It was soon after their wedding that his father had begun to look over his shoulder, Charlie's mother had told him. But who had been following them then?

Mrs. Bone now took a route through the narrow alleys that was completely new to Charlie. "I haven't been this way for a long time, but it hasn't changed much. Ah, here we are!" As she said this, they emerged into the small square in front of the cathedral. "Oh!"

she exclaimed, and she put her hand to her heart, as if the sight of the huge building had taken her breath away. "Your father used to play the organ here," she murmured. "But I haven't been back since . . . since he stopped."

She increased her pace, as if she could hardly wait to get away from the place and, of course, they found themselves passing Ingledew's bookshop.

"I know the lady who lives here," Charlie said, stopping to peer into the window. "Can we go in?"

"It's closed," his mother said quickly, "Look at the sign." And then, as they hurried on, she added, "Paton was here last night. He came home with a bag full of books. Something has gotten into your uncle lately — he's not himself at all."

Was Uncle Paton raising his head at last?

Maisie had seen them coming long before they climbed the steps to number nine. When Charlie stepped through the kitchen door, the kettle was on and a feast was laid out on the table.

"They'd no right to keep you from us for another

whole day," cried Maisie, giving Charlie a suffocating hug.

"He broke the rules," said a voice from the rocker by the stove. "He's got to learn." Grandma Bone frowned at Charlie. "Look at your hair, boy! Didn't you take a comb to school?"

"Yes," said Charlie, "but the matron's not too fussy about our hair, and you know who I mean by the matron!"

"Aunt Lucretia, of course," snapped Grandma Bone.

This was a great surprise to Maisie and Amy, who gaped at Grandma Bone in amazement.

"Why didn't you tell us?" exclaimed Charlie's mother.

"Why should I?" sniffed the old woman. She returned to the book she'd been reading as though nothing had happened.

"Well," said Maisie. "Some people take the cake."

Grandma Bone ignored this remark, just as she ignored the hearty tea that the other members of the house were settling into, excluding Paton, of course.

Charlie thought to ask after his uncle, but Grandma

Bone looked so frosty he decided not to. He didn't want any more arguments, he just wanted to fill himself with good food and then go and see Benjamin.

"And where are you off to?" Grandma Bone demanded after tea when Charlie made for the front door.

"He's going to see his friend, of course," said Maisie.

"And why is that?" asked Grandma Bone. "It's his duty to stay with his family on his weekends at home."

"Don't be silly, Grizelda," said Maisie. "Off you go, Charlie."

Charlie shot out the door before Grandma Bone could open her mouth again. He ran across to number twelve, where he found not only Benjamin, but Fidelio as well. They seemed very excited and immediately dragged Charlie into the kitchen where the remains of pizza, chips, bananas, and cookies littered the kitchen table. Runner Bean was enjoying the bits that had fallen to the floor, but he made a great fuss over Charlie when he came in, jumping up and licking his face with a very sticky tongue.

Charlie managed to break away from Runner Bean, while Benjamin began to explain what had happened. It seemed that an important discovery had been made.

"It was Fidelio," said Benjamin. "You know the voice in the dog you gave me, well, Fidelio said perhaps if we ran the tape forward there might be more. And there was. A lot more."

"So that's what you were trying to tell me this morning," said Charlie. His friends' strange antics suddenly made sense. "You were pretending to pull a dog's tail."

"Didn't you realize?" Fidelio grinned. "Sit down, Charlie, and listen to an amazing story."

Charlie noticed that his friends had already managed to haul Dr. Tolly's case out of the cellar. He pulled up a chair and sat at the table. The metal dog stood in the center, surrounded by cardboard and crumbs.

"Listen," said Fidelio. He pulled the dog's tail and, as soon as Dr. Tolly's familiar voice began to give instructions, Fidelio pressed the dog's left ear and forwarded the tape. "Now," he said. "Here it comes."

When Dr. Tolly spoke again, his voice sounded different, more urgent and sorrowful. Charlie pulled his chair closer.

My dear Julia, the voice began, *if you are listening to this you have discovered the secret of my beloved child; the child who was once Emma Tolly and now has another name. I hope you have found a safe place for the box marked Tolly Twelve Bells. I could not send the key or instruct you how to open it because I can trust no one, Julia. They listen at my door, they steal my letters, and, by the time you hear this message they will have stolen my life. I know it. I am already weak. I cannot leave my bed. My enemies have poisoned me, Julia, and it is just punishment for what I did to my child.*

And so now I shall tell you how it came about, how I found myself in this sorry predicament. As you know, I decided to hand over our little Emma. It was greed that drove me. What they offered in return for my daughter was the most exciting challenge of my life. They gave me a replica of my ancestor, the knight from Toledo with the sharpest sword in the world. I was to bring it to life—how arrogant I was to believe that I could. For five years I toiled. To no avail. I am only a scientist, not a magician. When Emma was seven, I asked them to return her. They refused. I had failed in my task, they said.

At this point Benjamin sneezed, breaking the spell that Dr. Tolly's compelling voice had cast over them.

"Well, it's interesting," said Charlie. "But it doesn't tell us very much."

"Poisoning is very interesting," said Benjamin.

"Listen," commanded Fidelio, stopping the tape. "The next part is the best. It's where everything happens."

Benjamin and Charlie were dutifully silent while Fidelio started the tape again. Once more Dr. Tolly's deep voice resounded from the metal dog.

Julia, they promised I could see her, visit her. I thought it would be a good life for little Emma, surrounded by a loving family — a mother, a father, and a brother — rather than remaining with me, a crusty, absentminded man. But they were supposed to tell her who she really was so that one day, she might choose to return to me, and to you, dear Julia. That was my hope. That was before I knew what Manfred could do.

Charlie looked at Fidelio, who rolled his eyes. Benjamin whispered, "Is that the . . . ?"

"Shh!" said Fidelio.

Remember the day, continued Dr. Tolly, *remember I came to the shop first, and you dressed little Emma in her new white dress and tied a ribbon in her hair. But you wouldn't come with us to the square in front of the cathedral. If only you had.*

There were four of them — Bloor and his wife and son, and the old man. The boy was about eight at the time. They placed a case at my feet and, indeed, there was a figure in it; then I lifted my little girl and the old man held out his arms.

That's when it happened, Julia. When everything went wrong. As the great clock above us began to chime, a man came out of the cathedral. I recognized him immediately. It was the young organist. The choir was still singing when he came toward us. He lifted his hand and said, "Stop! You can't do this!"

As he stepped in front of me, the old man struck him in the face. The organist struck back, and the old man fell on the stones, hitting his head. He screamed with pain. And then I noticed Manfred staring at the young man; his eyes were like fiery coals. The organist covered his face with his hands and sank to his knees.

By this time Emma was crying with fright, but Manfred turned his terrible eyes on me, and I found myself putting my screaming child into his arms. As the cathedral clock struck twelve, he looked at her and she stopped crying. She seemed to be transfixed.

I was a coward, Julia. I did a terrible thing then. I ran away. I picked up the case and fled down those narrow alleys as though all the fiends of hell were behind me.

Later, I found out that they'd sent Emma to another family. They refused to tell me where. The old man was crippled for life by his fall. As for the young organist, I never saw him again. I realized that both he and my little Emma had been worse than hypnotized. They were spellbound for life, unless I could find a way to wake them up. And so I did, Julia. At least I believe I did. In the case marked Tolly Twelve Bells there is a *sound that might wake our little Emma. The Bloors found out what I was doing and, of course, they want to destroy my invention. If you press the letters on the side, one by one, firmly and carefully, it will open.*

"So that's how it opens," said Charlie.

"Wait!" Fidelio raised his hand. "Listen to this!"

I almost forgot, said Dr. Tolly's voice. Why did they want my child? We were students together, Dr. Bloor and I. It was natural that I confide in my old friend. Certainly, I could tell no one else. Emma can fly. It happened only once, when she was a few months old. But who knows . . . ?

Take care, Julia. This recording is finished. The courier is at the door. Farewell.

"What do you think?" asked Fidelio. "Quite a story, isn't it? Imagine! That girl, whoever she is, can fly."

"We think it's Emilia Moon," Charlie murmured. "And the organist . . ."

"What about the organist?" said Fidelio.

"Nothing," said Charlie. The young organist might have been his father, but how could they find him now? He could be anywhere. First they must wake Emma Tolly, and then, perhaps, one day his father.

Fidelio was eager to put plans into action as soon as possible. "We've got to get that case out of here, tonight," he said. "Now we know what it can do."

"Asa's on my trail again," said Charlie. "He'll be watching every move we make."

"No problem," said Fidelio. He showed Charlie the huge xylophone case he'd brought along. "My dad said he'd pick me up from here by car. If you and Benjamin start walking around the block, Asa will probably follow you. Dad's coming in about ten minutes, so with any luck, Asa won't be around to see me take the xylophone case out to the car. If he does, he might think it's just a musical instrument."

They all agreed this was a very good plan. Dr. Tolly's case was lifted into the empty xylophone case and Charlie and Benjamin set off for the park. It was dark by now, but with Runner Bean bounding beside them they felt quite safe. They soon became aware of Asa's badly disguised figure, sneaking from tree to tree on the other side of the road, but they tried not to show that they had seen him.

After twenty minutes of walking around, Charlie and Benjamin returned to number twelve, Filbert Street. Fidelio and the big case had disappeared.

"We did it!" cheered Benjamin.

"Good old Fidelio," said Charlie. "I'd better get home now. See you tomorrow."

"We'll take the tape to Miss Ingledew, shall we?"

"Good idea," said Charlie.

He ran back across the street, eager to tell his uncle everything that had happened. Paton was standing, very conveniently, alone in the hall, but he was in no mood for secrets. He was about to go out. He was wearing a very smart black suit and, amazingly, a purple bow tie. His hair had been cut and his face looked very white and freshly shaven. He smelled of something spicy, rather than the usual mixture of ink and old paper.

"Wow!" said Charlie. "Where are you going, Uncle Paton?"

Paton looked embarrassed. "You asked me to get a key for you," he said, "from Miss Ingledew."

"We don't need it now," whispered Charlie.

Paton took no notice. "I er. . ." he cleared his throat. "I'm taking Miss Ingledew out to dinner."

"Really!" This was news indeed. As far as Charlie could remember, Paton had never, ever taken anyone out to dinner.

His uncle lowered his voice and, leaning close to Charlie, he said, "Grizelda's not very happy about it."

"She wouldn't be," said Charlie with a grin.

Uncle Paton patted him on the shoulder, winked, and left. It was a very dark night.

Charlie felt quite excited for his uncle. He silently wished him good luck and an accident-free night.

Grandma Bone had shut herself in her room, so there was a nice peaceful atmosphere in the kitchen. Maisie and Charlie's mother were both reading maga- zines. They looked up when Charlie came in, eager to hear all about his first week at the new school. Charlie told them the funny, interesting bits. He left out Gabriel Silk and his strange assertion that Charlie's father was not dead. He also left out the part about the cape. He would have to find an explanation for that later.

He was allowed to stay up much later than usual. With Grandma Bone out of the way there was no one to insist on an early bedtime. Besides, it was Sunday the next day, and his mother assured him he could stay in bed as long as he wanted. But at length Charlie's eyes began to close, he yawned several times, and had to admit that he was in danger of falling asleep. Kissing Maisie and his mother good night, he went to bed.

Charlie couldn't have said how long he'd been asleep before he became aware of something strange going on. There were slow steps outside his door. Up and down. Up and down. The stairs creaked and someone crossed the hall. Tired as he was, Charlie slipped out of bed and tiptoed downstairs.

Uncle Paton was sitting at the kitchen table, where a single candle flickered mournfully. He had flung his coat and tie on the floor and his face was buried in his folded arms.

"Uncle Paton, what is it?" Charlie whispered. "What happened?"

His uncle wouldn't reply. He just groaned. Charlie pulled out a chair and sat opposite his uncle, waiting for him to recover from whatever it was that had caused such terrible despair.

At last Paton lifted his head and said, "Charlie, it's all over."

"What is?" said Charlie.

"I couldn't help myself," Paton said pensively. "It was bound to happen. Our friend, Miss Ingledew, looked so stunning. She wore a black dress and her hair was piled on her head, and her neck was as white as a swan's . . . well, I was bowled over."

"Of course," said Charlie.

"I restrained myself until the pudding."

"Oh. That was good."

"No, it wasn't," moaned Paton, "although I suppose she did enjoy most of the meal."

"What did you have?"

"Oysters. A Caesar salad. Roast duck, and a pavlova pudding."

"Yum!" said Charlie, who didn't know what any of it was, except the duck.

"But the wine went to my head, and I was so intoxicated, so happy," Paton sighed hugely. "There was a candle on our table, so that was all right, but behind Julia, on the wall, there was a light in a red shade and—poof—off it went. Glass everywhere. All over her hair and her lovely black dress. I jumped up and another one went off at the next table. Imagine my distress."

"But they didn't know it was you," said Charlie.

"Ah, that's when I made a fool of myself. 'Sorry, sorry,' I cried, and another lamp shattered. Then another. I rushed out, still apologizing. I was so embarrassed. I couldn't stay in there, every light in the restaurant would have exploded."

"Never mind," said Charlie soothingly. "I'm sure you'll think of an explanation for Miss Ingledew."

"But, Charlie, I didn't pay the bill!" cried Paton. "Imagine her disgust. She thinks I'm a coward, frightened of a few popping lightbulbs, and I left her to pay the bill."

"You'll just have to tell her the truth," said Charlie.

"Nooo!" Uncle Paton gave a thundering moan of despair. "We're doomed, Charlie. You and I. Doomed in our differences. In our horrible family afflictions."

"We're not," said Charlie fiercely. "Please pull yourself together, Uncle Paton. I've got something very important to tell you, and I really need you to concentrate." Uncle Paton laid his head on his folded arms again, and this time he didn't seem inclined to move. So Charlie began to recount everything Dr. Tolly had said on the tape. At last Paton lifted his head, and Charlie had his full attention.

"Good Lord," said Paton, as Charlie came to the part that concerned the organist, "Lyell!"

"It was my father, wasn't it?"

"Must've been," said Paton. "Go on, Charlie."

257

By the time Charlie had finished the strange story of Dr. Tolly, Paton was beginning to look much more lively.

"My dear boy, this is all too extraordinary for words," he said. "Tragic, too. So tragic. That poor child. And your father—how I wish I could have prevented that. There's no doubt at all, in my mind, that in trying to save the child, he sealed his own fate."

"But Uncle Paton, my father's still alive," said Charlie.

"What? No, I'm sorry, Charlie, you must be wrong."

Charlie told his uncle about Gabriel Silk, the blue cape, and his father's tie. "I don't see why he would lie," said Charlie. "You should have seen him, Uncle Paton. He knows these things. Just like I hear voices and Manfred can hypnotize . . . and you can explode light-bulbs."

"I suppose I must believe you, Charlie. But I saw the place where the car went into the quarry. Your father couldn't have gotten out, and if he did, where is he now?"

Charlie gave a gloomy shrug. He didn't know the

answer, but it was interesting to learn that no one had found his father's body. "I think Grandma stopped them from finishing Dad off because he was her son. But she let it happen, the accident and everything, because she couldn't make him do what she wanted. They were all in it, the Bloors and the Yewbeams, all except you, Uncle Paton. If anyone stands in their way or does something they don't like, they finish them off, or hide them, or make them forget who they are."

"Oh, dear boy!" Paton suddenly banged the table with his fist. "I blame myself. Keeping one's head down is just not good enough. I knew something was going on, I can't deny it. Those sisters of mine were plotting and whispering; they had secret meetings, and there were visits from Dr. Bloor and his ghastly grandfather Ezekiel, and I took no notice."

"Grandfather?" said Charlie, somewhat surprised.

"Yes, grandfather," said Paton. "An evil old man if ever there was one. He must be over a hundred by now. One evening I got a phone call from Lyell. He had discovered that something was going on and he wanted my advice. In those days he lived on the other side of the city with you and your mother. I said I would meet him outside the cathedral." Paton covered his face with his hands. "I didn't go, Charlie," he moaned. "I forgot. I was working on my book, you see. But what's a book compared with a life? I never saw your father again."

In spite of the dreadful and mysterious events surrounding his father's disappearance, Charlie felt rather proud. His father had tried to prevent something evil from happening.

"Uncle Paton, tomorrow, I'm going to take Dr. Tolly's tape to Miss Ingledew," he said. "And while I'm there, I'll try and explain things for you about the exploding glass and everything."

"It's very good of you," Paton said sadly, "but I'm afraid my prospects there are doomed."

"'Course they're not," Charlie retorted. He suddenly realized that he and his uncle had been making quite a noise. Why wasn't Grandma Bone thumping the floor or stomping downstairs to poke her nose into things?

"What's happened to Grandma?" he asked.

Paton smiled for the first time that night. "I put something in her milk. She won't wake up for hours. Probably not until teatime tomorrow."

Charlie burst out giggling. He couldn't help himself. Laughing merrily, he and his uncle climbed the stairs together, their problems forgotten. For now.

BILLY'S DARK BARGAIN

When Billy Raven told Charlie that he didn't mind being alone in the long dormitory, it wasn't strictly true. In fact, Billy dreaded Saturday nights. He found it difficult to sleep knowing he would have to spend another whole day and night on his own.

True, Blessed kept him company, in his way, but the old dog's knowledge of humans was limited. His conversation was full of animal events and animal feelings and, now that he was getting old, he moaned constantly about his ailments. Billy sympathized, but he would rather have had another boy to talk to, or even a girl.

There were other orphans at the academy, Billy knew this, but they had all been adopted by nice, friendly families. Billy often wondered why no one had ever wanted to adopt him. He decided it was because he looked so strange; perhaps people were afraid of his white hair and dark red eyes.

Across the courtyard, the candles in Manfred's room shone like eerie little stars. Billy watched them for a while, then, leaving the curtains open, he climbed over Blessed and got into bed. His head had barely touched the pillow when the old dog gave a snort and sat up.

"Billy's wanted," said Blessed.

"Who wants me?" asked Billy, slightly alarmed.

"Old man. Now. I show."

"Now? But it's dark and...and...why does he want me?"

"Blessed not know. Come now."

Billy put on his slippers, took his flashlight from a drawer, then, wrapping himself in his bathrobe, followed Blessed out of the dormitory.

The battery in Billy's flashlight had run very low and he could barely see Blessed's tail as it swung in front of him. Billy kept meaning to ask one of the other boys to get him a battery, but he wasn't sure who to ask. Next weekend he would be going home with Charlie. Charlie would get him a new battery, he was sure.

Blessed was walking much faster than usual and Billy had to run a few paces to keep up with the old dog. When Blessed came to a staircase, however, he slowed down. He heaved himself upward, panting desperately. At the top of the staircase the air was thick and warm. Now they were entering the Bloors' family quarters. Billy shuddered to think what would happen if Manfred found him outside his door.

"Are you sure this isn't a mistake?" Billy asked the dog. "Do you think you could be wrong?"

"Blessed never wrong," snorted the dog. "Follow."

Billy followed, along passages that reeked of candles, and then up another staircase and into a shadowy area where flickering gas jets hissed and popped from the wall, and cobwebs hung limply from the dark, crumbling ceiling.

"Nice smell," Blessed commented.

"Nice?" said Billy. "It's like bad eggs and . . . and dead things."

"Nice," said Blessed. He had reached a black door with a huge brass handle. The paint was scarred by a patch of deeply scored lines and, as Blessed lifted a paw and began to scratch at the door, Billy realized what they were. Obviously the old dog came here often.

After three scratches, a cracked and haughty voice said, "Enter!"

Billy turned the handle and went in. He found himself in an extraordinary room. The only light came from a fire that burned in a massive stone fireplace at the end of the room. Beside the fire sat an old man in a wheelchair. Strands of thin white hair hung limply from a red woolen cap, and beneath the cap the old man's bony face protruded like a skull; the eyes were so deep and dark, the cheeks so hollow, and the lips so thin they were hardly there, and yet the dreadful mouth smiled when Billy came in.

"Come closer, Billy Raven," the old man beckoned with a long twisted finger.

Billy swallowed and approached. The heat in the room was stifling and Billy couldn't imagine why the old man wore a woolen shawl around his shoulders.

He took a few steps into the room and stopped. Blessed waddled past him and lay beside the fire, panting.

"It's very hot in here, sir," Billy said, gasping for air.

"You'll get used to it. My doggie loves a fire, don't you, Percy?" The old man grinned fondly at the dog, though it was hard to tell. He might have been scowling.

"I thought he was Cook's dog, sir."

"He thinks he's Cook's dog because I can't take him for walks anymore. Can I, Percy?"

"He told me his name was Blessed." Billy ventured a little farther into the room.

"His name is Percival Pettigrew Pennington Pitt. He just thinks he's Blessed." The old man gave a cackle. "Do you want some cocoa, Billy?"

Billy had never had cocoa. He didn't know what to say.

"It's hot and sweet and gives you wonderful dreams." The old man's crooked finger beckoned again. "There's a saucepan of milk warming by the fire. And on my little table there, you'll find two blue mugs with cocoa and sugar in them, already mixed. You just pour that milk into the cups and stir away, and then we can have a nice little chat, can't we, Billy?"

"Yes," said Billy. He carried out the old man's instructions and soon he was sitting in a big, comfortable chair, very much enjoying his first cup of cocoa.

The old man took a few noisy slurps and then said, "Well now, Billy, I expect you're wondering who I am. I'm Mr. Bloor Senior Senior. Ha, ha!" There came another unhealthy-sounding cackle. "But I am also Ezekiel. You can call me Mr. Ezekiel."

"Thank you," said Billy.

"Good! Good! Now, Billy, you've got a problem, haven't you? You haven't been adopted, have you? No. And that's a pity isn't it? Would you like to be adopted, Billy? Have nice, kind, cheerful parents?"

Billy sat up. "Yes!" he said.

There seemed to be a small flicker in the fathomless eyes. "Then you shall, Billy. I've got just the mom and dad for you. They're wonderful people and they're very, very excited to have you."

267

"Really?" Billy could hardly believe it. "But how do they know me?"

"We've told them all about you. They know how clever you are, and what a good boy you've been, and they've seen your school photo."

"So they know about . . ." Billy touched his white hair.

Mr. Ezekiel gave one of his sinister smiles. "They know you're an albino, and it doesn't worry them at all."

"Oh." Billy felt quite dizzy with excitement. He took a long gulp of the sweet, rich cocoa to steady his nerves.

Mr. Ezekiel was now staring at him intently. "If we arrange this adoption for you, Billy, you will be expected to do something for us in return."

"I see," Billy said uncertainly.

"You've made a new friend, haven't you? A boy in your dormitory called Charlie Bone?"

The old man's tone was kind and gentle, and Billy was reassured. "Yes," he said.

"I want you to tell me everything he does; where

he goes, who he talks to, and, most important of all, what he says. Do you think you can do that?" The old man leaned forward and fixed Billy with his chilling black eyes.

"Yes," Billy whispered. "I'm going to stay with him next weekend, if I'm allowed."

"You will be allowed, Billy. It would be perfect. And now you can tell me everything that you have learned about him so far."

With the prospect of living forever with kind and wonderful parents, Billy eagerly told the old man everything he wanted to know. He didn't think that it would hurt Charlie, and even admitted his own part in spying on Dr. Bloor in the Da Vinci tower.

Mr. Ezekiel frowned when he heard this and cursed under his breath; but he quickly assumed an expression of kindly interest while Billy continued to recount all the details he could remember. There was one thing about Charlie that he didn't tell the old man. He couldn't tell him that Charlie knew his father was alive because Billy had been asleep when Gabriel Silk wrapped the blue silk tie around his neck.

"Thank you, Billy," said Mr. Ezekiel when Billy had finished. "You may go now. The dog will take you back to your dormitory. Percy, get up!"

Blessed blinked and stood up, rather shakily.

Billy slid out of the comfortable chair and put his empty mug on the table. "When will I see my new parents, sir?" he asked.

"All in good time." The old man's voice had lost any trace of warmth. "You have to keep your part of the bargain first."

"Yes, sir." With Blessed panting at his side, Billy walked to the door where he turned and said, "Goodnight, sir. When shall I . . ."

"The dog will bring you." Mr. Ezekiel dismissed him with an impatient wave.

When the old man was alone, he pointed his deformed finger at the saucepan. Slowly the pan lifted into the air and, as the old man beckoned, it flew gently toward an empty mug. "Pour," said Mr. Ezekiel.

The pan tipped forward and poured a few drops of warm milk into the mug, the rest dripped on the old man's woolen shawl.

"Fool!" shouted Mr. Ezekiel. "Will you never learn?"

The hot room seemed to have exhausted Blessed. It took him a long time to reach the dormitory, by which time, Billy's flashlight had lost all its remaining strength, and he had to walk with his hand on the old dog's head. Blessed knew the way even in the utter darkness and stopped only once, to say, "Ears bad. Don't touch."

"Sorry," said Billy.

"Need drops," muttered Blessed. "Billy get some?"

Billy didn't see how he could. "I'll try," he said.

When they reached the dormitory they found Cook pacing anxiously outside. She was a small round person with dark, graying hair and very rosy cheeks. The sort of person you would expect a cook to be.

"I've been looking everywhere for that blessed dog," said Cook. "He's got to have his medicine."

"He says he needs drops for his ears," Billy told her.

"Does he?" Cook knew about Billy's relationship with Blessed. "He needs drops for just about everything, doesn't he? Where've you been, young Billy?"

"I've been to see the old man."

"You poor thing." Cook gave a kindly sigh. "I'd get back to bed if I were you."

Billy said good night to Cook and Blessed and went to bed. He lay awake for a long time, trying to imagine what his new parents would be like.

A RINGING, CHANTING,
SHINING KNIGHT

It was a real joy to get up on Sunday morning, knowing that Grandma Bone would still be asleep. Charlie leaped out of bed and went down to eat a huge breakfast with Maisie and his mother.

"I expect you've had a lot of nasty breakfasts lately, haven't you, Charlie dear?" asked Maisie.

"Five," said Charlie. He told them he was going to be spending some time with Benjamin and to make up for it, he would wash up his breakfast things.

His mother wouldn't hear of it. "You go and have a good time while you can," she said cheerfully waving him away.

Benjamin looked worried when he let Charlie in. "I've had a letter from my parents," he said.

"I thought they lived here," said Charlie.

"So did I. But they must have left early this morning. I sort of remember Mom coming in to give me a kiss when it was still dark. When I woke up I found the letter on my pillow." Benjamin led Charlie into the kitchen where Runner Bean was finishing off his cornflakes.

"Can I read it?" asked Charlie.

Benjamin handed him the letter. It had obviously been written in haste because the writing rushed across the page in big, looping scrawls. It said:

Our dear Benjamin,

As you know, we are private detectives. Just lately we have both been working on the same case. The case of the missing window cleaner. It has taken up all our time and quite exhausted us, and we are so sorry, dear Benjamin, that we've had to leave you all on your own so often. We will make up for it when we come home.

This brings us to the reason for our letter. The strange case of the missing window cleaner has just taken an exciting turn. We've received information that he may be trapped in a cave in Scotland, so we

*are going up there right now, before he disappears
again.*

Take care of yourself, dear Benjamin.

Lots of love,

Mom and Dad.

*P.S. A nice lady from social services is coming to
look after you until we get back.*

"I don't like the part about the nice lady," said Charlie,
when he had finished the letter. "People have different
ideas about nice."

"As long as she's nice to Runner, I don't mind," said
Benjamin.

The two boys decided to go to Ingledew's immediately. Benjamin had taken the precaution of copying
the tape twice, in case Manfred turned up to search
them, or something equally horrible. He had also
pushed a large suitcase into the cellar and dropped a
rug over it, so that anyone searching for Dr. Tolly's case
would be temporarily fooled.

"You have been busy," said Charlie admiringly.

275

With Runner Bean leading the way they set off for the bookshop. Being Sunday, they found it closed, of course, but after several knocks and a few shouts, Miss Ingledew opened the door. She was wearing a long green bathrobe and looked a bit down in the dumps.

"What do you want?" she asked. "It's Sunday morning, for goodness sake."

"I'm sorry Miss Ingledew," said Charlie. He told her about the tape they'd found in the metal dog. "It's meant for you," he said, "so we brought it for you. It'll tell you everything about your niece. She's in the academy, and we think we can wake her up."

"Wake her up? What are you talking about? You'd-better come in, both of you." She glanced at Runner Bean. "He doesn't eat books, does he?"

"Never," said Benjamin.

They followed Miss Ingledew through the curtains and into her cozy book-lined living room, Runner Bean taking great care not to knock over the little towers of books scattered on the floor.

Miss Ingledew put the tape into a dusty-looking

tape recorder and motioned the boys to sit. They squeezed themselves into the only empty armchair — the others being full of books and papers — while Miss Ingledew perched on the edge of her desk. She pressed play and Dr. Tolly's voice rumbled out into the room.

The boys watched Miss Ingledew's face as she listened. Several times she shook her head, and often she wiped her eyes. Now and again she exclaimed, "Oh no," and when the tape finally ended, she murmured, "I remember that day so well. A very strange thing happened — I should have guessed."

"What sort of strange thing?" asked Charlie.

"Cats," said Miss Ingledew.

"Cats?" Charlie sat up.

"I don't know where they came from, but the day little Emma was due to leave they suddenly appeared in my kitchen. They caused a fire by knocking a dishcloth onto the gas burner. It took a while to put it out. Their coats were very bright — red, orange, and yellow — and they kept circling the baby, as if they were

277

trying to protect her. They gave Dr. Tolly a nasty scratch on his face when he finally lifted the baby away."

"One of them is in the photo," Charlie said.

"I dare say it is," said Miss Ingledew. "They were everywhere. But when Emma left, they vanished." She rubbed her forehead. "So poor little Emma is asleep. This is all so extraordinary!"

"She's hypnotized," said Charlie. "Manfred did it to me. Only he's done it much worse to her. But it's wearing off, Miss Ingledew. I heard them talking about your niece and Manfred said he was getting fed up because he had to keep 'putting her under.' So it won't take much to wake her up, and we think we've got the thing that'll do it."

"But who is she, Charlie?"

"We think she's a girl called Emilia Moon," said Charlie. "She has fair hair and her eyes are very blue and sort of dreamy. She doesn't say much, but she's very good at drawing."

"Nancy," murmured Miss Ingledew. "She sounds just like my sister, Nancy. Oh, I wish I could see her."

"Leave it to us, Miss Ingledew," said Charlie, jumping up. "We'll find a way to wake her up, and then she can come and live with you."

Miss Ingledew gasped. "Is that possible? Perhaps she's happy where she is, living with the Moon people."

"She doesn't look very happy," said Charlie. "She probably doesn't even know she can fly."

"That's something isn't it?" Benjamin remarked. "I wish I could fly."

"I think it's very unlikely that Emma can fly. Dr. Tolly certainly never mentioned it before." Miss Ingledew pushed herself off the desk. "I can't thank you enough, Charlie, and you, Benjamin," she said. "You've given me hope. Let me know as soon as you need me, won't you?"

"You bet," said Charlie. He had just glimpsed a tiny bit of glass shining in her hair and wondered how he could bring up the subject of the unfortunate glass popping. He had to do it, for his uncle's sake. But Runner Bean was barking excitedly and they were already through the curtains and heading for the door.

Charlie stopped suddenly, cleared his throat and said, "About my uncle, Miss Ingledew."

She went very red. "I'd rather not talk about that," she said.

"But it was an accident."

"Accident? It was most embarrassing."

"I mean the lightbulbs, Miss Ingledew. My uncle couldn't help himself."

"Lightbulbs?" She didn't understand. "Your uncle walked out on me. Well, ran out, to be precise. Anyone would have thought I was an ogress."

"Not at all. Quite the opposite. It was because he thought you were beautiful that it happened."

Seeing Miss Ingledew's puzzled expression, Charlie plunged straight in and told her the truth about his uncle's peculiar gift.

She stared at Charlie, first in disbelief, and then horror. Finally a sort of alarm crossed her face. "I see," she muttered. "How unusual."

"He'd really like to see you again," Charlie went on hopefully.

"Hm," said Miss Ingledew. "I'm feeling sort of tired now, boys." She opened the door and they dutifully stepped out. The door was closed very firmly behind them.

"I didn't know your uncle did that kind of thing," said Benjamin.

"Don't tell anyone," said Charlie. "Perhaps I shouldn't have told Miss Ingledew, but Uncle Paton is desperate to see her again, so I thought it would be best to tell the truth."

"If you ask me it's scared her off," said Benjamin cheerfully. "Next stop Fidelio's. Come on. I've got a map of where he lives."

Benjamin and Runner Bean raced ahead while Charlie jogged along behind, feeling bad about Miss Ingledew and his uncle. It seemed that he had made the situation even worse.

Fidelio's house was quite a sight or, to be more precise, a sound. It was a large and, luckily, detached old house sitting in the middle of a cobbled square. The only garden to speak of was some wispy grass that surrounded the house inside a low brick wall. As Benjamin and Charlie approached, the noise coming from inside the house was so great that they saw the oak beams, supporting the porch, tremble, and two slates slid down the roof and smashed on the brick path.

The noise was made up of many instruments: violins, cellos, a flute, a harp, and a piano could be heard. A brass plaque on the door told them that the place was called Gunn House. Many guns, they thought, as a drumroll echoed out of a lower window.

Charlie wondered how the people inside were going to hear the doorbell. He soon found out. When he pressed the bell, a loud recorded voice boomed, "DOOR! DOOR! DOOR!"

The two boys jumped backward and Runner Bean gave a long howl of fright. Seconds later Fidelio opened the door and Charlie and Benjamin found themselves stepping into a sort of hive of music. Children rushed up and down the stairs, in and out of rooms, carrying sheets of music and a variety of instruments.

"Is this...I mean are they all your family?" Charlie asked in amazement.

"Most of them," said Fidelio. "There are ten of us including Mom and Dad. But some of our musical friends have come by. My oldest brother, Felix, is starting a rock band."

A large bearded man crossed the landing at the top of the stairs and Fidelio called out, "This is Benjamin, and this is Charlie, Dad!"

Mr. Gunn beamed down at them and sang out, "Benjamin and Charlie, eating barley, welcome both of you, however early." He gave a booming laugh and disappeared into a room that was full of violin sounds.

"Sorry about that," said Fidelio. "Dad likes to turn everything into a song. I've put the case in a room at the top of the house. Come on." He led his friends and a quaking Runner Bean up the stairs and past doors that shook with sound. The rock band room caused Runner Bean to whine so pitifully, Benjamin had to cover the dog's ears with his hands.

Whenever they passed a child with the same bright

hair and freckles as Fidelio, he would say, "This is Benjamin and this is Charlie," and the two boys would be welcomed with beaming smiles and a "Hi!" or "Hello!" or sometimes a "How ya doin'?"

At last they reached a door at the very top of the house and Fidelio showed them into a room full to bursting with music cases of various sizes. "Our instrument cemetery," said Fidelio. "It's where we keep everything that's broken and might one day be fixed." He pulled the long xylophone case into the light, snapped it open, and lifted out Dr. Tolly's metal case.

"Shall we open it?" he asked, setting the case on the floor.

Suddenly, Charlie wasn't sure. He couldn't wait to find out what was in the case and yet he was a little afraid. Uncle Paton had suggested he should be there, to help if something went wrong. But what could go wrong in such a friendly, noisy house? No one would hear the sounds that Dr. Tolly had arranged, and if they did, they would think nothing of it.

"OK," said Charlie.

"You do it, Charlie," said Benjamin.

Charlie stepped forward and knelt beside the case. He could see the letters quite clearly now: TOLLY TWELVE BELLS. He touched the first "T," gently but firmly. Next came the "O," and now Charlie found that he could hardly stop himself. It was easy, really. One by one he pressed the letters and, as he came to the last one, an "S," a light tap came from inside the lid.

Charlie quickly stood up and took a few steps back.

With a loud crack, the lid swung back and a figure began to rise out of the case.

It was certainly not what Charlie had expected. He had imagined Dr. Tolly's ancestor to be an old man, dressed in velvet. The figure that rose out of the case was a knight. Its arms and legs were encased in shining chain mail, and on its head it wore a flat-topped hood, also of chain mail. There was a small opening for the face, but only the eyes and nose could be seen. It was an eerie, awesome sight, this tall shining figure, rising up like a fast-growing flower. Most awesome of all was the gleaming sword held in the knight's right hand.

When the figure had achieved its full height it suddenly raised the sword, and three boys and a dog jumped back with yelps, screams, and furious barks. And then they were silent, for somewhere inside the knight, a bell began to ring. One, two, three … on it went, and while the bell rang out, a chorus of deep male voices chanted an ancient-sounding hymn.

"It's Latin," whispered Fidelio. "I've heard them practicing in the cathedral."

All at once, Charlie understood what Dr. Tolly had done. He had used the sounds that swam around little Emma Tolly, just at the moment when she was hypnotized — or spellbound. Dr. Tolly believed these sounds would wake his daughter, and even if she couldn't remember who she was, she would at least be aware that something had happened to her.

The bell inside the shining knight tolled for the twelfth time. The knight lowered his sword and began to sink back into the case. It was strange to watch how he dropped and dwindled, bending his head and sub-siding until he lay in his silk-lined bed, no bigger now than the length of his gleaming sword.

"Wow!" gasped Benjamin.

"Amazing!" said Fidelio.

"I wonder if it really will wake Emilia up," mur-mured Charlie.

Fidelio was still shaking his head in disbelief. "How did he do it?" he muttered. "What's it made of?"

"The face looks real," said Benjamin. "The eyes are so shiny."

"Glass," said Charlie. "And the rest is just a sort of poly-something." He thought of all the strange metal shapes in Dr. Bloor's workshop. "I bet Dr. Tolly had been fooling the Bloors for years, sending them robots and metal figures and dressed-up skeletons, pretending they held the secret to waking Emilia up. Just to keep them off his back. But they got him in the end."

"They got him, but not Tolly Twelve Bells," said Ben-jamin.

Charlie closed the case. "Do you think it'll be safe here until next weekend?" he asked Fidelio.

"'Course it will. But we'll need a girl to help us if we're going to get Emilia here."

"No problem," said Charlie. "Olivia Vertigo loves this kind of thing."

The three boys made their way back through the musical house, and this time they met Mrs. Gunn, who had the same bright hair and freckles as everyone else in the family. She was carrying a double bass across the hall, but took the time to pat each boy fondly on the head as he passed.

When they left Gunn House, Benjamin and Charlie headed for number nine, where Maisie had promised a big lunch would be waiting for them.

Soon Charlie and Benjamin were sitting down to roast chicken, potatoes, parsnips, and several other more unusual vegetables from Mrs. Bone's greengrocer. There were three dessert choices and the boys had all three: ice cream, pudding, and mango crumble.

Uncle Paton called down that he wasn't at all hungry, so Runner Bean had his portion. Maisie wondered about keeping some food for Grandma Bone. It was most unlike her to stay in bed so long, she remarked. Charlie smiled to himself. "Why don't you give what's left to Runner Bean?" he asked. "I'm sure he's hungrier than Grandma Bone."

"Good idea," said Maisie, and Runner Bean happily polished off his second lunch.

Benjamin stayed for tea as well. That's when Grandma Bone woke up. She came staggering downstairs in a gray bathrobe. "What's going on?" she barked. "It's four o'clock. Why didn't someone wake me up?"

"You were tired, Grizelda," said Maisie. "We didn't want to wake you."

"Tired? Tired? I'm never tired," said Grandma Bone.

Benjamin and Charlie escaped into the garden where they played all Runner Bean's favorite games. For a while it seemed just like every other weekend, as if nothing had changed since they met, when they were both five years old. Runner Bean had seemed a lot bigger then.

But, of course, things had changed. Tomorrow Charlie had to go back to Bloor's Academy, and tonight a complete stranger was coming to look after Benjamin.

"Do you want me to come with you?" Charlie asked, when his friend decided he'd better go home.

Benjamin shook his head. "It'll be OK," he said. "I've got Runner."

"Look, if anything happens while I'm away, I mean, if you need help, go to my Uncle Paton. He's not like the other Yewbeams. He's on my side."

"OK," said Benjamin.

As Charlie watched Benjamin and Runner Bean cross the street, he had a nasty feeling in the pit of his stomach. Something was wrong, but he couldn't say what it was.

Benjamin climbed the steps, put his key in the lock, and went into number twelve. Charlie stared at the closed door and wished he had gone with his friend. And then he put Benjamin out of his mind, because there was something he had to tell his mother.

He found her in the tiny bedroom at the back of the house. She had obviously gone there to escape Grandma Bone's ranting. She patted the bed and Charlie bounced up and sat among the piles of clothes that she'd been mending. He waited until his mother was sitting in her favorite chair — one of the few things she'd managed to save from their old house — and then he told her about Dr. Tolly's strange message.

Mrs. Bone's expression of amazement turned to sadness as Charlie recounted the story of Emma Tolly. He wished he could make her smile by telling her that his father was still alive, but he had no proof, yet. Sometimes he thought a little of the spell that had captured his father had reached out and caught his mother as well. She was so quiet and remote.

One day he would find Lyell and rescue him. But first there was Emma Tolly to rescue. And that was something Charlie could do. Next week he would make sure Manfred found no excuses to give him detention. He would keep his head down, like Uncle

Paton, and on Saturday they would find a way to get Emilia Moon to Gunn House.

As he slipped out of his mother's room, she looked up and said, "Take care, Charlie. Don't do anything . . . dangerous."

Charlie grinned and shook his head. But he made no promises.

WAR

If Charlie had gone with Benjamin to number twelve, what happened that night might have been stopped. But who can say for sure? After all, the Yewbeams were a powerful family.

As Benjamin and his dog walked up the steps to their front door, Runner Bean gave an anxious whine and Benjamin wondered who the "nice" person might be that his parents had arranged to look after him.

They stepped into the hall together. There was a smart black bag at the bottom of the staircase, but no sign of a sitter.

"Hello!" Benjamin called out, tentatively.

Someone walked out of the kitchen, someone tall, all in black, with gray hair piled on her head and big round pearls dangling from her ears. She didn't have red shoes, but Benjamin knew who she was. Or rather he knew she was related to the woman with the red shoes.

"Are you—?" he didn't know how to finish the question.

"I'm your sitter, dear," she said.

"But aren't you . . . ?"

"Yes, I'm one of Charlie's great-aunts. So that makes it all very cozy, doesn't it? You can call me Aunt Eustacia."

"Thank you," Benjamin said nervously. "Did my mom and dad really ask you to come?"

"Of course." She spoke a little impatiently. "Why else would I be here?"

"It's just a bit peculiar," said Benjamin.

Aunt Eustacia ignored this. "You'd better come and have your dinner," she said. "I've made some nice hot broth."

Benjamin followed her into the kitchen and drew a chair up to the table. Runner Bean gave a small grunt and sat beside him.

"Dogs shouldn't be in kitchens," said Aunt Eustacia. She poured some steamy brown liquid into a bowl and set it in front of Benjamin. "Shoo!" she said to Runner Bean. "Out!"

Runner Bean growled, showing his teeth.

Aunt Eustacia took a step backward. "What a horrible dog," she said. "Benjamin, get it out of the kitchen at once."

"I can't," said Benjamin. "He likes to eat at the same time as me."

"Ha!" Aunt Eustacia flung open the cabinets and, finding a can of dog food, she spooned some into a bowl marked DOG and put the bowl outside in the hallway. "Now," she commanded, shaking a finger at Runner Bean, "eat!" She pointed at the bowl.

The dog rolled his eyes and moved closer to Benjamin.

Benjamin decided it would be best to avoid an argument with Aunt Eustacia this early on, so he leaned down to Runner Bean and said, "Runner, go and eat your dinner. I'm OK."

Runner Bean grunted and padded out to the hall, where he could be heard gobbling up the dog food. Benjamin wished he could have eaten dog food. It had to be tastier than the disgusting brown broth that he'd been given.

When he'd finally managed to get all the broth down his throat, Benjamin was sent to bed.

"School tomorrow," said Aunt Eustacia. "You'd better get in early tonight."

"Are you going to sleep here?" asked Benjamin.

"Naturally," said the grim-looking woman. "I'm your sitter."

Benjamin remembered that he had to pretend Tolly Twelve Bells was still in the house. "You stay down here, tonight," he told Runner Bean. He got the dog's basket and put it beside the cellar door.

Runner Bean looked puzzled, but stepped obediently in his basket.

Benjamin went to bed, but he lay awake, waiting for Aunt Eustacia to come upstairs. When he was sure she was in bed at last, he crept down to the phone in the hall and dialed Charlie's number.

"Hello!" said Maisie's cheerful voice.

"It's..." Benjamin got no further for a dark figure had appeared at the top of the stairs.

"And what do you think you're doing?" asked Aunt Eustacia.

At the other end of the line, Maisie's voice went on saying, "Hello! Hello! Who is it?"

"Put down that phone," commanded Aunt Eustacia.

"I just wanted to call my friend," Benjamin said. At this point, Runner Bean began to bark.

"It's nearly midnight," shouted Aunt Eustacia. "Get to bed at once!"

"Yes," said Benjamin miserably. He replaced the receiver and trudged up to bed.

On Monday morning, Charlie had to leave the house early. A blue academy bus stopped at the top of Filbert Street at seven forty-five precisely; it spent another hour collecting musical children from various parts of the city.

So Charlie didn't see Benjamin before he left, and barely heard Maisie when she called after him, "Benjamin called last night. At least I think it was him because of the barking." It was only when he was sitting on the bus that Charlie recalled Maisie's words and wondered what Benjamin had wanted.

He ran into Fidelio as they were filing through the academy entrance, and they agreed to meet during the break and talk to Olivia Vertigo.

Charlie didn't feel like a new boy any more. Today he knew exactly where to go and how to find things. His music lesson with Mr. Paltry—Winds—didn't go too well, but he managed to avoid detention and he actually got a few things right in the English lesson.

At break time, in the great misty garden, Charlie and Fidelio spied Olivia talking to a group of girls who all looked very dramatic; they had white faces and wore dangerous-looking boots, and they all had either bleached or colored hair. Today Olivia's hair was indigo.

When Charlie beckoned to her, she came striding over the grass in enormous, thick-soled boots with metal toe-caps.

"I bet Manfred will make you take those off," Charlie remarked.

"I'll try to keep out of his way," said Olivia. "So, what's new?"

"Let's start walking," Fidelio suggested. "We don't want to look like conspirators."

With Olivia clomping between them, the two boys took turns relating all that had happened over the weekend. Olivia was very excited. "You'll need me to get Emilia over to Gunn House, won't you?" she asked. "She'd never go with either of you."

"That's it exactly!" said Charlie.

He had noticed Billy Raven following them a short distance behind and wondered if he should tell the albino what was going on. But he decided against it. For now, the fewer people who knew their secret, the better. Billy would be coming home with him for the weekend. He would find out then.

Olivia agreed to spend the rest of the week making friends with Emilia, so that she could visit her on the weekend. "It won't be easy," said Olivia, "because Emilia's so sort of far away, if you know what I mean. But I suppose she would be if she's in a trance." She strode off with a wave, so that she could spend the last two minutes of break with her drama friends.

Charlie didn't meet with Gabriel Silk until he went into the cafeteria. The older boy rushed up to the table Charlie was sharing with Fidelio, spilling half his glass of water into his plate of chips. "Hi!" he said. "Everything OK? Anything I can do to help?"

"Not at the moment, thanks," said Charlie.

Gabriel looked unusually cheerful. Obviously he was wearing all new or very happy-feeling clothes. Charlie realized that Gabriel could be a very useful friend to have on his side. Already he was beginning to think of people as being on his side or against him. He wondered why this was.

He didn't see Manfred until dinnertime, but to his great relief the older boy took no notice of him. Asa, however, kept darting sly looks across the long table. The meal was exactly the same as last Monday's: soup, egg and chips, and a pear.

"It's always the same," said Fidelio. "Tomorrow it will be soup, sausage and potatoes, cabbage, and an apple."

Charlie wished he could swap his gift for hearing voices to one of turning bad food into good. He closed his eyes and pretended that he could. He found that the flat, old egg actually tasted better.

Now that he knew the way to the King's room, he found that he was the first one there. Almost. Zelda and Beth were playing some sort of game. They ignored Charlie. Zelda was dark and spiteful looking, and Beth was large and muscular with pale, frizzy hair. They were glaring at each other from either side of the table. In the center a wooden pencil box moved first one way, then the other.

Charlie sat down in the large space between them and plonked his books on the table.

"Shhh!" hissed Zelda.

The pencil box shot toward her.

"Sorry," said Charlie.

The pencil box hovered and then moved toward Beth. She growled and, glaring at the box, sent it back to Zelda. Charlie realized they both had the same endowment, moving things with their minds.

Other children began to drift into the room, ruining the girls' concentration. Tancred and Lysander came in together. This time Tancred grinned at Charlie. His hair looked more electrified than ever and Charlie noticed that it crackled slightly when Tancred tried to pat it down.

"How're you doing, Charlie Bone?" asked Lysander with a big smile.

"OK, thanks." Charlie smiled back.

"Shut up!" said Zelda as the pencil box shot sideways, lifted into the air, and crashed onto the floor.

"Crazy game," said Lysander.

"It's not a game!" snarled Zelda, retrieving the pencil case.

Charlie had managed to get a seat on the same side of the table as Manfred, so he didn't have to worry about the awful stare. He had a much better view of the Red King from this angle, and he found himself gazing up at the dark, mysterious face several times. It had a strange, calming effect on him and he was aware that his homework seemed much easier than usual. In fact he got it all done before the bell rang.

Fidelio and Charlie had agreed not even to whisper about Tolly Twelve Bells in the dormitory. Billy was watching Charlie intently, and just before lights out he came and stood at the end of Charlie's bed.

"Is it still all right me coming for the weekend?" asked Billy.

"Of course," said Charlie. "My mom says it'll be fine."

"And . . . and are you going to do anything about Emilia Moon?" Billy sounded a bit awkward.

Charlie said, "Not sure yet." There was something not quite right about Billy.

Billy crept back to bed as a voice barked, "Lights out." A large hand came around the door and snapped off the lights. Knowing who the hand belonged to didn't help. Charlie imagined Aunt Lucretia sneaking along the passages, listening at doors.

Before he finally drifted off to sleep he remembered what Maisie had said. "Benjamin called last night. At least I think it was him because of the barking."

Why was Benjamin calling so late, and why didn't he leave a message? And why was Runner Bean barking? Charlie fell asleep before he could figure it out.

Benjamin was not asleep. He'd had a very unpleasant day. It was cold and windy and, as he walked home from school, he thought of all the good, hot things he could cook for himself and Runner Bean: sausages, chips, toasted cheese, chicken nuggets, and grilled bananas. "Yum! Yum!" Benjamin said to himself. He'd managed to forget Eustacia Yewbeam.

But there she was, banging pots and pans in Benjamin's kitchen as though she were preparing a feast, not a measly bowl of broth. When Benjamin asked for a sausage she gave him a glassy stare and said, "Whatever for? It's not as if it's Christmas."

Runner Bean leaped out of his basket, barking with joy and licking every bit of Benjamin that he could find: his face, his hands, his ears, and his neck.

"That dog hasn't moved all day," grumbled Miss Yewbeam. "I couldn't even get into the broom closet."

"He's a very good guard dog," said Benjamin. Later he was bitterly to regret those words.

That night he listened to Miss Yewbeam walking through the rooms. What could she be doing? She'd had all day to explore. He had an uncanny feeling that someone else was in the house. Eventually, Benjamin closed his eyes and fell into an uneasy sleep.

He was woken up by a terrible noise: a howling, screaming, whining sound. Benjamin leaped out of bed and ran to the top of the stairs.

"Runner?" he called. "Is that you?"

He was answered by a low snarl and then a series of earsplitting growls and barks. Something was attacking Runner Bean. Benjamin tore downstairs.

"Runner! Runner, I'm coming," he shouted.

There was a horrible scream, and a bang as the back door crashed open.

Benjamin ran down the passage toward the open door. He almost fell over Runner Bean's motionless body.

"Runner!" cried Benjamin, kneeling beside the dog's shaggy head.

Runner Bean gave a sad little whine, and Benjamin, stroking the rough fur, found that it was covered in something sticky.

The hall light was switched on and Miss Yewbeam marched down the stairs. "What's going on?" she demanded.

"My dog's been attacked," cried Benjamin. "He's all covered in blood."

"My, my, what a mess!" declared Miss Yewbeam. "We'll call the vet in the morning."

"I can't leave him like this," said Benjamin. He ran into the kitchen and came back with a bowl of water and some old cloths. Miss Yewbeam stood and watched as Benjamin washed off the blood and applied anti-septic. Runner Bean's wounds were like huge bite marks. But what sort of animal could have gotten into the house? And why?

Miss Yewbeam told Benjamin to go to bed. He refused. "I'm going to sleep down here with Runner," he said. He got a cushion and a blanket and lay beside the injured dog all night.

In the cold light of Tuesday morning, Runner Bean looked very ill. Benjamin wouldn't go to school. "He might die while I'm away," he cried.

"Nonsense." Miss Yewbeam tried to drag Benjamin up to his room.

"No! No! No!" he shouted.

She brought his clothes downstairs and tried to make him get dressed. He struggled and fought. She slapped and pushed and pulled.

"Help!" cried Benjamin, though he didn't know who he was calling to. And then he remembered what Charlie had said, and he dashed to the front door, bounced down the steps and, still in pajamas, rushed across the road to number nine, where he pounded on the door.

The door flew open and Benjamin fell into the hall. He found himself looking up into the grim face of Grandma Bone.

"And what do you think you're doing, Benjamin Brown?" asked Grandma Bone.

"I want to see Mr. Paton," said Benjamin, struggling to his feet. "Mr. Paton Yewbeam."

"He's not available," said Grandma Bone.

"He's got to be," Benjamin shouted. "Mr. Paton! Mr. Paton!"

"Shhhh!" ordered Grandma Bone.

Several doors opened upstairs, and Maisie and Charlie's mother looked down from the landing.

"Benjamin, what's happened?" asked Amy Bone.

"My dog's been attacked and I want Charlie's uncle Paton," cried Benjamin.

As the two women began to run down to Benjamin, Paton appeared at the top of the stairs in a red velvet bathrobe. "Who wants me?" he asked.

"Me! Me, Mr. Yewbeam!" said Benjamin. "My dog's hurt. He won't wake up. Please can you help me?"

Paton descended and strode to the front door.

"Paton, you're not dressed," said Grandma Bone.

"Nonsense!" said Paton.

"Sun's up," murmured Maisie.

"Don't worry about the sun," said Paton. "Come on, Benjamin." He opened the front door and marched down the steps with Benjamin beside him.

Traffic had begun its usual rush up Filbert Street toward the center of the city, but Paton took no notice. Looking neither to the left nor to the right, he walked straight across to number twelve. Cars screeched to a halt, and drivers hooted and swore at the tall man in his bright red bathrobe, and the small boy in blue-striped pajamas.

When Paton entered number twelve, he came face-to-face with his sister.

"Ah, it's you, Eustacia," said Paton. "I might have known."

"And what do you mean by that?" Eustacia asked coldly.

"Benjamin, where are your parents?" asked Paton.

"I think they're in Scotland, looking for a missing window cleaner," said Benjamin.

"We'll soon see about that," said Paton. "Now, where's the dog?"

Benjamin led Paton down the hallway to Runner Bean's basket. The big dog lay in an awkward huddle, his torn nose resting on his paws. His eyes were closed and he was hardly breathing.

"Good heavens," Paton exclaimed, bending over the dog. "A wild beast has attacked your dog, Benjamin. Something with exceptional teeth and claws."

"It's my fault," sobbed Benjamin. "I told him to guard the cellar. But it was silly, really, because there's nothing in . . ." He stopped, remembering, too late, that Eustacia Yewbeam was hovering by the front door. "How could a wild beast get in?" he asked Paton. "All the doors are locked at night."

"Someone let it in," said Paton, glancing at his sister. "We'll have to get Runner Bean to a vet," he told Benjamin. "And very soon. It looks to me as if time's running out for this poor dog."

Benjamin had an idea. He remembered how Mr. Onimous said he had a special way with animals.

"I know someone who'll come here," he said. "Mr. Onimous, the mouse man. I've got his card. He's got these amazing cats, like flames." Benjamin jumped up and ran into the kitchen.

"I'm off," said Eustacia, and she slid out the front door so fast, they hardly saw her go.

"What's going on, Mr. Yewbeam?" asked Benjamin. "Why did someone let this happen to Runner? And why are your sisters so mean and angry?"

"It's war, Benjamin," said Paton. "Something that's been waiting to happen for a long time. Until now, they've had it all their own way, but they've gone too far, and some of us are just not going to stand for it!"

THE INVENTOR'S DAUGHTER

"Olivia's really working on Emilia," Fidelio told Charlie.

It was Friday and they were walking together around the frosty garden. Just ahead they could see Olivia and Emilia, deep in conversation, or rather, Olivia was talking and Emilia appeared to be listening.

In a few hours they would all be in their own homes. Even Olivia had managed to stay out of trouble for a whole week. At that moment she darted back to the boys, or rather, she stomped in her huge boots.

"It's worked," she said in an undertone. "I'm going to visit Emilia tomorrow afternoon. So expect us around teatime."

"How're you going to get her away from the Moons?" asked Charlie.

"I'll think of something." Olivia strode away.

The bell went off and they began to wander back toward the academy. Billy Raven brushed past them as they reached the door.

"See you later, Billy," said Charlie. "Remember, you're coming home with me."

"Just for one night," said Billy. "I've got to come back on Saturday."

Charlie was puzzled. "I thought you wanted to stay the whole weekend," he said.

"I have to get back. Matron said." Billy gave him a strange awkward glance and rushed off.

"He's been behaving very oddly this week," Fidelio remarked. "Last night he left the dormitory for hours. The smell of that awful dog, Blessed, or whatever it's called, woke me up. I couldn't get to sleep afterward."

"Perhaps he's sleepwalking," Charlie said. "He looks pretty tired."

Neither of them thought about Billy again. At half past three they packed their cases and at four o'clock they were on their way home on one of the academy buses: blue for music, purple for drama, and green for art. Charlie noticed that Olivia had managed to get into a green bus with Emilia. Olivia wore a big green hat and had turned her purple cape inside out; the lining was a dirty green color.

"Trust Olivia!" Charlie grinned to himself.

"What's she done?" asked Billy, who was sitting beside him.

"Oh, nothing. She's just funny, that's all."

"Oh," said Billy.

Maisie made a great fuss over Billy. She'd baked a chocolate cake, especially for him, and made up a comfortable bed in Charlie's room. "Poor little thing," she kept muttering, as she hovered around the table, pouring orange juice, slicing cake, and trying to tempt Billy with iced biscuits and jam tarts. Billy enjoyed the fuss. He had never seen so many good things to eat all on one table.

"We had a bit of excitement here this week," Charlie's mother said, as she poured the tea. "Benjamin's dog was attacked and your uncle Paton took charge. I've never seen him so active. He went out in broad daylight."

"In his bathrobe," Maisie added.

"Runner Bean was attacked?" Charlie said anxiously. "Where's Uncle Paton, now? And where's Grandma Bone?"

"Locked in their rooms," said Maisie. "There have been terrible fights, every night. Shouting and stamping and slamming doors. I don't know how many lightbulbs we've lost."

As soon as tea was over, Charlie took Billy across the road to meet Benjamin. The door was opened by a woman with short blonde hair and glasses. She was wearing a gray suit and, although she looked very businesslike, she had a warm and welcoming smile.

"Hello, Charlie," she said. "You don't recognize me, do you? I'm Mrs. Brown, Benjamin's mom."

Charlie was amazed. He hadn't seen Mrs. Brown for ages. He was sure she'd once had long dark hair. "This is Billy," he said.

"Come in! Come in!" said Mrs. Brown. "Runner Bean's having his treatment."

"His treatment?" said Charlie, stepping into the hall. There were suitcases on the stairs, rubber boots on

315

the floor, and coats and raincoats draped over chairs and banisters. What on earth had been going on?

"Benjamin's in the living room, Charlie," said Mrs. Brown. "He'll be pleased to see you."

Charlie led Billy to a room at the back of the house. He hadn't been in it very often. Benjamin usually preferred the kitchen.

When he opened the door he was met by a loud hiss and a long, warning meow. He could hardly believe his eyes. Aries, the copper-colored cat, stood on the back of an armchair; Sagittarius stood on the back of another; and Leo was perched on the arm of the sofa. They stared fiercely at Charlie, and then relaxed. Aries even gave a soft purr.

Benjamin was sitting on the sofa beside Leo. "Come in, Charlie," he whispered. "Mr. Onimous is treating Runner."

Runner Bean was lying on the floor with Mr. Onimous kneeling beside him. He had a bottle of green liquid in one hand and a cotton ball in the other. Runner Bean had a bandage on his nose and a stitched-up ear. Nasty scars could be seen on his body where the fur had either been torn or fallen out.

"He's getting better," Benjamin whispered.

Charlie slipped into the room and sat beside Benjamin, but as soon as Billy came in the three cats set up a low, warning growl.

Mr. Onimous looked up. "What's going on?" he asked. "I gotta have quiet."

Billy stood with his back against the wall. He looked terrified.

"Who's that?" asked Benjamin.

"It's Billy Raven," Charlie whispered. "He's from the academy. He hasn't got a home so he's staying with me for the weekend."

"Hello, Billy," said Benjamin in a hushed voice. "Have a seat!"

Mr. Onimous was now changing the bandage on Runner Bean's nose. The dog gave a little whimper. At that moment Billy took a step forward and all three cats leaped to the floor, grumbling and yowling.

"They don't like me," squeaked Billy.

Mr. Onimous frowned at him. "Why ever not?" he asked. "I think you boys had better leave the room. Old Runner here is getting a little bit excited."

Charlie, Benjamin, and Billy went into the kitchen, which was wonderfully tidy, for a change.

"So what's been happening?" asked Charlie.

"A lot," said Benjamin. He began with the terrible discovery of Aunt Eustacia in his house, and then went on to describe the mysterious attack on Runner Bean; how he'd run across to ask Charlie's uncle for help; and how, since that moment, his life had changed, because Paton had somehow located his parents and insisted they come home.

"I think he got the police to find them," said Benjamin. "Mom wears this yellow raincoat sometimes, so she's easy to spot. Anyway, Mom and Dad came home, just like that. Your uncle said they'd been tricked and sent on a wild goose chase. I think your grandma had something to do with it. Anyway, when they came home, your Uncle Paton had this big long private talk with them, and since then, Mom says she's only going to work while I'm at school, never at night, and never on the weekends."

Charlie could hardly believe it. Uncle Paton had put his head up at last. He could obviously make things happen when he wanted to.

Mr. Onimous popped his head into the kitchen. "We'll be off now, boys," he said. "Runner Bean's doing very well, considering. I'll be back on Monday." He was off in a flash, as usual, with the three cats whizzing after him like fiery-colored rockets.

"What a funny man," Billy murmured. "He's a bit like a mouse."

The others agreed, although Benjamin pointed out that Mr. Onimous had extraordinary powers. "I thought Runner Bean was dead," he said, "but Mr. Onimous just put his funny hands on him and he began to get better. And the cats kept him warm by walking around and around him, even though they don't like dogs."

"They didn't like me either," Billy said quietly. "Animals always like me, but they didn't."

Charlie had an idea. "Billy can understand animals,"

he told Benjamin. "Do you want him to talk to Runner? He could tell us what really happened."

Benjamin wasn't sure. He gave Billy a funny look. "Is he one of those kids like you?" he asked Charlie.

"Yes," said Charlie. "You could do it, couldn't you Billy?"

Billy nodded.

"All right." Benjamin led them back to the living room where Runner Bean was licking one of his wounded paws. He seemed a bit afraid of Billy, but when the albino boy started making his funny little grunts and hums, the dog relaxed. He pricked up his ears and listened.

When Billy had finished, Runner Bean began to talk, or rather to grunt, and then he gave a tired sort of groan and lay down.

"Well?" said Charlie. "What did he say?"

"He says he was attacked by a wolf," said Billy.

"What?" cried Benjamin.

"It wasn't an ordinary wolf," Billy went on. "It was a

boy as well as a wolf. I think he meant that the boy turned into a wolf."

"Whew!" Benjamin collapsed into a chair. "A wolf!"

"It was one of us," Charlie murmured. "It had to be. One of those boys at the academy can turn into a wolf—a kind of werewolf—and Aunt Eustacia let him in, so that he could get Runner Bean away from the cellar door. Because she thought Dr. Tolly's case was still there."

"Isn't it?" asked Billy.

The other two boys looked at him. Could they trust Billy? They would have to, Charlie realized, because tomorrow they would all be going to Gunn House together. They couldn't leave Billy behind.

"Dr. Tolly's case is somewhere else," said Charlie. "I'll tell you about it when we get home."

Benjamin looked very cheerful as he waved goodbye from the steps of his house. His mom came out and waved too, and then she put her arm around Benjamin's shoulders and they went inside together.

"My Uncle Paton's a genius," Charlie said proudly.

"Before this week Benjamin hardly ever saw his parents. I'd even forgotten what his mom looked like."

"I'm going to have new parents," said Billy.

"Really? That's fantastic! When did you find out?" asked Charlie.

"Oh, just the other day," said Billy. "Only I have to be . . . good."

"I'll help you to stay out of trouble," Charlie promised.

That night, before they went to sleep, Charlie told Billy everything that he hoped would happen the next day.

"But what will Emilia do, when she wakes up?" asked Billy.

"We don't know," Charlie admitted. "We don't even know if she really is Emma Tolly, or if she'll come to Gunn House. It's all up to Olivia now."

Olivia had very obliging parents. When she told them she had to see a girl called Emilia Moon, who lived miles away on Washford Road, her mom drove her to

Emilia's home and agreed to collect her and Emilia from a Gunn House at five o'clock.

"Are you sure you don't want me to come in with you?" Mrs. Vertigo called from her car.

Olivia stood at the gate of a house called Moonshine. "No, Mom." She gave a wave. "I'll be OK."

Nevertheless, Mrs. Vertigo waited until she saw Olivia press the bell. A gray-haired woman opened the door, and Mrs. Vertigo called, "Bye-eee!" and drove off.

"What do you want?" the gray-haired woman asked Olivia.

"I've come to see Emilia," said Olivia. "She invited me."

"Emilia never said." The thin, angry-looking woman made no attempt to invite Olivia in.

"Well, then she forgot," said Olivia. "You can't send me away now, because my mom's gone and I live miles away."

"Tch!" The woman clicked her teeth. "Emilia!" she shouted. "Come here!"

Emilia appeared. She looked rather gloomy.

"Did you invite this girl here?" demanded the woman.

Olivia waved and smiled at Emilia, until Emilia said, "Yes."

"You'd no right," said the woman. "I suppose you'd better come in," she said grudgingly.

Olivia stepped into a cold, exceptionally tidy house. Emilia gave her a weak smile and led the way upstairs to her room. It was a rather sad room. There were no pictures on the walls, and everything that Emilia owned must have been packed away in the numerous drawers and closets that lined the room. The bed was covered with a spotless white blanket, and on the pillow sat a very neat-looking stuffed duck.

"That's nice," said Olivia, for want of anything better to say.

Emilia smiled.

"Shall we go out?" asked Olivia. "There might be more to do in the garden."

Emilia agreed.

The garden consisted of a neat lawn surrounded

by large, bushy shrubs. Beyond a swing at the far end, Olivia spotted a promising-looking wall.

"What's on the other side of that wall?" she asked Emilia.

"Just an alley," said Emilia. "It leads to the main road."

"Let's climb over it."

"Why?"

"Because I want to show you something," said Olivia. "It's very special. I can't tell you what it is, but it's in Fidelio Gunn's house."

"Is this a trick?" Emilia looked anxious.

"Emilia, trust me," said Olivia. "I'm your friend."

Olivia's gentle tone was so persuasive, Emilia was soon climbing over the wall behind her.

"We'll be back before your mom has noticed we're gone," Olivia promised.

Meanwhile in the attic at Gunn House, Fidelio, Charlie, Benjamin, and Billy were munching their way through a second plate of sandwiches. They were sitting on various piles of boxes and music cases, while blasts of music reverberated beneath them.

Charlie decided he was just eating to forget his anxiety. Was he doing the right thing? Would Olivia find the house? Would Emilia wake up? And if she did would she scream and freak out, or faint . . . or turn into something else? A bird maybe? He took another sandwich.

"For a singer, your mom makes amazing sandwiches," he told Fidelio, as he munched into banana and peanut butter.

"Fidelio!" Mr. Gunn sang out from the hall. "There are two young ladies to see you!"

"Show them up, Dad!" called Fidelio.

"Up you go, right to the top, mind your heads and please don't hop!" sang Mr. Gunn.

Olivia burst out laughing but Emilia was silent—as far as Charlie could tell—there was so much noise in the musical house.

"Here we are!" said Olivia striding into the room.

Emilia followed her. She looked puzzled, but not frightened.

"Did Olivia explain?" Charlie asked her.

"You've got something to show me," said Emilia slowly.

"Yes. It's something your father made," said Charlie.

Emilia frowned. "My father's an accountant. He doesn't make things," she said.

"Well, actually, he was an inventor," said Fidelio. "But he died and he left you this case." He pointed to the metal case that lay in the center of the room.

"How do you know?" asked Emilia, her frown deepening.

Fidelio looked at Charlie, and Charlie said, "It all happened when I met your aunt."

"I've got an aunt? I never knew I had an aunt."

"She's a very nice person, and she's been wanting to see you for years and years," Charlie told Emilia. "She gave me the case, and then I found out what was in it and how it could—er—wake you up."

Emilia looked even more confused. Olivia sat on a large trunk and pulled Emilia down beside her. "It's going to be OK. We won't let anything bad happen to you," she said.

"I didn't know I wasn't awake," Emilia murmured.

"I think we'd better do it now," said Fidelio. "Time's running out. Go on, Charlie."

Charlie stepped forward. He ran his fingers firmly but carefully over the letters on the side of the case. TOLLY TWELVE BELLS. As he reached the last letter he looked around the room. Everyone was staring at his fingers. He noticed that Billy Raven's eyes had gone wide and dark, and that they completely filled the round frames of his glasses. It gave him a blank, hidden look.

When the last letter had been pressed, the lid began to open. Charlie stood to one side and watched Emilia's face, but it was Olivia who cried out in amazement. Emilia just looked baffled.

When the knight raised his sword, everyone jumped up and backed away, even Emilia. And then the bell began to chime, and the voices of the chanting choir filled the room.

For a moment, Emilia looked as if she were in intense pain. She hunched her shoulders and put one hand over her mouth. She closed her eyes and sank back onto a box. Tears began to trickle down her cheeks.

The others watched, fearfully, as the tears grew into a stream and Emilia began to sob helplessly. She rocked back and forth, moaning and sighing until the knight lowered his sword and descended into the case. When the chanting ceased and the bell chimed for the last time, Emilia was silent. Both hands now covered her face and she was completely motionless.

No one in the room spoke. Charlie closed the case, wondering what to do next.

At last Emilia said, in a very small voice, "I didn't know that I was so unhappy. All my life I've lived with people who didn't love me."

Olivia flung her arms around her, saying, "It's going to be OK, Emilia. You're going to be happy now. You'll see. Charlie, tell her."

So Charlie told Emilia about her poor mother who died, and her father, Dr. Tolly, the inventor. And then he described Julia Ingledew, who lived in a bookshop and longed to see Emilia, longed to look after her forever and ever, in fact. And then Charlie told Emilia the strangest thing of all. "Your father said you could fly, Emilia. That's why they wanted you at Bloor's."

"Me?" said Emilia. "I can't fly."

"Well, you did once," said Charlie. "Perhaps it only happens when you need to."

"Like, if you're frightened," said Olivia.

"Tomorrow I'm going to take you to see your aunt," Charlie told Emilia.

"But how?" she asked.

"I'll find a way," he said confidently. "You know you can just walk away from the Moons whenever you want to, now that you know who you are."

Suddenly a voice called up through the singing flutes and violins, the drumming and piano exercises, "A Mrs. Vertigo is here!"

"Well timed, Mom," said Olivia. "Come on, Emilia."

Emilia followed Olivia downstairs where Mrs. Vertigo was comfortably chatting with Mrs. Gunn. At Olivia's insistence, she broke off her interesting conversation about lungs and drove the two girls back to an alley behind Washford Road. Mrs. Vertigo was rather surprised to see Olivia and Emilia climb over a wall, but did as she was asked and drove around to the front of the house, where she waited for Olivia to come out of the front door. This happened about two minutes after she'd parked the car.

"You're a star, Mom," said Olivia, climbing into the car. "It all worked perfectly."

"You do lead an exciting life, Olivia," said Mrs. Vertigo, who was, in fact, a real star. A film star, as it happened.

For a few moments after the girls left, the four boys sat in a bemused silence. Charlie was enormously relieved that their plan had worked. Now it was up to him to see that Emilia found a home where she truly belonged.

"What shall I do with the case?" asked Fidelio.

"Can you keep it up here?" Charlie asked. "I think I'm going to need it again."

"It's safe with me," said Fidelio.

Billy Raven stood up. "I'd better go back now," he

said. "They're sending a car for me." His voice was a bit shaky and he looked at the floor as he spoke.

Charlie wondered if he was feeling ill. He agreed to take Billy home immediately. Fidelio had to do his violin practice, and by the time the three boys left Gunn House, they could hear their friend adding to the musical racket behind them.

As they wandered back to Filbert Street, Charlie and Billy were wrapped in their own thoughts, but Benjamin hopped along, whistling and chattering, eager to be back with his returned parents and his precious dog.

A black car sat outside number nine. When the boys tried to peer through the smoked-glass windows, a door opened and an elegant cane shot out, whacking Charlie on the knee.

"Ouch!" He leaped back. "Who's in there, Billy?"

"It must be old Mr. Bloor," he said.

Something made Charlie anxious. "Billy, you won't tell anyone about Emilia, will you?" he said. "No one can know until we're ready."

Billy shook his head.

Charlie took him in to collect his bag and, after a brief thank you to Maisie and Mrs. Bone, Billy ran out and jumped into the black car.

"What a strange boy," said Maisie, as the black car pulled away from the curb.

Emilia Moon lay in bed in her tidy, white room. "Emma Tolly," she said to herself. She repeated the name and decided she liked it much better than Emilia Moon.

The telephone in the hall rang several times. This was unusual. The Moons never got phone calls at night. But Emilia thought nothing of it. She was so excited. She'd never really felt excited about anything before. Her life had been dull and cold and organized. Nothing had ever surprised or delighted her. But all that was about to change. "Now I am Emma," she murmured.

Her door suddenly opened and Mrs. Moon looked in. "Get dressed and pack your things," she said. "We're going out."

"Where are we going?" Emma asked nervously.

"Back to the academy. We've just had a call."

"Why?" asked Emma. Could they have found out about her visit to Gunn House?

"You've broken the rules, Emilia," Mrs. Moon said coldly. "Now, hurry up."

With shaking hands, Emilia put on her clothes and went downstairs. Mrs. Moon grabbed her arm and took her out to the car, where Mr. Moon, a thin bespectacled man, sat waiting in the driver's seat. Emma and her bag were pushed into the back of the car and they drove off.

Bloor's Academy looked huge and forbidding from the outside. A single light showed at the top of the tall, grim building, but otherwise it seemed silent and deserted.

Emma walked between Mr. and Mrs. Moon, across the courtyard and up the wide steps. Mr. Moon pulled a chain that hung beside the massive doors, and a bell rang somewhere, deep within the building.

Emma's heart sank when Manfred Bloor opened the door. She glanced away from his coal-black eyes, expecting one of the horrible, numbing stares. But he didn't even try to make her look at him.

"Thank you," he said to the Moons. "Come in, Emilia!"

"Good-bye, Emilia," said Mrs. Moon. She put Emilia's bag on the floor beside her. "Be good."

The heavy doors closed and Emma was alone with Manfred. "Why did you bring me here?" she asked. "In the middle of the night?"

"You broke the rules, didn't you, Emilia? You must be punished."

Emma felt suddenly brave. It was a very unusual sensation. She also found that she was angry. "I'm not Emilia," she said. "I'm Emma Tolly."

Manfred laughed. It was a horrible, vicious sound. "We'll soon knock that nonsense out of you. Emma Tolly! I never heard such garbage. Pick up your bag and follow me."

Something inside Emma wanted to fight, but she didn't see how she could. She was alone with Manfred, as far as she could see. Perhaps, later, she could find a way to escape.

Manfred led her down passages she'd never seen, up dangerously narrow spiral steps, and through empty rooms hung with cobwebs. He carried a lantern in each hand, but Emma could barely see where she was going. There was obviously no electricity in this part of the building. Bats screeched and flittered across the crumbling ceilings, and the wind moaned through broken windows. At last they reached a small room where a narrow bed had been pushed against the wall. There was a pillow and a blanket, nothing else. The floor was bare, the walls great slabs of stone.

Manfred put one of the lanterns on the floor. "Night, night!" he said. "Sleep well, Emilia Moon."

He closed the heavy door behind him, and Emma heard a loud click as a key was turned in the lock. When Manfred's footsteps had receded, she tried to open the door. It was locked, just as she expected.

Emma sat on the bed. She didn't cry. She'd done enough crying for one day. She just sat and thought about all the wonderful things she was never going to have after all. The kind aunt, the friends, the adventures and the amazing feeling of being happy.

"They'll say I've disappeared," she said to herself, "and no one will ever find me."

She looked around her dreadful, dingy cell. Would she be kept here for ever and ever? Until she was very old?

"No," she said to herself. "I'm Emma Tolly now, and Emma won't stand for it. Emma is a persevering person." And with that she leaped up and screamed for all she was worth. "Help! Help! Help!"

She could hear her own voice echoing through the empty rooms beyond the door. But there was no answer.

So Emma called out again, and this time she banged on the door. She rattled and knocked and kicked until her toes were bruised and her knuckles were red and raw. And then she retreated and lay on the narrow bed, exhausted by her efforts.

She was just about to close her eyes, when there

was a soft creak outside the door. Emma sat up. The key turned in the lock, the latch was lifted, and the door swung open.

Emma rushed across the room and looked out. There was no one to be seen. She picked up the lantern and swung it across the passage outside. No one — nothing — unless you counted the bat that hung from a beam. Bats can't open doors, thought Emma.

Holding the lantern as high as she could, she began to walk down the passage. "Who's there?" she whispered. "Who let me out?" This time she didn't dare to raise her voice in case Manfred came storming back.

At the end of the passage she came to a staircase. Cautiously she began to climb down. At the bottom of the stairs, passages branched right and left. Emma hesitated and then took the right. It was very smelly. Gaslight flickered from the walls and she wondered whether it was this that caused the smell.

And then she saw the monster. Or was it a dog? It was low and fat, like a pillow on very short legs, and its face had all but disappeared, except for a long sagging nose.

Emma gasped and shrank against the wall. But the dog hadn't seen her. She was about to creep in the other direction when a voice screeched, "Stop. You there! Come back!"

Before tearing away, Emma cast one quick look over her shoulder. She saw a man in a wheelchair, so old that his face was almost a skull. He had a woolen shawl over his shoulders and his long white hair dripped like wax from a small woolen cap.

"It got out!" he shrieked. "The inventor's brat! Manfred, get it!"

Stifling a scream, Emma ran. She crashed up the stairs, banging her lantern against the wall, along the passage and into the cell-like room, slamming the door behind her. And then she waited, knowing that very soon something bad would happen.

It wasn't long before Manfred's unpleasant face peered through the door. "Ah, you're there," he said. "You'd better not try that again."

He closed the door with a bang and locked it, say-ing, "I'm taking the key, so don't think you can let her out again. Any more trouble, and you won't get jam for a week." Obviously, he wasn't speaking to Emma.

Something hard crashed against a wall and Man-fred yelled, "Stop it!"

Another door banged and then there was silence.

Emma tiptoed to the door. "Who are you?" she asked. There was no answer.

"I'm sorry I got you into trouble," she said.

Still no answer. Whoever was out there had either crept away or jam was so important to them, they didn't want to risk being deprived of it.

"Well, anyway, thank you for trying to help," said Emma.

She sat back on the bed. The candle in her lantern had almost burned out and she could hardly bear the thought of being in complete darkness in that cold creepy room. She stared up at the grim, gray walls, and then, in the dying candlelight, she noticed a small win-dow behind the bed. If she climbed on her pillow she could reach it, and yet she knew the window must be very high up. Far too high for her to jump.

"Charlie said I could fly," she murmured. As she said these words her fingers began to tingle and a strange throbbing passed through her arms, making them almost weightless.

Paton Yewbeam was taking his midnight stroll. He walked with a purposeful stride, and yet his mind was in a turmoil. On one hand he was feeling very positive; at last he was beginning to put things right, and his sisters knew where he stood.

A bulb exploded as he passed a lamppost. There was the usual clatter of falling glass, and then another sound, the patter of light footsteps. Paton sighed, but he didn't look back. If someone was following him, let them. They couldn't prove a thing. He began to mutter to himself. "If only I hadn't insisted on dinner. If we'd stayed at home, eaten by candlelight....She thinks I'm a freak. Forget her, Paton. She'll never forgive you."

Paton became aware that the footsteps had caught up with him. A girl was walking by his side; she had a small, pale face and long, rather straggly fair hair.

"Excuse me," said the girl. "Can you tell me the way to Ingledew's Bookshop?"

"Indeed I can," said Paton. "I believe I was just on my way there."

"Oh, good," said the girl. "My name's Emma Tolly."

THE RED KING

It was half past midnight when Paton rang the bell of Ingledew's Bookshop. Of course, no one answered the door. And yet Paton happened to know that Julia Ingledew went to bed very late. She had admitted that she often read a book until two in the morning. He rang again.

A window above the door flew open with a bang, and Julia Ingledew looked out. "Who is it?" she asked angrily. She saw Paton. "Oh, it's you. This is a fine time to come calling."

"Julia . . . er, Miss Ingledew, it's not really me. Or rather it is me, of course, but there's someone else who wants to see you." Paton stepped back from the door, gently drawing Emma with him. "Her name's Emma Tolly."

"What? I don't . . . I can't . . ." The window slammed shut. Hasty footsteps descended a creaking staircase, and the door flew open with a loud tinkle.

"Hello!" said Emma.

"Nancy? Oh, you're so like Nancy," cried Miss Ingledew. "Come in, come in, and you, Paton. Oh, I can't believe this. I just...oh, my goodness, I'm lost for words."

Julia drew Emma into the shop. She stared at her, touched her hair, her face, and then she hugged her. "It's really you. Oh, Emma, how did this happen?"

"I woke up," said Emma. "Charlie Bone and his friends helped me, and then this nice man brought me here."

"Thank you, Paton," Julia said fervently. "Come and have a cup of tea or something. This is a celebration."

She took them through to her cozy room behind the bookshop, and Emma stared at the shelves of rich, mellow books, their gold-tooled letters glowing in the soft light. She breathed in the smell of old paper and leather and print and, with a deep sigh, she declared it to be the most wonderful room in the world.

"It could be your home, Emma," said Miss Ingledew

happily. "If all goes well. Unless you want to stay with the people who adopted you."

"No, no, no!" cried Emma. "I never want to see that horrible house again."

"You must tell me all about it," said Miss Ingledew. "I want to know everything. And you, Paton, I'm sure you've got a lot to do with this. Sit down, sit down." She rushed around the room removing books and papers from the chairs, plumping up cushions, and flicking dust from the lamp shades.

An hour later, Paton made his way home. He whistled a merry tune as the street lamps flickered and crackled above him. He hadn't been so happy since he was seven years old.

Early on Sunday morning, Charlie woke up to find his uncle standing at the foot of his bed.

"Great news, Charlie," said Uncle Paton. "I haven't been able to sleep a wink. Emma Tolly is with her aunt, and we're going to make sure she stays there."

Charlie sat up. "How did it happen?" he asked.

Paton told him how the Moons had taken Emma to the academy in the middle of the night. And how Manfred had locked her up.

"But she got out," said Charlie.

"Yes," Paton said slowly, "and, at the moment, she won't say how. But, Charlie someone got wind of your little experiment, someone betrayed you, and I think you ought to find out who it is."

Charlie had a horrible feeling he knew. It couldn't possibly have been Benjamin or Fidelio, or even Olivia. He would trust all three with his life. That only left Billy Raven. "It's Billy Raven," he said. "I feel sorry for him, Uncle Paton. He hasn't got any sort of home, and I think he's frightened of something. Did you see the car that arrived for him? It had smoked windows, and somebody inside stuck out a cane and hit me."

"The old man," Paton murmured.

"What old man? You mean Manfred's great-grandfather!"

"I've got a few things to show you, Charlie. Come and see me after breakfast."

Charlie got dressed and ran down to breakfast. He was surprised to find Grandma Bone in the kitchen and even more surprised when she actually smiled as he dug into his sausage and fried eggs. Charlie was suspicious. He thought he'd get a lecture about breaking the rules. But perhaps she hadn't yet heard about Emma Tolly's escape.

As soon as breakfast was over, Charlie went upstairs and tapped on his uncle's door.

"Come in, Charlie!" Uncle Paton's voice didn't sound weary and angry anymore.

Charlie could hardly open the door. There were books all over the floor. He had to tiptoe into the few empty spaces, while his uncle directed him; "Not there! Yes, that's right . . . Mind that one, Charlie! I don't want to lose my place."

"What's going on, Uncle Paton," said Charlie, sitting in a small gap in the papers strewn across his uncle's bed.

"You asked me about the Red King, Charlie, and I've made strides — great strides. Miss Ingledew helped me to find some of these books," he indicated the huge ancient-looking books beside his desk. "They're priceless, treasures really. I've yet to translate them all, but a great deal has already come to light. I've made notes. Listen."

"They're in another language?" asked Charlie.

"Many languages. Now, listen. The Red King came to these islands, meaning Britain, in the thirteenth century. They say he came from Africa, though from which part I can't be sure. He was called red because of his scarlet cloak and the blazing red sun on his shield. One of his companions was a knight from Toledo, the city of swords. The Red King married this knight's daughter, but sadly she died when their tenth child was born.

"The Red King left his castle and traveled the land, mourning his wife. There are many accounts of his strange deeds during this period: of the storms he invoked, of his gift for healing, and for his accurate prediction of future events. It says here," Paton heaved a book onto his lap, "'the Red King could, with his black eye, render powerless any adversary,' in other words, he could hypnotize." Paton put down the book. "I could quote hundreds of instances of mysterious happenings, but what it all boils down to is that the Red King was a magician."

"And all of us endowed ones are somehow descended from him?" asked Charlie.

"Yes. But that isn't the end of the story." Paton leaned forward, cupping his chin in one hand and staring earnestly at Charlie. "The king was absent from his castle for fifteen years. He neglected his children who had, in various ways, inherited some, but not all, of his many talents. When the king returned, he found that his children were at war."

"At war?"

"At war with their neighbors. They were using their talents to trick and to steal, to plunder, maim, and kill. The people in the surrounding countryside were terrified of them."

"Were they all bad then, those children?" asked Charlie.

"Indeed no. Only five were intent on achieving power. The others left the castle, they disappeared into the country. Some even sailed to other lands, hoping to escape their terrible siblings and reluctant to use their strange endowments. But they couldn't escape, Charlie, because some of their children became wicked too, and often the children of the bad were born good. In this way the families were bound together, forever, never able to break free from their past; and so it has continued until today. Just when a family thinks it is clear of wickedness, up pops a thoroughly bad one, with a talent to cause havoc." Paton shook his head. "So many warring families, so much heartache, so much distress."

"I'm glad I'm an only child," said Charlie.

Paton laughed. "If we stick together, we'll win in the end, Charlie!" He swung around to face his desk again.

"Yeah!" Charlie stood up and began the precarious journey across the floor. When he reached the door he turned and said, "What happened to the Red King,

Uncle Paton? Couldn't he put things right, seeing as he had all that power?"

"He'd waited too long," Paton said solemnly. "He would have had to kill his children, and that he couldn't do. With his three leopards, the Red King departed from his castle, and was never seen again. Although there are accounts of an invisible presence in various parts of the country."

"You never said anything about leopards," said Charlie.

"Didn't I? Well, there we are. I forgot." Paton gave Charlie a mysterious smile. "This afternoon, I'm going to Ingledew's to help Julia with her arrangements for keeping Emma."

"Do you think it'll work? Will Emma really be able to stay there forever?"

"We'll make it work. The Bloors won't want the world to find out what they've been up to. They'll have to give Emma up. As for the Moons, it doesn't sound as if they enjoyed being parents at all." Uncle Paton looked very confident. In fact, he looked like a new man altogether.

Charlie left his uncle to his books and went across to see Benjamin. To his surprise, there was no one in at number twelve, not even Runner Bean. It gradually dawned on Charlie that the Brown family had gone out for the day. All together. This had never happened before. Benjamin had always been at home, whenever Charlie wanted him.

Charlie wandered down to the park, just in case Benjamin had taken his dog out for his first walk since the attack, but there was no sign of them.

When he got home he found Maisie sitting in the rocker by the stove. "I don't feel very well, Charlie," Maisie said. "I think I'll skip lunch today, and take a little nap."

This was unheard of. Maisie was never ill. Charlie watched his grandmother plod across the kitchen. What had happened to her?

Over lunch, he and his mother had a long chat about Emma Tolly.

"It's like a fairytale," sighed Mrs. Bone. "I hope it'll have a happy ending."

"She doesn't belong to the Moons," said Charlie. "She hates them. She belongs to Miss Ingledew."

"But can they prove it?" Amy Bone shook her head. "Who's going to believe stories about hypnotism and . . . shining knights and ringing bells . . . and Dr. Tolly's message."

"No one will have to know. Uncle Paton says the Bloors won't want other people to know what they've been up to, so they'll give up without a fight."

"I don't believe that," said Amy Bone. "Someone will have to pay for what's happened. Be careful, Charlie."

"Don't worry about me, Mom."

After lunch, Mrs. Bone had to go down to the greengrocer's. She'd promised to help with some packaging. "I won't be long, Charlie," she said. "Maisie's upstairs if you need her."

The house was very quiet. Uncle Paton had already gone out. When Charlie peeked into Maisie's room he found she was fast asleep. He crept past Grandma Bone's door. He certainly didn't want to wake her up. He ran across to number twelve and found that the Brown family was still out. The air was very still and cold and, as Charlie crossed the road again, tiny snowflakes began to settle on his head.

And then he saw them: three dark figures marching down the street. The Yewbeam sisters walked shoulder to shoulder, refusing to give way, so that, in order to avoid them, other people had to duck into the road. Charlie thought he might be able to run into the park before they saw him, but it was too late, they had increased their pace.

They met outside number nine.

"Charlie, how convenient," said Aunt Lucretia. "We wanted to have a little chat."

"In private," added Aunt Eustacia.

"Oh," said Charlie. As he climbed the steps he heard them whispering behind him.

They stepped into the hall and pressed their damp coats into Charlie's arms.

"Nasty snow," Aunt Venetia remarked, as she flicked Charlie's hair with her long nails.

"Come in," called Grandma Bone from the back room. "Hurry up, Charlie. We haven't got all day."

"I know," said Charlie, "seeing as Aunt Lucretia's a matron, and Aunt Eustacia's a sitter."

The two aunts gave him very nasty looks but didn't say anything. It crossed Charlie's mind that he could quite easily run upstairs and lock himself in his room, but he decided he'd better get this unpleasant "chat" over with. So he dutifully hung up the moleskin coats and took his place at the table, opposite his three Yew-beam aunts.

"Well, Charlie," began Aunt Lucretia. "You've been very busy lately, haven't you?"

"Poking your nose in where you shouldn't," added Aunt Eustacia.

"I hope you're not going to make a habit of it," said Grandma Bone.

"I'm sure he's not," said Aunt Venetia with a sickly smile. She folded her arms and, leaning them on the table, stuck her long neck out toward Charlie. "You were just trying to help a friend, weren't you, Charlie? We know all about Emma Tolly. And we know where Tolly Twelve Bells can be found. It belongs to Dr. Bloor, you know."

"It doesn't," said Charlie. "It belongs to Miss In-gledew and you're not going to get it."

"Oh my!" Aunt Venetia threw up her hands in mock horror. "What a fierce boy. Tolly Twelve Bells can stay where it is. We have no more interest in it, do we sisters?"

"None at all," they said.

Charlie didn't believe them. Tolly Twelve Bells had played its part in waking Emma, and there seemed to be no reason to keep it. But, at the back of his mind, Charlie knew there was a reason. There was someone else to be woken up.

He suddenly found himself saying, "My father isn't dead, you know."

Grandma Bone's face went white. "What are you talking about?" she exclaimed. "Of course he's dead."

"No, he's not. One day I'm going to find him."

"Is this what your uncle's been saying?" asked Aunt Lucretia. "Paton is mad you know, quite crazy. He doesn't know what he's talking about. You mustn't have anything more to do with him."

"Promise you won't," said Aunt Eustacia.

"No," said Charlie.

Grandma Bone banged her fist on the table. This was followed by several seconds of deadly silence. Charlie thought it was about time he left. He pushed back his chair and stood up.

"Wait!" said Aunt Venetia. "I've got a present for you, Charlie." She bent down and pulled something out of the large bag at her side. "Here you are."

A brown paper parcel came sliding across the polished table. Charlie stared at it. "What is it?" he asked.

"Open up!" Aunt Venetia winked at him.

Charlie swallowed. It had to be something nasty. He pulled at the string and the paper fell open, revealing a folded blue cape.

"A cape," said Charlie. "But I've got one."

"A dreadful ratty thing," said Grandma Bone. "Dr. Bloor said you were to have a new one, and Aunt Venetia has kindly made one for you."

"She's very good with her hands," said Aunt Lucretia.

Aunt Venetia's smile was so wide, Charlie could see the lipstick that had come off on her teeth.

"Thank you," he said uncertainly.

"A pleasure." Aunt Venetia waved him away. "You can go now, Charlie."

Charlie left, clutching his new cape. He ran upstairs and found that the ratty blue cape had been removed from his wardrobe. He examined Aunt Venetia's gift, but there seemed to be nothing wrong or different about it.

Charlie mentioned the cape to his mother when she came to help him pack his bag.

"It's very kind of Aunt Venetia," she said thoughtfully, "but not at all like her. I've never known her to give anyone a present, even at Christmas."

"Perhaps they don't want to be ashamed of me,"

said Charlie, "seeing as Aunt Lucretia's a matron at the academy."

"That must be it," said his mother. "The Yewbeams are a proud family."

But Charlie couldn't help wondering.

INTO THE RUIN

When Charlie got to the academy the next morning, he noticed that there was a buzz of excitement in the hall. Children were finding it very hard not to talk, they kept nudging one another and pointing to the long table that had been placed against one of the paneled walls. It was covered with small glass lanterns.

"It's the ruin game tonight," Fidelio told Charlie. They had reached the coatroom, which was full of chattering children.

"What happens?" asked Charlie, thinking of the girl who never came out. "I don't know how to play it."

"It's not really a game," said Fidelio. "It's more of a hunt. At the center of the ruin a medal has been hidden. The winner has to find the medal and get out of the ruin before an hour has passed. Each department takes it in turn. Tonight it's drama, tomorrow it'll be art, and it's us on Wednesday. It's not easy. Last year no one found the medal, and the year before someone found it, but it took them three hours to get out, so it didn't count."

"Is it worth it?" asked Charlie. "It's just a medal."

"The winner gets a whole year free of detention — unless they do something really bad. They also get days off, and free stuff like new instruments, or paint boxes or dressing-up clothes. Plus, it just makes you feel good."

"Oh." Charlie had a sinking feeling. He told himself he was silly. There would be a hundred children in the ruin. How could anyone get lost? And yet people had disappeared in there. And someone could turn into a wild beast and go in to find prey.

"Don't look so grim, Charlie," said Fidelio. "Tonight, we'll watch from the gallery in the art department. It overlooks the garden. You'll enjoy it, I promise you."

After supper that night, the children from the drama department filed into the hall and collected their lanterns. The gallery overlooking the garden began to fill up with spectators as, one by one, the children with purple capes emerged into the garden. Charlie was glad that Olivia had decided to wear sensible shoes — the sort of shoes she could run in, if anything chased her.

The single file of flickering lanterns moved across the grass like a long glittering snake. And then, gradually, the head of the snake began to disappear, as children were swallowed by the dark walls of the ruin.

"Now what?" breathed Charlie.

"We wait," said Fidelio.

They didn't have to wait long. Some of the younger children began to run out of the ruin very soon after going in. They were either scared of the dark or of getting lost. Their names were ticked off as they ran back into the hall. Lanterns were nervously returned and sheepish children went eagerly to bed.

Olivia was one of the last to come back. Fidelio and Charlie were waiting on the stairs that led to her dormitory.

"I didn't like it out there tonight," she said. "There was something behind those walls that gave me the creeps. I kept seeing this shadow — it was there one minute and then it was gone."

"What sort of shadow?" asked Fidelio.

"An animal," said Olivia. "Maybe a dog—I don't know. I didn't get to the center, no one did."

"Well, I'm glad you got out," said Charlie, glancing at Olivia's sensible shoes.

"I kept close to Bindi," said Olivia. "I feel safe with her because she's endowed. Manfred gave me such a nasty look when he was handing out the lanterns, I thought I'd had it."

"Not you, Olivia," said Charlie.

The next night it was the art department's turn to play the ruin game. Fidelio and Charlie were joined by Olivia in the gallery. Charlie was relieved to know that Emma Tolly wouldn't be among the medal hunters. He wondered if she was still with Miss Ingledew. If his uncle had anything to do with it, she would be. Uncle Paton was a very powerful person, in his way.

Nothing eventful happened in the second ruin game. No one found the medal. And everyone came out safely.

And then it was Wednesday night. As the line of

children in blue collected their lanterns, an icy wind swept across the hall. It was going to be freezing outside and Charlie was glad of his warm cape. This time it was Dr. Bloor himself who stood by the table, handing out the lanterns. He gave Charlie a grim nod as their hands touched, and with sudden insight, Charlie guessed that it wasn't Dr. Bloor he had to fear. In fact the big man seemed almost wary of him.

The door into the garden was opened and the first children stepped out into the night. There was no moon or even any stars, and they looked up into a sky that was entirely black. The ground, however, had a pale glow, and lifting his lantern Charlie saw that snow had settled and frozen into a thin crust. It crunched beneath their feet like broken glass.

"I'm right behind you, Charlie," Fidelio whispered. "Keep going."

Charlie turned and saw Fidelio's cheerful face illumined in the lantern light.

"Good luck!" Charlie whispered. "Hope you find the medal."

"Silence," said a stern voice. "Talking or whispering will be punished."

They had reached the entrance of the ruin. Manfred stood to one side, ticking off names on a long scroll as children passed him. Above his head swung a large lantern, and Charlie saw that Zelda Dobinski was standing behind Manfred, holding the pole that supported the lantern. She gave Charlie a chilly stare as he stepped through the stone arch.

He found himself in a paved courtyard surrounded by tall, thick hedges. Facing him were five stone arches, separated by four stone seats. Fidelio nudged Charlie and nodded to the middle arch. They set off. At first it appeared that they were the only ones to have chosen the middle arch, but gradually they began to find little groups of children, hurrying across their path or scurrying beside them. Some of the children were even running in the opposite direction.

"Do you think we're going the right way?" Charlie whispered.

"Who knows?" replied Fidelio.

They turned a sharp corner and made their way through a passage so narrow that the walls brushed their elbows as they passed.

Now and again they would emerge into a glade where a fountain splashed into an icy pool. A great stone fish was Charlie's favorite and Fidelio had to pull at his cape to get him away from it. Sometimes they would stumble against a crumbling statue or a mildewed urn, and as time went on, a deep silence began to fall about them. They could no longer hear the swish and patter of hurrying feet, or the hushed muttering of other children.

"How do we know we've reached the center?" Charlie whispered.

"There's a tomb," said Fidelio. "That's all I know."

"A tomb? I wonder whose?"

"Charlie!" Fidelio said out loud. "Stand still. There's something wrong with your cape."

"What?" Charlie swung around and stared at his cape. It was glowing. Tiny brilliant threads ran everywhere through the fabric, giving it the appearance of a strange, sparkling cloud.

"My aunt made it," said Charlie. "But why did she do this?"

"Maybe so someone could follow you in the dark," said Fidelio, "or hunt you."

Charlie pulled off the cape and flung it to the ground. "Well, they're not going to get me," he declared. "I might freeze to death but I'm not going to be caught."

"You can share mine if it gets too cold," said Fidelio.

The next passage they chose was more like a tunnel. They had to almost bend in half to avoid bumping their heads on the low-beamed ceiling. Charlie began to feel breathless in such a confined space. He hurried forward and emerged into a circular glade. Three statues stood in the center, though by now Charlie could hardly make out what they were. He realized his candle had nearly burned through.

Expecting his friend to come out of the tunnel behind him, he called, "Hey, Fidelio, look at this."

There was no answer. Charlie peered into the tunnel. There was no light, no Fidelio.

"Hey, come on. Stop fooling around!" Charlie dashed back into the tunnel. With his free hand he groped at the walls and at the dark space in front of him. Had his friend fallen or slipped into another passage?

"Fidelio! Fidelio!" called Charlie, not caring about punishments.

His calls were met by silence. And then his candle went out.

Charlie realized that he had known, all along, this would happen. He had broken the rules, like his father before him. He had rescued Emma Tolly and now he was to be punished. But he wasn't going to give in without a fight. Flinging down his useless lantern, Charlie began to feel his way back through the tunnel. At some stage it must have branched off into another open passage because he could smell fresh air again, though it wasn't exactly fresh, but more a mixture of leaf-mold and damp stone.

Turning a sharp corner, he caught sight of a light and, hardly able to believe his luck, he ran toward it. The lantern was standing on a great stone tomb.

Someone bobbed up from behind it, and Charlie saw Billy Raven's white head. The round frames in his spectacles glowed like tiny moons.

"I found it," cried Billy. He held up a shiny gold disk on a chain.

"Well done," said Charlie. "I've lost my lantern, Billy. "Can I come with you?"

"It's mine," said Billy. He grabbed his lantern and leaped away.

"It's OK. I won't take it, Billy!"

Charlie watched the light bob away from him, and then it vanished. He had no idea which way Billy had gone. It was impossible to guess. There wasn't even a sound to guide him.

And then there was a sound, the soft tread of hurrying feet, four of them. And there was the low breath of a panting animal. Charlie leaped forward. Stumbling and reeling he ran from the soft footfalls and the sour smell of a beast.

Fidelio had given up looking for Charlie. He thought perhaps his friend had found his way out of the ruin already. Something strange had happened in that narrow tunnel. He'd been pushed through a gap into another passage, but he couldn't see who had pushed him. He asked several children if they'd seen Charlie. They hadn't. "Billy Raven found the medal," someone said.

Hm, thought Fidelio. I wonder how?

He seemed to be the last one to leave the ruin. "Has Charlie Bone come out?" he asked Manfred, who was now crossing names off the scroll.

"Ages ago," said Manfred.

"Are you sure?"

"Of course I'm sure," Manfred snarled.

Fidelio ran indoors. He asked everyone he met if they'd seen Charlie Bone. Everyone who knew Charlie by sight swore they hadn't seen him.

"What's up?" asked Olivia when she saw Fidelio's grim expression.

"Charlie's still in the ruin," he told her.

"No. But it's been ages. They said everyone was out."

"Not true," said Fidelio. He ran up to the dormitory.

Billy Raven was sitting on his bed. Several boys stood around him, admiring the medal that hung from a chain around his neck.

"Have you seen Charlie Bone?" Fidelio asked them.

"No," they all replied.

Billy Raven just shook his head.

"Congratulations," said Fidelio. "I see that you won." He sank onto his bed. He didn't know what to do.

Half an hour later, a voice called, "Lights out in five minutes."

Fidelio dashed into the passage. "Matron," he said. "Charlie Bone hasn't come in."

The tall woman in her starched blue uniform didn't even turn around. "Oh dear," she said and marched on.

Fidelio clutched his hair. "Don't you care?" he shouted.

She ignored him. "You're late," she said as Gabriel Silk came hurrying down the passage.

"Sorry, Matron," he muttered. "I ask you," he said to Fidelio, "even after tramping around that dingy ruin for hours, they made me finish my homework." He noticed Fidelio's distraught face. "What's going on?"

"Charlie's still in the ruin," Fidelio told him.

"What?" A change came over Gabriel Silk. There was a determined glint in his gray eyes, and he appeared taller and more upright than before. "We'll see about that," he said gravely, and he began to march back down the passage.

Fidelio followed, wondering what Gabriel was going to do. At the top of the stairs Gabriel turned and said, "Fidelio, go back to the dormitory. You can't help now."

"I want to come with you," said Fidelio. "Charlie's my friend."

"No," said Gabriel solemnly. "It's not your place. It would be dangerous. You must leave it to us."

Gabriel seemed to have acquired a very compelling stare. Fidelio stepped back. "Who do you mean by 'us'?" he asked.

"The children of the Red King," said Gabriel, and he ran down the stairs.

THE BATTLE OF THE ENDOWED

Where do you think you're going?" called Mr. Paltry as Gabriel walked across the hall. "You should be in your dormitory."

Gabriel ignored him. He ran through a doorway, up a staircase, and along the hallway leading to the King's room. There were only two people in the room when Gabriel burst in: Lysander and Tancred. They were both reading.

"Charlie Bone's still in the ruin!" Gabriel announced.

Lysander and Tancred looked up.

"Manfred and Zelda are there," said Gabriel.

"And Asa?" asked Lysander.

"I think he's changed already," said Gabriel. "He must have gone in."

"Then it's time," said Lysander.

They made a strange trio: the African, the boy with yellow electrified hair, and the skinny one with the long, solemn face. Shoulder to shoulder they walked past Dr. Bloor locking his office, past Dr. Saltweather carrying a music stand, and past Mr. Paltry tidying up the lanterns. None of the teachers could stop the three boys.

They stepped out into the cold night and walked across the frozen ground toward the ruin.

Behind them, children had gathered at the long windows of the gallery. Disobedience was rife that night. Olivia Vertigo had spread the word; a boy was lost in the ruin. Ignoring rules and Matron's commands, children slipped out of bed and ran down the dark passages, whispering anxiously.

Fidelio found himself standing next to Olivia by the windows. "Can you feel it?" she asked.

A wind was stirring. It swirled around the three figures marching toward the tall stone walls, lifting their capes into great billowing shadows. None of the three carried a lantern, and Fidelio saw that the black clouds had blown away and a full moon now filled the garden with silver light.

"It's Tancred," Olivia murmured. "I've been asking

around. Tancred can bring the wind, they say, and storms, too."

"What about Lysander?" asked Fidelio.

"No one's quite sure," said Olivia. "But he's powerful. Someone said he can summon spirits. Everyone agrees on one thing though. Asa Pike can change his shape, but only after dark."

"So that's who it was," said Fidelio. He already knew what Manfred could do, and he had heard that Zelda Dobinski could move things with her mind. But what sort of things, he wondered. Could she move people?

Deep in the ruin, Charlie was crouching beside a wall. He thought he had escaped the beast but it was getting close again. He could hear the rattle of loose stones as it leaped around the crumbling courtyards.

Charlie dragged himself upright. He took a few steps forward and something crashed into his path. He bent down and felt the rough contours of a statue. It had almost killed him. He crawled over the statue and crept forward. There was a crack and a mighty splash as a fountain toppled into its pool. A great wave

MIDNIGHT FOR CHARLIE BONE

of water knocked Charlie to the ground and stones from the broken fountain rained down on him.

He rolled onto his stomach, shielding his head with his hands. "I won't give up, I won't! I won't!" he muttered. But how long could he last? His enemies were very powerful. Was there no one strong enough to help him?

Like an answer, a breeze whistled through the undergrowth. It grew stronger and became a mighty wind howling around the ancient stones and roaring through the sky. It rocked the great cathedral bell so that it rang continuously across the town, like a warning of some imminent catastrophe. Looking up, Charlie saw the full moon emerging from the clouds. Its brilliant light filled the ruin so that all the dangers could be clearly seen. Some of the huge stones began to tumble out of the walls and now Charlie could walk straight through them. But which way should he go?

The beast, too, could see its way. It was getting angrier. Its snarl seemed to come from everywhere and, suddenly, there it was, standing only a few meters in front of Charlie. Its eyes were a glowing, luminous yellow and its bristling snout was drawn back to reveal long, shining fangs.

Charlie stood motionless, waiting for the beast to leap, but, all at once, something pale and ghostly slipped between them. Charlie could make out a spear and a shield. Another figure emerged, and then another. They surrounded the beast and the cornered animal gave a howl of fear.

As Charlie backed away from the ghostly figures, his foot caught on a grass-covered stone and he fell sideways, landing in a bed of thorns. Seeing its victim lying helpless, the beast lunged forward, but two bright spears came down, barring its way and almost slicing through the black snout. The beast growled and its furious eyes glared at Charlie, unable to reach him; it was afraid of those glittering spears and dared not pass them.

Charlie got to his feet and stumbled away. The thorns had torn into his face and hands and he could taste blood on his lips and feel it trickling over his fingers. He found that he was shivering violently. His feet were growing numb and he felt so light-headed he could hardly think. "I've got to get out before I freeze to death," he muttered, his jaw shaking with cold.

Something warm brushed against his legs and, looking down, he saw the copper-colored cat, Aries. Sagittarius appeared on his other side, and then Leo slipped from behind a statue just ahead of him. Nose to tail the cats began to circle Charlie, and the heat from their glowing fur seeped through his body, right into his aching bones.

As he increased his pace, the cats stepped in front of him and, like a single bright flame, began to lead the way through the ruined castle.

Gradually Charlie became aware that he was passing statues he recognized; many of them had fallen to the ground, but he was glad to see that the stone fish fountain was still standing.

At last they reached the courtyard with the five entrances. The wind died and the distant bells stopped ringing. The three cats jumped onto a stone seat and began to wash themselves.

"Aren't you coming out with me?" asked Charlie.

They looked at him and purred.

"Thank you, anyway," said Charlie.

He could see the sweep of white, frozen grass beyond the last arch. But who, or what, was out there? Was he really free? Charlie hesitated, took a breath, and walked through the arch.

Someone stepped up beside him.

"Hi there, Charlie," said Gabriel Silk. "You're safe."

Charlie's relief was so enormous he thought he was going to faint. But before he could fall, strong arms lifted him upright, and Tancred and Lysander peered anxiously into his face.

"Whoa!" said Tancred.

"You OK?" asked Lysander.

"Yes," said Charlie. "Thanks." He noticed that twigs and branches littered the ground and that frozen snow had been swept into great icy banks.

"There's been a storm," he said.

"Among other things," said Lysander with a laugh.

"Too much for some people," added Tancred, laughing even louder than his friend.

Charlie saw two figures kneeling on the ground. He recognized Manfred and Zelda.

"Come on," said Gabriel. "Cook will be preparing a midnight feast."

"A feast?" said Charlie. "Is that allowed?"

"Tonight is an exceptional night," said Lysander. "Everything is allowed."

As they approached the dark mass of Bloor's Academy, Charlie noticed that some of the windows were blazing with light. In front of a great crowd of children, he could make out Olivia and Fidelio, dancing and waving.

Charlie waved back. "It's my friends, they look so funny."

"Fidelio told me you were missing," said Gabriel. "If he hadn't, you might still be in the ruin."

Charlie shuddered.

Tancred opened the garden door and they walked into a wall of children, all talking and shouting at once.

"How did you get out, Charlie?"

"What happened in there?"

"Did you see the beast?"

"Why did you get lost?"

"Make way," shouted Lysander, pushing through the crowd.

"Come on, you guys," urged Tancred, "Let Charlie through."

The crowd obediently gave way before Tancred and Lysander, and Charlie found himself walking down a narrow path between rows of children. When he finally got through into the hall, he saw that the long table of lanterns was now spread with plates of sandwiches, pies, hot dogs, and chips. Cook was bustling about beside the table, doling out the food.

"Ah, the guest of honor," she said when she saw Charlie. "Now then, you poor frozen child, what do you want to eat?"

Charlie was overwhelmed. "Er — well," he muttered, eyeing the food. "I don't — uh . . ."

"Everything," said Lysander. "He wants it all."

"Everything coming up," said Cook, piling a plate with food.

Charlie spied Fidelio and Olivia trying to get through the crowd. "Can my friends have some next?" he asked Cook. "They're just . . ."

"No," said Cook, handing him his plate. "These three first." She pointed to Charlie's rescuers. "If it weren't for them, you wouldn't be here at all, would you?"

"Uh, I suppose not," said Charlie. "Sorry."

Cook gave him a big wink and handed out plates of food to Gabriel and Tancred, who had everything, and Lysander, who just wanted chips.

Charlie saw that all the teachers from the music department were in the hall. They were trying to organize the children into groups. Mr. Paltry looked flustered and angry, but Dr. Saltweather seemed to be enjoying himself. Now and again, he would burst into song as he shepherded children toward the table.

Miss Chrystal beamed at Charlie and gave him the thumbs-up sign. She was helping Mrs. Dance keep some of the younger children out of the hall. With the exception of Tancred and Lysander, only children from the music department were allowed at the feast.

Olivia had managed to find a blue cape and, so far, none of the staff had noticed that she didn't belong in music. She came running up to Charlie with two plates of hot dogs.

"I got an extra one for you. You poor thing, you're covered in bruises and just look at your hair!"

Charlie patted his mop of hair, which had collected so many leaves and twigs it felt like a real hedge. "Oh, I forgot," he said. He was rather full, but he couldn't bring himself to refuse Olivia's offering. "Let's share it," he suggested, then, lowering his voice, he asked, "How did you get hold of that blue cape?"

"It's Billy's," she said. "He was too tired to come down, poor little fellow. He found the medal, you know."

"Yes, I did," said Charlie.

Fidelio darted him a quick look and raised one eyebrow. They would have to have a talk with Billy Raven, Charlie decided. Somebody or something was making him act very strangely.

"I can't believe all this food was put out, just because I got stuck in a ruin," he murmured.

"It's Cook," said Fidelio. "When Cook makes up her mind about something, none of the teachers can stop her. Not even Dr. Bloor. Last year, a boy called Ollie Sparks disappeared for three days. He got lost in the old part of the building and no one could find him. He finally got out by crawling through a hole in the floor. He was covered in cuts and bruises, his hair was full of spiders, and for a while he couldn't even speak. Anyway, Cook gave him a big midnight feast, and after that he went home. He never came back."

"I don't blame..." Charlie's next words died on his lips, for the door into the garden suddenly flew open and Dr. Bloor and Aunt Lucretia appeared. Between them they were dragging the drooping figure of

Manfred Bloor. He certainly didn't look threatening anymore. His head hung forward and his dreadful eyes were half closed. Aunt Lucretia threw a withering glance in Charlie's direction before she disappeared through the door into the west wing.

Silence descended on the hall as Mr. Carp and another teacher appeared, carrying the limp form of Zelda Dobinski.

Even though everyone was scared of Zelda and Manfred, seeing them looking half-dead took all the fun out of the party. Very soon most of the children began to drift off to bed.

All the boys in the dormitory seemed to be asleep when Charlie, Gabriel, and Fidelio crept in, but there was a snuffling noise coming from Billy's side of the room. In the darkness, Charlie made his way to the end of Billy's bed.

"Billy," he whispered. "Are you awake?"

"I'm sorry I left you in the ruin," Billy mumbled. "I didn't mean for you to get hurt."

"It's OK," said Charlie. "But you betrayed Emilia,

didn't you? You told someone about her waking up. Why did you do it, Billy?"

There was no reply.

"Did someone make you do it?" asked Charlie.

There was a long silence before Billy murmured, "I just want to be adopted. Is that so wrong?"

Charlie didn't have an answer.

Next day, life returned to normal. The only difference was that most of the teachers were more understanding than usual. They tended to ignore Charlie's yawns and forgetfulness. He actually fell asleep during the English lesson. Only Mr. Paltry was his usual bad-tempered self.

And then, at lunchtime, Fidelio came bouncing up to Charlie with the most amazing news. His brother Felix had arrived, on the pretext of delivering a repaired violin, but really to let Fidelio know what had been happening in the outside world.

"Emma and Miss Ingledew have locked themselves in the bookshop," said Fidelio. "They won't let anyone in. The Moons have been pounding on the door and demanding that Emma come back to them. They say that Dr. Tolly's tapes don't prove anything. Without papers and a signature, they don't believe that Emma is the inventor's daughter."

Charlie sat up. "You mean after everything we've done, Miss Ingledew can't get Emma back for good?"

"Seems not," said Fidelio. "Unless the papers are found."

"What papers?" said Charlie.

"You know, the stuff that proves who you are. Your birth certificate, adoption papers — stuff like that."

Charlie groaned. "They've got them, haven't they? The Bloors. I bet they've hidden them somewhere."

"Must have," agreed Fidelio. "Next thing we've got to do is find them."

Charlie had horrible visions of being caught climbing into dark attics and getting detention for years and years. "That's not going to be easy," he muttered.

As it happened, Fidelio and Charlie didn't have to

do anything. Someone else did it for them. In a very dramatic way.

The explosions began half an hour before lights out. The first one was hardly noticed. The lantern above the main doors gave a little pop and a few pieces of glass fell out. The next one was louder. A pane in one of the windows in the west wing cracked and smashed onto the cobblestones in the courtyard.

Children leaped out of bed, or ran from bathrooms, dropping towels and toothbrushes in the rush to see what was going on.

Charlie opened the window in his dormitory and twelve heads poked out over the sill. Beneath them, the boys saw a tall man in a long dark coat. He wore black gloves and a white scarf and his abundant black hair glistened like polished stone.

"Wow!"

"Who is he?"

"What's he doing?"

Whispers ran around Charlie's head, and he saw

that other windows had opened and children were peering down into the courtyard.

"He's my uncle," said Charlie, with a slightly proud smile.

"Your uncle?"

"What does he want?"

"Did he smash that window?"

"How did he do it?"

"He doesn't look like someone who breaks windows."

The whispers grew louder and Matron could be heard marching down corridors shouting, "Shut those windows! Get into bed! Lights out! Lights out!"

Some of the children scuttled back to bed, but others still watched the man in the courtyard. He was turning in slow circles now, and staring up at the children. When he saw Charlie, he grinned. Charlie held his breath. He could feel the strange humming that always preceded his uncle's lightbulb accidents.

"Bloor!" Paton suddenly shouted. "You know what I'm here for. Let me in."

The bronze-studded doors remained closed. The whispers died. Everyone waited to see what would happen.

"Very well," roared Paton. He had his back to the children now and was facing the Bloors' private rooms in the west wing.

There was a bang, and the panes of a lighted window flew out into the air. Another followed and then another. Each time the explosion was louder, and the flying glass hit the ground with greater force.

Charlie was amazed. He hadn't realized how powerful his uncle's talent could become when he really wanted to use it.

"Yewbeam!" a voice bellowed. "Stop it, or I'll call the police."

"Oh, I don't think so," Paton shouted back. "There are things going on here that you wouldn't want them to know. Now give me Emma Tolly's papers before I break every light in the building."

Charlie saw a window in the west wing close quickly.

The room beyond it was in darkness, but a second later another window shattered. And now Paton turned his attention to the east wing, where some of the teachers, unaware that electric lights were the cause of the explosions, were still busily tidying up the classrooms.

BANG! BANG! BANG! Three windows in the science lab blew out. But this time the situation was more serious. Something in the lab had caught on fire. Black smoke and the stink of burning chemicals drifted up to the watching children.

"Stop it!" cried Dr. Bloor. "Paton, I implore you!"

"Give me the papers," Paton demanded.

Silence.

And then a shower of jewel-like colors burst over the glass already littering the ground. Someone had forgotten to turn off the lights in the chapel, and the beautiful stained glass windows were now only a memory.

"All right!" screamed a voice.

In the silence that followed, a cloud of paper

floated gently from an upstairs window. Slowly it spun and hovered, before falling to earth like playful, giant snowflakes.

As he ran to catch the falling papers, Paton began to chuckle. The chuckle became a full-throated laugh, and then a resounding roar, a great big *Ha! Ha! Ha!* of triumph.

The watching children couldn't stop themselves from joining in, and soon the courtyard of Bloor's Academy was so filled with laughter, the echo could still be heard at Christmas.

THE LONGEST NIGHT
OF THE YEAR

The newspapers reported the breaking window incident as MYSTERIOUS EXPLOSIONS IN ANCIENT SCHOOL. No one would have believed the truth, even if they'd been told.

Paton took Emma Tolly's papers to Miss Ingledew and when it was proved, beyond a doubt, that Emilia Moon was really Emma Tolly, the Moons gave her up. They were mildly fond of Emma, but it was the money they would miss, more than the child. Dr. Bloor had paid them well to look after her.

It was quite clear that Dr. Tolly's signature on the adoption papers had been forged, but Miss Ingledew let that pass. She just wanted Emma, and Emma wanted nothing more than to live with her aunt forever, in the wonderful house of books.

On the morning after the explosions, the courtyard of Bloor's Academy was a sight to behold. Glass littered the ground. Large gleaming panes, diamond-bright spears, and glinting fragments of color were all covered with a fine silvery dust that flashed and blazed in the morning sunlight.

The workmen who came to clean up the mess could hardly believe their eyes. They gazed at the old stone walls and the dark, gaping windows, and scratched their heads. Whatever had been going on in Bloor's Academy?

"I wouldn't like my boy to go to this school," said one.

"Nor me," said another.

"Creepy place," said a third.

At number nine Filbert Street, Maisie was busy making Christmas cakes. The war between Uncle Paton and his sisters was over. For the moment. Paton had won a battle, but Charlie knew there'd be another. Paton had lifted his head at last, and the Yewbeam sisters were worried. Sooner or later they would try to even the score.

For a whole weekend, the rocker by the stove

remained empty. Not once did Charlie see Grandma Bone. But he could feel her, seething, sulking, and brooding in her room. He didn't care. He felt quite safe. He had good friends and an uncle who wouldn't stand for any wickedness. He thought he might even buy Grandma Bone a pair of socks for Christmas. She certainly needed them.

When his mother suggested it might be better if Charlie didn't go back to Bloor's (all those bruises gave her a shock), Charlie found himself disagreeing.

"Mom, I have to go back," he said, "to keep the balance."

She looked puzzled.

"It's difficult to explain," said Charlie. "I know there are some really bad things going on at Bloor's, but there are good things too. And I think I might be needed, to kind of help out."

"I see," she said.

At that moment, his mother looked so wistful Charlie longed to tell her that, one day, she might see his father. But he held his tongue. It was too early to raise her hopes. Instead he asked her what she wanted for Christmas.

"Oh, I forgot," she exclaimed. "Miss Ingledew is having a party and we're all invited. It's a welcome home for Emma. Isn't that great?" She was all smiles again.

The rest of the semester passed in a flash of feverish activity. There were plays to rehearse, exhibitions to put up, songs to practice, and concerts to arrange. Wherever you went you couldn't get away from the humming, jangling, and thumping of music.

It took Manfred and Zelda a week to recover from whatever it was that Tancred and Lysander had done to them. The surly pair were still not themselves. Manfred kept his sinister gaze on the floor, and Zelda had such bad headaches she couldn't even play push the pencil box. Asa was his old self, however. There wasn't a hint of anything wolfish about him, except, perhaps, his eyes.

On the last day of the semester, the drama department put on a production of *Snow White*. Maisie and

Charlie's mother were in the audience, but Uncle Paton stayed away. He felt he might not be welcome. Charlie agreed.

Olivia played the wicked stepmother. She was superb. No one would have guessed that she was only eleven. When she came on stage for the final curtain, the applause was deafening.

Charlie found her surrounded by admirers when he went to say good-bye. But Olivia caught sight of him, hovering at the edge of the crowd, and called out, "See you at the party, Charlie!"

Miss Ingledew's party took place on the longest night of the year—three days before Christmas. Charlie and his family were the last to arrive, because Maisie had changed her clothes five times before deciding to wear a mauve satin dress with frills. Grandma Bone, who was still sulking, hadn't been invited.

It was surprising how many people Miss Ingledew had managed to fit into her small living room. Fidelio had come with his large father, and Olivia with her film-star mother. Benjamin had brought Runner Bean, now completely recovered, and both his parents. Mr. Onimous had been followed by the three flames. The cats had refused to stay behind once they'd sniffed a party in the air. And, after all, they had played a large part in Emma's rescue.

Bottles and glasses and a great many dishes of delicious-looking food had been placed on the shop counter. Uncle Paton helped himself to a whole plateful as he passed, and there was a certain gleam in his eye when he said, "Julia, my dear, what a wonderful cook you are."

"Oh, they're just snacks," said Miss Ingledew, blushing slightly.

Her cozy living room was lit by an enormous number of candles; tall, short, wide, and thin, they danced and flickered from every surface. Charlie noticed that all the lightbulbs had been removed. Miss Ingledew wasn't taking any chances.

After a while the children decided to have their own party in the shop, because there were so many talkative and over-merry adults in the living room. But shortly before midnight, Miss Ingledew called them all back in. She wanted to make a little speech.

It didn't last long. With tears in her eyes, she thanked everyone who had helped find her dear sister Nancy's daughter. "It was the happiest day of my life when Mr. Yewbeam—er—Paton, brought Emma to my door," she said. And then she had to sit down and blow her nose because the tears had turned into a flood.

There were murmurs of sympathy and congratulation, and Emma ran to hug her, but any awkwardness was relieved by Mr. Onimous, who looked extremely smart in a fake-fur waistcoat. He leaped onto a chair and said how pleased he was to have started the search for Emma. And how proud he was of his three cats.

At this point a small disagreement broke out between Runner Bean and the flames. But it was mostly a matter of low-key growling and griping and soon settled by a word from Mr. Onimous.

Emma Tolly made the last speech of the night. She

looked completely different from Emilia Moon. Her blonde hair had been tied in a bouncing ponytail and her cheeks were flushed with excitement. It was almost as if pale Emilia hadn't been a real person at all, but a sad figure borrowed from a fairytale.

"I'm so happy," she began. "I still can't really believe I'm here. I have to keep pinching myself. Before I say anything else I just want to let everyone know that I'll be going back to Bloor's Academy next semester."

Miss Ingledew looked up with a start. She began to rise, saying, "No..." but Paton gently restrained her.

"I'm sorry, Auntie," Emma went on. "I know I said I wouldn't, but I've changed my mind. It's a good school, after all, and I've got a really great art teacher. And Fidelio and Olivia are still there, and Charlie, of course. They're not scared of anything, besides..." she frowned, almost to herself, "there are things...other children I mean, who might need me. So I'm going back." She gave a bright smile. "And now I'd like to thank everyone who helped me find out who I really was, especially Charlie, who started it all."

"To Charlie," said Miss Ingledew, holding up her glass for a refill.

"To Charlie!" Everyone cheered and raised their glasses, and somewhere a clock began to chime.

It took Charlie several minutes to realize that the whole room was looking at him. His thoughts had been far away, with someone else who had fallen asleep at twelve o'clock.

TO BE CONTINUED...

SNEAK PREVIEW OF

THE TIME TWISTER
BY JENNY NIMMO
CHILDREN OF THE RED KING SERIES BOOK 2

JANUARY 1916

FOR THE LAST FEW DAYS OF THE CHRISTMAS HOLIDAY, HENRY YEWBEAM AND HIS YOUNGER BROTHER, JAMES, HAVE BEEN SENT TO STAY WITH THEIR COUSINS, THE BLOORS, IN BLOOR'S ACADEMY.

THE COURTYARD AT BLOOR'S IS FULL OF SNOW. THE WINDOWS ARE FROSTED. THE TEMPERATURE IS BEGINNING TO DROP EVEN FURTHER. IT GETS COLDER AND COLDER. IT HASN'T BEEN THIS COLD FOR A HUNDRED YEARS.

HENRY YEWBEAM DOESN'T CARE ABOUT THE COLD. HE HAS TO GET AWAY FROM THE BLOORS, ESPECIALLY EZEKIEL, WHO IS CONSTANTLY TORMENTING HIM. HENRY PUTS ON HIS BLUE SCHOOL CAPE AND TAKES HIS BAG OF MARBLES DOWN TO THE FREEZING HALL. THIS IS A WONDERFUL PLACE TO PLAY MARBLES; SUCH A LONG, SMOOTH FLOOR AND NO INTERRUPTIONS. HALFWAY THROUGH HIS GAME, HENRY SEES A MARBLE ROLLING TOWARD HIM. IT'S NOT ONE OF HIS; IT'S BIGGER, SHINIER. HE PICKS IT UP. IT'S FULL OF BEAUTIFUL COLORS. SUDDENLY, HENRY KNOWS HE SHOULDN'T HAVE TOUCHED THE STRANGE MARBLE.

THE WALLS ARE FADING; THE LIGHT IS GOING; HE FEELS HIMSELF DISAPPEARING. QUICKLY HE PULLS A PIECE OF CHALK OUT OF HIS POCKET AND WRITES ON THE FLOOR: *GIVE THE MARBLES TO JAMES.*

HENRY HAS NOW VANISHED FROM 1916.

January 2002

IT'S FREEZING COLD, THE COLDEST DAY FOR NEARLY A HUNDRED YEARS. CHARLIE BONE IS CROSSING THE HALL ON HIS WAY TO A LESSON AT BLOOR'S ACADEMY. IT'S DESERTED EXCEPT FOR BLESSED THE DOG, WHO IS SNIFFING IN A CORNER. SOMETHING BEGINS TO HAPPEN A FEW FEET IN FRONT OF CHARLIE. A BOY IN A BLUE CAPE MATERIALIZES. HE RUBS HIS EYES AND SAYS, "OH, MY WORD! WHAT HAPPENED?"

CHARLIE TAKES THE BEWILDERED HENRY YEWBEAM INTO THE BLUE COATROOM. CHARLIE CONFIDES IN GABRIEL SILK AND TOGETHER THEY TRY TO KEEP HENRY HIDDEN, BUT IT BECOMES IMPOSSIBLE. BLESSED HAS TOLD BILLY RAVEN, WHO IN TURN HAS ALERTED OLD EZEKIEL. MANFRED, ZELDA, AND THE MATRON ARE ON THE HUNT FOR HENRY.

WHY DID HENRY DISAPPEAR? CAN CHARLIE HELP KEEP HIM SAFE FROM OLD EZEKIEL?

WILL HENRY EVER BE REUNITED WITH HIS BROTHER JAMES?

JENNY NIMMO

I was born in Windsor, Berkshire, England, and educated at boarding schools in Kent and Surrey from the age of six until I was sixteen, when I ran away from school to become a drama student/assistant stage manager with Theatre South East. I graduated and acted in repertory theatre in various towns and cities: Eastbourne, Tunbridge Wells, Brighton, Hastings, and Bexhill.

I left Britain to teach English to three Italian boys in Amalfi, Italy. On my return I joined the BBC, first as a picture researcher, then assistant floor manager, studio manager (news), and finally director/adaptor with *Jackanory* (a BBC storytelling program for children). I left the BBC to marry the Welsh artist David Wynn Millward and went to live in Wales in my husband's family home. We live in a very old converted watermill, and the river is constantly threatening to break in, which it has done several times in the past, most dramatically on my youngest child's first birthday. During the summer we run a residential school of art, and I have to move my office, put down tools (typewriter and pencils), and don an apron and cook! We have three grown-up children, Myfanwy, Ianto and Gwenhwyfar.